Electricity

Ray Robinson was born in North Yorkshire in 1971.
An award-winning short-story writer,
Electricity is his first novel.

www.rayrobinson.co.uk

Ray Robinson

ELECTRICITY

PICADOR

First published 2006 by Picador

First published in paperback 2006 by Picador

This edition published 2007 by Picador
an imprint of Pan Macmillan Ltd
Pan Macmillan, 20 New Wharf Road, London N1 9RR
Basingstoke and Oxford
Associated companies throughout the world
www.panmacmillan.com

ISBN 978-0-330-44069-1

Copyright © Ray Robinson 2006

The right of Ray Robinson to be identified as the
author of this work has been asserted by him in accordance
with the Copyright, Designs and Patents Act 1988.

The acknowledgements on page 334 constitute an extension of
this copyright page.

3 5 7 9 8 6 4 2

A CIP catalogue record for this book is available from
the British Library.

Printed and bound in Great Britain by
Mackays of Chatham plc, Chatham, Kent

Visit **www.panmacmillan.com** to read more about all our books
and to buy them. You will also find features, author interviews and
news of any author events, and you can sign up for e-newsletters
so that you're always first to hear about our new releases.

for

CHARLIE ROBINSON
1918–1998

and

BELLA ROBINSON
1910–2005

Confusion in her eyes that says it all,
She's lost control.
And she's clinging to the nearest passer by,
She's lost control.
And she gave away the secrets of her past,
And said I've lost control again.
And a voice that told her when and where to act,
She said I've lost control again.

'She's Lost Control', Joy Division

*and their hairs stand on end to a shimmer of leaves
or the movement of clouds, and the way that the tense
has been thrown like a switch, where the land turns
to dreams*

'Electricity', Paul Farley

ERRRRmmmmg

MMMMMMg
mmmmm greeeee heeeeey aaaaa
NEEEEE MMMMMMgreegreegree gree heeeeeeeey
aaaaa ERRRGH ERRRGH hernyerrrGGGHHH
hergh HERRR hergh mmmmm
greeeheeeee yaaaaa
NEEEEE MMMMMM greegreegree gree
heeeeeyaaaaa ERRRGHERRRGH
MMMMMg ERRRR mmmmg
mmmmm greeeee heeeeey aaaaa NEEEEEEE
MMMMM gree gree gree gree
heeeeeeeey aaaaa ERRRGHERRRGH
hernyerrrGGGHHH hergh HERRR
hergh mmmmmgreeeee
heeeee yaaaaa NEEEEE MMMMM gree
greegree heeeeyaaaaa ERRRGH ERRRGH
MMMMMg ERRRR mmmmg
mmmm greeeee heeeeey aaaaa NEEEEE
MMMMMMgreegreegree gree heeeeeeeey
aaaaa ERRRGH ERRRGH hernyerrrGGG
HHH hergh HERRR hergh mmmmm
greeeeheeeee
greeeeheeeee yaaaaa NEEEEE
greegree gree
gree ERRRR
MMMMMg aaaaa NEEEEE
greeeee heeeey
MMMMMgreegree gree gree
heeeeeeeey aaaaa ERRRGH ERRRGH hernyerrr
GGGHHH hergh HERRR hergh mmmm-
mmgreeeheeeee yaaaaa NEEEEEEE
MMM greegreegree gree heeeeeyaaaaa
ERRRGHERRRGH mmmmg mmmmmmm

ERRRRmmmmg
MMMMMg
mmmmm greeee heeeeey aaaaa
NEEEEE MMMMMgreegreegree gree heeeeeeey
aaaaa ERRRGH ERRRGH hernyerrrGGGHHH
hergh HERRR hergh mmmmm
greeeheeeee yaaaaa
NEEEEE MMMMM greegreegree gree
heeeeeyaaaa ERRRGHERRRGH
MMMMMg ERRRGH mmmg
mmmm greeee heeeeey aaaaa NEEEEEEE
MMMMM gree gree gree gree
heeeeeeey aaaaa ERRRGH ERRRGH
hernyerrGGGHHH hergh HERRR
mmmmmgreeee
heeeee yaaaaa NEEEEE MMMMM gree
greegree heeeeyaaaa ERRRGH ERRRGH
MMMMMg ERRRR mmmmg
mmmm greeee heeeeey aaaaa NEEEEE
MMMMMgreegreegree gree heeeeeeey
aaaaa ERRRGH ERRRGH hernyerrGGG
HHH hergh HERRR hergh mmmmm
greeeeheeee NEEEEE
yaaaaa gree
gree greegree gree
heeeeeyaaaa ERRRGHERRRGH
MMMMMg ERRRR mmmmg mmmmm
greeee heeeeey NEEEEE
MMMMMgreegree gree gree
heeeeeeey aaaaa ERRRGH ERRRGH hernyerrr
GGGHHH hergh HERRR hergh mmm-
mmgreeeeheeeee yaaaaa NEEEEEEEE
MMM greegreegree gree heeeeeyaaaaa
ERRRGH ERRRGH mmmmg mmmmmm

and here's the breath
here's the breeze
here's the shimmer

I grab on to the side, fingernails scratch-scratching the wood.
— Sorry?
She looks at me and we smile and the bolt, it snaps my hand away like fire and the planet tilts, burnt wind blowing around inside me, skin suck-sucking the dust in and the crackles, the coughing . . .
They're here again.
Shadows moving all around me, breathing static breath, smell them in the buzzing as they sliiiiiide their long fingers in, tickling the switch and the colours, the sweet colours are here
wrapping their arms around me like they love me

ERRRRmmmmg

MMMMMMg
mmmmm greeeee heeeeey aaaaa
NEEEEE MMMMMgreegreegree gree heeeeeeeey
aaaaa ERRRGH ERRRGH hernyerrrGGGHHH
hergh HERRR hergh mmmmmm
greeeeeheeeee yaaaaa
NEEEEE MMMMMM greegreegree gree
heeeeeyaaaa ERRRGH ERRRGH
MMMMMg ERRRR mmmmg
mmmmm greeeee heeeeey aaaaa NEEEEEEE
MMMMMM gree gree gree gree
heeeeeeey aaaaa ERRRGHERRRGH
hernyerrrGGGHHH hergh HERRR
mmmmmmgreeeeee
heeeee yaaaaa NEEEEE MMMMMM gree
greegree heeeeyaaaaa NEEEEE MMMMMM gree
MMMMMMg ERRRR mmmmg
mmmm greeeee heeeeey aaaaa NEEEEE
MMMMMMgreegreegree gree heeeeeeeey
aaaaa ERRRGH ERRRGH hernyerrrGGG
HHH hergh HERRR hergh mmmmmm
greeeeeheeeee
gree yaaaaa NEEEEE
greegree gree gree
MMMMg heeeeyaaaaa ERRRGHERRRGH
greeeee heeeey ERRRR mmmmg mmmmm
MMMMMMgreegree gree gree
heeeeeeeey aaaaa ERRRGH ERRRGH hernyerrr
GGGHHH hergh HERRR hergh mmmm-
mmgreeeeheeeee yaaaaa NEEEEEEEE
MMM greegreegree gree heeeeeyaaaaaa
ERRRGH ERRRGH mmmmg mmmmmmmm

ERRRRmmmmg
MMMMMg
mmmmm greeeee heeeeey aaaaa
NEEEEE MMMMMgreegreegree gree heeeeeeey
aaaaa ERRRGH ERRRGH hernyerrrGGGHHH
hergh HERRR hergh mmmmm
greee heeeee yaaaaa
NEEEEE MMMMM greegreegree gree
heegreeyaaaa ERRRGHERRRGH
MMMMMg ERRRR mmmmg
NEEEEEEE
mmmmm greeeee heeeeey aaaaa
MMMMM gree gree gree gree
heeeeeeeey aaaaa ERRRGHERRRGH
hernyerrrGGGHHH hergh HERRR
heeeee yaaaaa NEEEEE MMMMM
mmmmmmgreeeee
greegree heeeeyaaaaa ERRRGH ERRRGH
MMMMMg ERRRR mmmmg
mmmmm greeeee heeeeey aaaaa NEEEEE
MMMMMgreegreegree gree heeeeeeeey
aaaaa ERRRGH ERRRGH hernyerrrGGG
HHH hergh HERRR hergh mmmmm
greeeeeheeeee
yaaaaa NEEEEE
greegreegree gree
gree
MMMMMg ERRRR mmmmg mmmmm
greeeee heeeeey aaaaa NEEEEE
MMMMM greegreegree gree gree
heeeeeeeey aaaaa ERRRGHERRRGH hernyerrr
GGGHHH hergh HERRR hergh mmm-
mmgreeeeheeeee yaaaaa NEEEEEEEE
MMM greegreegree gree heeeeeyaaaaa
ERRRGHERRRGH mmmmg mmmmmmm

26

I was thirty years old when they came to take me away again.

Sat in my booth having A Blank One, the din from the machines just getting too much and smothering me. Pulses and bleeps, whirrs and chug-chugs of slots spewing coins, the rat-a-tat-tats of guns and those lasers zapping away. Sounds sinking down the plugholes of my ears, making my eyes wander the signs on the walls:

UNDER 16S NOT ALLOWED IN WITHOUT AN ADULT

TAKE A SEAT, REST, PLAY BINGO!

CHECK IN, CASH OUT!

JACKPOT £50 FULL HOUSE FORTNIGHTLY

THESE MACHINES PAY UP TO £25 CASH!

The letters swimming in and out of my eyes, making me dizzy-as.

And that's when I saw them: two uniforms. They headed to Jim's office and I thought: here to warn us about some gyppos on the make, something like that. But next thing I know Jim's come round the Derby machine and he's pointing right at me.

I put my head down, pretending to count coins.

They tapped on the door and stepped in. The police-woman went Lily? and it looked like my name tasted proper bad in her mouth. The cloud on her face – it said it all.

I nodded, wondering what the fuck I'd done. Then the policeman asked me to confirm my full name and birth date and address, nodding away like he knew them all along.

And then one of them said it,

— Your mother's ill.

Mother.

I felt my head drop.

Then my eyes went and my arms were all heavy down my sides.

— She's been rushed into hospital. She's in a critical condition.

A hand squeezing me.

— She asked for you.

I wanted to lie down, right there and then. I wanted to go to sleep. Wanted these bastards to go back out of that door and leave me the fuck alone. Come on. Yes come on. An arm through the crook of mine. Come on, Lily. I wanted to smash them away. Find somewhere small and dark to curl up and hide. Never come out again. But something inside said you just couldn't.

They had me again.

I watched my trainers through the blur of my lashes. Moving out of the booth, over the carpet, over the pavement, into the car.

Sirens blared away like I was some kind of murderer.

— Do you really need to do that?

The policewoman turned around.

— We need to get there as soon as we can, I'm afraid. We did the full length of the promenade and I felt on show, people turning and staring. An old couple and some kids on bikes outside the chippy – their eyes on mine in the back seat. Their heads moved together, slow, and I wondered what they saw as I gawped back.

I curled up on the back seat and watched the upside-down sky outside the window. It was all murk up there, like dirty dishwater and the clouds were suds. I pictured my hands going into the water and felt cold, felt wet inside.

Because I knew where we were headed.

Over the moors. Along the same road that I'd come on when I was eleven years old. Brought to the care home down near the cliff-edge. Locked up until they could decide what to do with me. Taken away from her, from him, from that house. I remember my heart was hot with never wanting to see them again. The heat went from my chest to my body and I felt the warmth of myself because they were out of my life.

But that journey was in front of me now. I was going back in time.

A couple of hours of hills and cows and drystone fucking walls. The hills making me feel hemmed in. Like brackets in a sentence, but I couldn't find any words to put between them. And I knew I had to. Words that would make sense of the why-am-I-here?

I asked it when I was eleven and I was asking it now.

A couple of hours, then we'd start dropping down those steep roads and into the vale. And those places would be out there. The places that I dream about, though I don't want to dream about.

I hugged my legs. My lungs were folding over into themselves, tucking and pleating. I struggled to breathe. A rattling noise in the back of my throat. I took a quick look out: sheep with shitty arses staring at me, their eyes slitty and yellow like devils.

I grabbed the back of the headrest. I didn't want it all to go in reverse.

I didn't want to be that girl again.

25

It had that same stink in there. TCP and Germolene. Underneath you could still smell piss and shit and puke. Bodies turning against themselves. The air warm as blood. Sounds ping-ponged off the walls, squeaky trainers and heels clackety-clacking on the shiny floor. The corridors were long and narrow, strip lights running down the middle of the ceiling. Plastic rectangles of white light. Men mainly, wandering about in their scratchy smocks. One with a piss-coloured bag on a tall stand, wheeling it along, doddering in his slippers – he gave me a dark look.

I'd been there a thousand times as a girl and I tried to trick myself that I couldn't remember any of it. But that smell did it. Flick-flickers of memories on the back of my eyelids. Those lights above, burning my staring eyes that I couldn't close – they were the white lines on the road as the ambulance sped. And the swish of the trolley rushing me down to Emergency – I could still feel it on my skin. Sometimes I was too far gone. I got used to coming round to the blue haze of nurses, to blood pooled in my throat.

The police took me into a darkish passageway. A young man was stood talking to a nurse. He looked away when he saw me, greasy black hair hiding a beardy face, scummy-as. But there was something about him. I watched his hands held in front of him, like he was praying. The police took the nurse into a room. The young man sidled off.

5

And stood on my own in that corridor, I tried to remember what she looked like. Hair long. Down-the-back long. And dark, very dark. Or was I remembering it wet? Or did she dye it? No, it was greying and she always wore it up. Piled high in a queer way that made people stare. A fifties or sixties hairdo. A Bet Lynch beehive. And her eyes were pale blue like the sky in summer, like a seagull's. But a sky that always said rain. I saw the storm clouds in the snarly skin around them.

I could remember curlers and platforms, bright-as-fuck headscarves, and that it was always raining, always raging in that house. But I couldn't remember my mother's face.

They reappeared, all slumped and sagged, moving towards me with that look that says I'm sorry. I watched their mouths open and close. The nurse took my arm and led me down the corridor. We stopped beside a door.

— I'll be just out here if you need me.

I stepped in.

The walls were orange from daylight coming through the yellowy curtains. In the corner of the room was a table on wheels. And – yes – a shape beneath the bedsheets.

They said there was something wrong with her insides. She'd had cancer for years and they'd removed most of her guts. She'd a bag thing on her side but she hadn't passed anything for three weeks and hadn't told anyone. What they meant was that her body had filled with shit and killed her.

Shat her insides to death.

A red plastic chair and a locker next to the bed. There was no name, nothing in the room to say that this lump under the sheets was her. I walked over to the locker and opened the drawer. The letters on the cover were cold on my fingers. Holy Bible. Some queer smell hung in the room.

Sweet, like gone-off fruit. I was trying not to think that it was her making the smell. I moved to her side and sat on the chair.

And then I did it.

The white hair. The shrunk, sunken face. She looked newborn. Her skin was almost see-through. The veins beneath a bluish colour, stuck up like tree roots around her neck and forehead. Like dying had been some massive struggle. Her fingers were a tangerine colour. Years of cigarettes. They were spread out on the bedsheet like she was drying her nails. One of them was chipped and there was something disgusting about it: bright red nail varnish on your deathbed. I looked at her and imagined her getting cold. Going hard.

Then I got this image of her in my head, from when I was a kid: she's vexed and I'm trying not to look at her eyes, so I look at the cigarette dangling from the corner of her lipsticked gob. The red end dances about as she speaks. The grey ash is getting longer – I'm waiting for it to drop off. She grabs my face, her hands cold slabs of meat. She pinches my face and a nail slices in and I try not to scream. Her words loop clear inside my head: ARE YOU FUCKING LISTENING TO ME YOU LITTLE FUCKING BITCH?

I stood, and leaned over her.

I felt my arm go up, high above my head, and heard the loud crack as I brought my palm down, hard, on the side of my dead mother's face.

The skin on her cheek moved slowly back. Like mud. And I swear that she smiled. An itty-bitty little smile like she was saying ha-fucking-ha you're too fucking late.

I left the room, the corridor, the hospital. I was in the outside world that didn't look any different but *should*

7

have. I felt a tingle of warmth on my skin and tilted my face up to the bright patch in the sky. The heat on my face and in my heart again and I smiled for the first time that day because she was dead.

And I was safe.

24

I got the coppers to drop me off at the phone box outside the Clarendon. I thought fuck work – Jim'll think I'm in mourning or something anyway. I took the crumpled bus ticket out of my purse, the ticket with Ridge Racer's number written on. He answered and I said he had to meet me, now or never and he said yes with surprise.

I put Blondie on loud and danced around my bedroom. I chose my push-up bra and some low-deniers. Then the Clarins face tint and Rimmel eyeliner and Revlon lippy that I got cheap off the market, and that posh smelly I only ever wore for special occasions – not that often. I pulled out my black shoes without the heels and my brand spanking new dress. I'd felt saucy when I bought it because I knew how nice it'd look. I imagined men's roving sex-eyes and I liked the feeling it gave me. I haggled the guy on the stall down to fifteen quid. He said he wished he could see it on and I went in your dreams mister. It was short and hugged me in all the right places, showed off my legs. I have great legs. They make up for what I lack in the boob department.

I necked my two evening pills ☻☻ early.

It's what I measure my days by. Six a day. Two in the morning, two in the afternoon, two at night. You can't miss them. Like full stops and my days are three sentences. Awake, two pills, two pills, two pills, asleep.

You just hope life happens in between.

I brushed my hair so many times that it popped with static. I looked electrified with the heat inside me. It made me look even taller than my six foot. I could feel my frizz bobbing soft on my shoulders as I took long-legged strides along the seafront. I had the surprise of a thrill-knot dancing around my belly, and the beam across my face was on full power. The dress felt like something explosive hidden under my coat. I couldn't remember a time when I'd felt better, more alive.

So there was Ridge Racer, waiting for me at Davy Jones Locker, and I was nervous-as. He'd asked me out the week before. He came up to the booth and handed me a fiver.

— Twenties and tens, please. What's your name? You want to go out sometime?

I started laughing and he scratched his head.

— Lily. My name's Lily.

Then he stood staring and went well?

I think I said something like I'm a very busy girl, you better give me your number. I pressed the levers and he scooped out the coins.

— I've got the top three now.

And he strutted off, proud as a dog with two cocks.

When he left, he dropped a piece of paper into the coin tray. He winked at me and smiled from the door. He looked proper made up.

I started marching fast, wishing some of the people inspecting the fresh air and gobbing like goldfish would just move. Hey you, hippopotamus arse, MOVE IT. Couldn't they see I was late, got a date with Ridge Racer?

And though I'd been back heeling it to the rear of my thoughts, it began.

Soft pounding.

Sparks.

Zigzaggedy lines.

Tiny fucking insects crawling in my arms.

Of all the times.

I stared down the street, through the blur of heads towards the sea. I smelt the chips and vinegar from Maggie's Plaice. I saw the band of puke-green sea with mucky seagulls dive-bombing. Heeling it back. Wishing.

No way.

And in my new bloody dress.

Sometimes it's the lights.

The world speeds up and you need to grab on to something like you've forgotten what gravity is. The Earth jumps away from you and you panic panic panic like fuck. You'll find somewhere to sit and take hold of someone's arm, pull at their hair, snatch the child's doll away and chew its face off, all the time screaming mmmmmgreeeee-heeeeeyaaaaaNEEEEE then panting like you're squeezing a baby elephant out of your fanny, and they don't know whether to run, cry, hide or shite themselves. Wondering if you're having a heart attack, having a baby. Wondering if you're just the latest Care in the Community fruit-loop. Your nails digging into the wooden bench, knuckles scraping the concrete steps until they bleed.

Sometimes God shouts BOO into your soul, his breath knocks you to the floor.

Sometimes it's like warm trickles running from your feet up to your head.

Sometimes people make no sense, you watch their mouths moving but all you hear is oooo eeee aaaaa.

Sometimes your jaw judders, opens and closes like a fish and your tongue's a lump of gristle in your gob that you can't chew.

Sometimes there's no feeling at all
just wham bam, inhale, and dark electricity.

I spotted a bench over by the fountain. A flat-capped old bloke was sitting there with his dog. He smiled when I sat down, trying to control the breathing, getting that kind of sick feeling, like you're going to puke and it doesn't matter what position you sit in the green waves come flooding over you.

I put my hands under my bum and bit my lips.

I could feel it sizzling away in my head. Static on a record. Egg being fried in a distant kitchen. Jesus it was coming. A strong one. And I knew: soon I'd be down on the concrete, legs and arms shaking, eyes rolling, tongue lolling about while Ridge Racer nursed his pint and watched the door. I checked the ground for dog shite – I didn't want to ruin the dress more than I had to. I wrapped my hands over my mouth.

MMMMMg   ERRRRmmmmg

They say I have the strength of ten men when fitting. How many women is that? It's just one of the stupid things the bright sparks say. Like: I'm afraid you'll be on these pills *indefinitely*. That's one of their favourites. And it makes me laugh how they always end with an *I'm afraid* like they really fucking care. And so I say you mean until I peg it? Then they try to baffle me out of the office with their big words. But I'm smarter than they give me credit. I've spent all my fucking life listening to them going on at me, all my life reminding me, as if I'd forget. For your own safety – how many times have I heard that? I can make people laugh and look away and cry though. But I don't blame them. It must look awful. The kids in the care home loved it. I'd come round and they would be leaning over me, chanting and stabbing their fingers.

Chucking an epi. Epi epi epi epi.

The bright sparks scanned my head when I was a bairn. I've got this large lump, just above my left ear. It's where Mam chucked me down the stairs when I was just a baby. Because I wouldn't stop crying. She wasn't bothered about admitting it. And that's when my fits started.

The bright sparks call it my epileptic focus.

And seven or eight I was, when they came up with this daft idea that they should somehow try and *pull me out* of the fit, because of the way my arms lock under my chin. They thought that by pulling my arms apart, I'd be cured. They haven't got a fucking clue. Not really. None of them have. And I could remember that when I started my squealing, all of a sudden there'd be Mam and whoever else was at hand, their arms open, ready to try and *pull me out*. But they never did. And they gave up after the day I chucked about fifty, one after the other, and they had to call an ambulance.

FIT-TASTIC SPASTIC. That's what the kids in the care home called me.

mmmmmgreeeeeheeeeeyaaaaaNEEEEE

The old man was fretting. He probably wanted to say something, if he could only find the words. But there aren't any. No magic spells. Head spinning backwards, I grabbed his jacket and pulled him into me, still looking straight ahead, staring at the fountain and the patterns the water was making. They reminded me of something – headlights, dancing across my bedroom ceiling at night. Cars driving down the seafront. They were like little explosions that left stars behind.

I wasn't imagining things.

A hundred tiny glow-in-the-dark stars on my ceiling. A Christmas present sent to me by a pen pal in Australia years ago. The care home set me up with him. His letters were the most exciting things in my life. It meant there was more out there than just the seafront and arcades and fish and chips wrapped in greasy newspaper. So on my bedroom ceiling, I marked out the shape I knew best of all, off by heart: the seven stars of the Big Dipper. That's my favourite. I even tried to colour one of them in with a red felt pen, because it said in my *Night Sky* book that it was a red dwarf.

The boy wrote to me that he'd never seen the Big Dipper. He said things were different down there. They had a constellation called the Southern Cross. I thought it sounded fantastic – an enormous cross floating in the black sky. He also wrote that the shadow went across the moon the other way and that everything was upside down and back to front. One time, I tried to write to him standing on my head.

I looked at the stars at night until I fell asleep. They swam my dreams like water snakes.

Forever staring at lights hanging from the ceiling. In the supermarket, the kitchen, the living room, the class-room, the change booth at work. Being wheeled on a trolley through hospital corridors, lights flashing, whirring past like on the machines in the arcade. The weight, the pressure, the buzz. Electricity passing through my body as if I'm trying to shit through my skin, my pores, shit all the bad stuff out.

MMMMMgreegreegree gree heeeeeyaaaaa ERRRGH ERRRGH

For a second I thought it was passing. A false alarm. It happens sometimes. A little lull. A stillness. I turned to see his old face mumbling and I tried to smile, to nod back, but it must have looked terrible. My brain felt lopsided. I started squeezing the thickness of his jacket and closed my eyes. I knew I was doing the squealing thing and that it was going to start speeding up soon. Then I heard that fucking noise: nee-naw of sirens, getting closer. They're the worst, fingers twitching on those buttons and you always feel like slapping them afterwards. JUST HANG ON A FUCKING SEC you want to shout. But of course you can't, your tongue fills your mouth. Then the paramedics give you such grief when you walk away, telling them to leave you the fuck alone, the crowd around you inter-fering and all you want is to be invisible, to get home. To get washed and changed into some dry knickers and skirt.

I knew that if I could just get my breathing sorted, it just might go, just might pass.

hernyerrrGGGHHH hergh HERRR hergh

I once threw one and fell into the fire. I was about to get my tea. I was walking across the living room over the rug next to the fireplace. Next to Don's chair, where he'd always be perched in front of the telly, the remote in one hand and a beer in the other.

Don. Mam's man.

He just stared. Sat there and stared as if he hadn't seen it before. My legs buckled and I fell. The burning of shirt and skin. The stench of burnedness. Pain bigger than pain so you can't feel it. My back melting and blood filling my mouth with its rust taste. It seemed to take him weeks to get out of his chair. He grabbed my arms and pulled me onto the hearthrug, struggling to turn me over.

I can still see the look in his eyes: he wanted me to burn.

ERRRGH ERRRGH

Four smooth scars, weaving across the bottom of my back. Don said they were like worms wriggling down into my arse, trying to get back into their hole. He thought it was hilarious; I almost puked. My body is covered with silver flecks, rips of scars. I have a long way to fall and I fall a lot.

mmmmmgreeeeeheeeeeyaaaaaNEEEEE

It was coming. Such strong motion. I squeezed somewhere deep inside. Told it to go away. The old man and some others had their hands on me. Dog spinning in circles, barking, howling away. A moonfaced woman above me was blowing bubbles fretting OH LOVE WHAT IS IT LOVE? and I knew.

I knew that soon I'd be down there, lying in a puddle of piss and sweat.

ERRRGH ERRRGH

People will be stood over me, faces looming out of the dark after-fuzz, not knowing what the fuck to do. The old man pulling the dog off from licking me. And I'm like if I don't piss myself, then maybe Ridge Racer won't mind me being late. Maybe he's late too. Or maybe I can rush home and change anyway, or just stick my knickers in my bag. Dry the back of my skirt under the blow-dryer in the ladies, spray some perfume on, right as rain.

I'm like use your head Lily – use your frazzled fucking head.

MMMMMgreegreegree gree

I stood up, took my jacket off, and laid it on the ground. I got down onto my knees and rolled onto my back.

heeeeeyaaaaa ERRRGH ERRRGH

I would wait for the fit to come. For my spirit to rip itself out of me and send me back to that moment when I couldn't walk but I could fly. Soaring down the stairs towards the bottom step. I would wait for that moment when I flap my elbows like stiff jaggy wings and that breeze of quietness and gorgeousness comes over me. And it was then, just before the blackness, that I saw the image of Mam behind a stack of tins in the supermarket, hiding from her little fucking embarrassment

PICK YOURSELF UP, YOU HEAR ME, PICK YOURSELF

23

I never made it to the Locker. Some bastard called an ambulance and I came through in the back of it. The paramedics knew me; they knew what to expect. They parked the meat wagon up in front of the flat and looked after me until I could speak. The woman, Sandra, she gave me a green blanket to wrap around myself. I'd made a right mess. She helped me up into the flat and said she'd help clean me up if I wanted. Then I didn't know who she was. I saw the writing on my walls and knew not to be rude and asked her to leave. I stuck the plastic shower thing on the taps, crouched down in the bathtub, and got cleaned.

Thrash, get up, get on with it. That's what I say.

I slept right through until the next morning. Nearly twenty hours of sleep, thin as paper. Felt like ten minutes. Because what follows is a slump. Like you've been wrung out. You feel at fault, empty. You can't look at yourself in the mirror, to see the bruises and cuts and scabs. You disgust yourself. You get this lump in your guts like you've killed someone. It can last an hour or it can last a week, but you can't escape it.

I flung the bedroom window open and rubbed my gammy eyes. Children were playing down on the beach. They made sharp sounds that hurt. Yellow light-shapes smoothed along the walls, onto the carpet. I passed through one of them and it caught my skin all warm. It made me sink even further. I wanted to be outside, out there on the cold wet sands, running with the kids and screaming my fucking head off. Looking for a target to hit. Looking for something to dig my nails and teeth into.

I wrote it all down in my Headache Book. I wrote the same thing three times but it didn't make me feel any better. I wrote it in different coloured inks. Blue and green and red. Nothing. I drew a picture of my face and I was like a giant with the children in my mouth and I was eating them all up. The little fuckers kept on screaming.

The doorbell buzzed. I went to the window and looked down and saw the thick rug of Al's wig. I put my mouth into the gap of the window and shouted down. The distant click, his slow thuddy steps coming up. He tapped on the door three times and came in with a hiya love, all out of breath.

Al owned the flat and Mr Santa, the shop downstairs – a proper grotto of cheap tat. Footballs, beach balls, plastic buckets and spades, blow windmills, chamois leathers, dishcloths, tea towels, value kitchen and toilet rolls, hula-hoops, plastic Union Jack flags, butterfly nets and tennis rackets, you name it. It hurt your eyes if you were in there too long.

It was a weekday so he was wearing his Business Wig – a sort of brown side flick that was too short at the back. He must've thought it looked sensible, but it always looked back-to-front to me. It was his best by miles though. The others were his Pulling Wig – a shiny black mullet that made him look sleazy-as – and his Party Wig – a silvery quiff that he always wore to the karaoke at the Clarendon every Thursday. He was the winner of the past three years' Grand Karaoke Competition. Three hundred and fifty quid he got each time. He always won with 'Love Me Tender'. He called it his pièce de resistance.

— Hiya, Al.

He stepped towards me, pulling out a small bunch of yellow flowers from behind his back. I looked down into his large Labrador's eyes, pooling up.

— Sorry to hear about your loss, love. Jim told us.

The flowers still had their Asda cellophane on. The thought of him trudging all the way to the other side of town to buy me them – I got that tingle at the tip of my nose. He told me one time: you're the nearest thing I've ever had to a daughter. I took the flowers into the kitchen and tried to keep the tears down.

I was eighteen when I first moved into that flat. The home set me up with it. The other part of the deal was a job in the supermarket. I remember I turned up that first day at daft o'clock in the morning, but when I saw the naff uniform, I told them to stick it. Besides, my funny-looking new landlord, Al, said he knew of a job going in the arcade, calling the bingo numbers out. He said I could wear what I liked in there. I said I'm good at numbers and he was like you'll make a good call girl. It sounded proper glamorous.

So I put the flowers in the sink, thinking what could I say? I heard him go you're a tidy bugger. I knew what he was looking at: the graffiti on the walls, the tiny pillows on the corners of everything. He never asked. Never said anything. Just gawped and looked confused. It was just another way I coped. Notes to myself. No sharp corners. Notes about my tablets and how to make food the safest way. What I should and shouldn't eat. Sounds stupid. I started doing it soon as I moved in. Had no one to remind me what to do any more. And the words – they made me feel safe, that's all. The biggest was the one I'd written with a black marker pen. It was on the wall facing you when you came in. I wrote it there because sometimes I forget who I am or where I am. I forget where I live.

DON'T WORRY HOME BED SLEEP BE OK LOVE LILY
I'd even put some kisses to myself X X X
Sometimes these things are a comfort.

I went back in and he touched my arm and looked up into my eyes.

— You ever need anything, I'm here lass. Don't be afraid to ask. I'm just downstairs. It breaks my heart to think of you upset.

I leaned down and squeezed him tight and said cheers mate. He smelt like a damp cloth. He goes anything, OK. Anytime. Day or night. Your old mate Al is all ears.

— See this?

He pointed at his shoulder.

— It's yours to cry on.

He opened the door, waved his hand, and disappeared down the stairs.

❧❧

I stayed in the flat for a few more days. The only time I got up was to go to the toilet. Mind you, it wasn't just the fit – I knew if I shut the world out, well, nothing could go wrong, could it. No more fucking surprises, I mean. So I hid. I was good at it. I ignored the front door, Al and Jim's shouts through the letter box. I drew the curtains and left the television on day and night. I ate nothing but jam on toast. Drank nothing but water to wash down my pills. I knew the adverts word for word.

I had thoughts, bad thoughts, they swirled around my room and I saw her again, sitting in the corner of my bedroom. I closed my eyes and put my face into my pillow, but I couldn't do it for long because I knew she was there and I had to look at her. I had to ask her to leave.

It was me. I'd come to visit myself again.

Sitting on the chair, swinging her legs. Her hair full of cotters. Hissing and dirty. I could see her scabbed knees. She picked at them and put the salty flakes into her mouth and chewed on them. She laughed because she knew it was dirty.

I knew that it was dirty.

She was wearing that skirt, the one that stank. Mam refused to wash it more than once a week. Said it would teach me to go pissing myself. They gave me my own chair at school, a grey plastic one with my name written on in black pen. They made me sit at the back, near the door, I stank that much. That'll fucking learn you.

I called out my name: Lily.

I whispered it: Lily Jane.

She didn't answer. She swung her legs and hummed a rhyme. It was the one Nana used to sing to me. My head against her large breasts, her Geordie accent – I hear it deep through her chest as she sings. Violet scent up near her neck and old hands covered in flour. Lily Jane, tall as a crane . . .

I got up and opened the curtains. Winter. The weather does something to you. It's the boredom. It's like the town's waiting. You can see it in the boarded-up shopfronts. Only the Golden Nugget was alive for the locals, neon flashing away like it was Vegas or something. And next door, the Sunshine Express Café. The sign outside said Jugs Of Tea For Ninety-Nine Pee. Inside the people smoked and smoked, supping the stewed tea that looked like ah Bisto.

The clouds above the sea were like brains. Lumpy grey brains with migraines.

I got back into bed and sleep came soft, and heavy, and dreamless.

It was the best cure. The only cure.

22

I was in the booth and I got that feeling: eyes on me. I looked up and he was stood there, staring at me with that smile of his. I copied it. I got off my stool and locked the door behind me.

It was the man I'd seen in the hospital corridor the week before, the one talking to the nurse. I'd told myself off every time I'd thought about it – don't be so fucking stupid. Couldn't have been.

— You're looking well.

He looked chuffed and said cheers.

And there we were, brother and sister. Face to face for the first time in twenty years. I wanted to throw my arms around him.

— You weren't at the funeral.

It took my breath away, the look on his face.

Jim wasn't in his office. I grabbed Barry's arm and dragged him in. It stank of whisky and sweaty balls in there. I turned off the radio and asked Barry to sit down. He looked miserable and cold. I leaned against the back of the door and we stared at each other. I can't tell you how I felt. The sole of his shoe was hanging off. It lolloped like a dog's tongue.

— How are you, then?

He just shrugged.

— Where you living now?

— Why weren't you there, Lily?

— I've got a flat just down the way, above Mr Santa's.

He rubbed the back of his hand across his mouth, muttered something. It dawned on me that he might be homeless. I reached over and flicked the kettle on.

— You thirsty? You eaten?

He cottoned on.

— I've a flat. At Paradise.

— You mean you live in town?

I felt myself sag. Paradise Mansions. So fucking ugly they hurt your eyes.

Barry just nodded.

— You mean you've lived in town all this time?

— I've been wanting to talk to you for years, Lily.

That's when I saw it: flickers. His eyes. I remembered him crying, yelling his heart out. He was always bawling. Always a crybaby.

— Years?

— Before you started work here. I used to see you now and then. Used to see you on the beach in summer. All the time. You drink at the Locker.

I wanted to hug him. I wanted to punch him for not talking to me back then.

— You used to dye your hair jet-black. One time you had it shaved at the sides and dyed red. You used to wear these funny booty things with fur on the tops.

I ran my fingers through my hair.

— Fucking hell.

— You were probably too young to remember. I wanted to talk to you, course I fucking did. But I was worried I'd scare you. You were just a bairn when we got took away. I thought you'd be better off without.

He looked at his grubby fingers. Little kiddie eyes set into an old beardy face – it didn't look right. Wrapped up in a greasy parka and masses of long curly hair dangling around his shoulders in coils you could've fried chips in. Tall as me but chubby with it, and his eyes – like mine. Almost see-through blue, like a seagull's. Squat and round-as. A face that looked like it'd never frowned. Happy as a pig in shit. I wanted to kiss him. My thoughts turned to the *we* he just said. We. He looked at me waiting, so I told him.

— I'm never going back to that place ever again. I'm sorry.

He said really quietly: it's OK.

The kettle rattled to the boil.

— Was our Mikey at the funeral?

It sounded so everyday, so plain and easy. Like the years we'd spent apart, like they were nothing, didn't even exist, had never happened. We were back in that house, the three of us living there.

Barry's eyes drilled into mine.

— No. He wasn't. No one's seen hide nor hair of him for years.

— He in trouble?

— You don't know, do you?

— Know what?

— What happened?

— *What* happened?

— You don't know?

— Jesus.

Like pulling teeth. Barry said Mikey had done well for himself. He used to own a place just down the coast, a reptile house.

— Lizards and snakes and stuff. It was crazy.

He said Mikey considered himself to be something of a Tarzan character. Barry said he used to parade around the place in a leopard-skin loincloth, all muscle and fake tan and a made-up accent, twenty-foot snakes around his shoulders.

And I got this memory of him, of our Mikey breeding mice when he was a kid. The shed full of wire cages, the stuffy stench of them breeding out of control because he couldn't sell them to the kids at school fast enough. Mam let them all go in a barn somewhere. So she said. But she didn't ask Mikey, she just did it. He went fucking ape. Smashed up his room and ran away.

And there was Mikey, run away, and Mam acting like she couldn't care less. But she paced the rooms at night, staring out the windows. I was only young, but I remember him being away. It was a strong feeling, missing him, him not being there to look after me. I used to sit up at night and peek out of the bedroom curtains, looking for him in the garden. I was going to sneak him sandwiches and biscuits and pop. I had it all planned. But he just reappeared one night when we were having tea. Like nothing had happened. Just came in and sat down at the kitchen table and got stuck into some bread and butter. Mam said I knew you'd be home when you were hungry. Later on, she beat him black and blue. But he fought back, cut her lip, and I think that was the last time she hit him. Too big for a good hiding. And things changed after that. He'd stand between us, give her a look, curl his hands into fists.

He protected me. He didn't have to say a word.

I went over to the kettle and put my hands around its warmness. I tried to take it all in. Barry's cheeks were flushed and he kept sniffing. I felt bad. Guilty. I wanted to ask him so many things, but fucking Jim goes and knocks on the glass and steps in. I said Jim, this is Barry my brother, and Jim sniggered like yeah right. I told Barry I better be getting back to work and he looked worried. I went,

— Meet me later at the Locker?

— I can't. I'm off back home.

— Oh.

He opened his mouth but nothing came. I noticed how brown his teeth were.

— Tomorrow, then? Eightish?

— Sure. There's stuff we need to sort out. I need to know you're OK with me sorting it, you know. Taking responsibility and that.

I didn't know what he was on about.

— Mam's stuff.

— You can do what you like with it. Burn the fucking lot for all I care.

He gave me a look and turned away. I watched him shuffle out of the arcade.

My brothers. I can't tell you how many times I'd wished them back into my life.

I went and sat back in the booth and cried like something had broke. I had to put my mouth over my sleeve to stop the noise. It felt like black stuff coming out of me. I spat on the floor and rubbed it in with my foot.

Then I just felt empty.

⊘⊘⊘⊘

The raised voices in the Indian next door, that's what usually woke me, middle of the night. The sounds and that stink in my room. Heavy smell of doner and shish and tikka and kofte and pakora and bhaji and samosas, chips and fucking garlic bread. The voices waking me at two or three every morning. Shouts, jeering. Sometimes they were fighting in the street outside. One week an ambulance came, a sixteen-year-old lass stabbed in the neck while I dozed.

But what woke me that night was the quiet.

I looked out the window at the snow falling down along the promenade and onto the beach. So thick everyone had been driven indoors. The dark sea disappeared into it. I sat in the chair next to the window and thought about Barry going back to Mam's house, stood in his old bedroom with his eyes closed, remembering.

Our house was disgusting. It stank of piss and fags and the wallpaper was coming off the walls. The carpet looked like vomit and was made up of scraps from other people's carpets off the estate, all threadbare and stained-as. The three-piece suite was a coffee-brown colour, worn out on the arms, springs gone. You could only sit one side of it. The walls were wood-chipped and painted lung-cancer yellow. Along the picture rail, she'd hung pictures of a gypsy boy crying and another of some dogs playing pool. I fucking hated those pictures. Most of the houses on the estate were the same. We're not proud, they all seemed to sing.

Why had he never spoken to me before? I knew they'd both been shipped off to borstal somewhere, but I'd thought it was miles away. He knew who I was and where I was. He knew that I probably wouldn't have recognized him.

I got into bed and watched the snow outside the window, so thick you couldn't tell whether it was going up or coming down.

I wanted to know what he was doing. I wanted to see inside his head.

I didn't know him at all.

⊘⊘⊘⊘

The snow had been replaced by slush and the front was dead apart from the screeches of gulls and pigeons cooing. Brian was down on the promenade. He was out with his shopping trolley again. Off-His-Trolley Brian. Full of loaves from God knows where. Someone he knew at Tesco's, maybe. I tapped his shoulder and it startled him.

— Jesus Aitch, it's you.

He had something like scrambled egg stuck in his beard. Pigeons clung and pecked at his arm. I looked at his missing fingers.

— Can I help, Brian?

— No-o. They'll have your face off.

I stood back and pigeons pestered my feet. He'd been doing this as long as I could remember. Brian lived somewhere on the edge of town. Al told me his house was condemned, that one of the walls had collapsed and there was a hole in another so big that you could see into his living room from the street outside. He slept on the floor and lived off cocoa. Bird Brain Brian, people called him.

— Do anything nice last weekend, Brian?

He tipped the rest of the bread on the ground and the birds attacked it. Brian moved backwards. He turned and peered up into my eyes.

— Went to York, I did.

— That's nice. Who with?

— Me own.

— Oh.

— There's a pub there, at the station like.

— So you travelled all the way to York, and you didn't even get out of the station? Sat on your own in the station pub getting pissed? You must have a woman there, Brian.

He looked hurt.

— No-o. Pints of Guinness for less than two quid? Worth the journey just for that.

He barged past me to get another loaf from his trolley and began ripping it into chunks. I left him to it.

Stuffy pubs in winter, I love them. A real fire burning somewhere, condensation running down the windows, shouts from folk sat near the gust of a door suddenly opened. When outside's all nippiness and soggy and you're all cosy inside and getting slowly pissed.

Barry turned up, an hour late but happy-as, and I remember thinking he looked smug. He ordered whiskies and knocked them back. He fidgeted and wouldn't let me buy a round. There was something that didn't make sense. I wanted him to tell me something that made sense.

He began talking about home, about how it had changed.

He said with the new motorway been built, wealthy folk from Newcastle and Leeds had moved in. This is what he was saying, like he was selling the place to me. Films had been made there. There'd been a transformation. Barry called it *an overhaul*. House prices had soared. When he used the word *alarmingly* his eyes got wide. He said he hardly recognized the place or the people. He said

32

that foreign movies were showing in the cinema. Galleries and stuff. Hippy shops. Organic food. Funny accents. Lesbians and snobs and crusties. I had to talk to myself in my head: look at him, smile, listen to the words.

I just wasn't interested.

But then he goes and tells me the story of a woman who used to live on our estate. She'd won the Lottery. His eyes got even bigger when he said the amount. Three and a half *million*. I'm thinking, Jesus he wants to rob her.

He downed his drink. He slapped the table and whooped. His mood changed; he called the woman a stupid inbred bitch over and over again.

— And do you know what she spent it on? Do you?

I shook my head.

— Nowt. Not a frigging thing. Still hasn't to this day. All she's bought is the fucking poxy show house off the new estate up near the high school. The *show* house. Like it's some big fucking deal. She hasn't even replaced the carpets or furniture. Bought it as it was. That means she bought *second-hand* carpets, Lily. The interest on her millions will be worth treble that fucking house already. Easy. Stupid bitch.

I said it as well: Stupid bitch.

— But this is the best: she *still* goes to fucking work every morning at six. Six days a week. Driving a fucking *taxi*.

He howled.

— Stupid cow.

Then he touched the back of my hand and looked into my eyes.

— We were really fucking poor, Lily. Do you know that? *Really* fucking poor.

33

He took his finger away.

— I know.

— I hated it. Hated free school meals and clothes from jumble sales.

I looked at his tattered shirt and wished he would touch me again.

— Rich fucking farm kids, looking at us like we were shit. Calling us the Scumtons. Pezzas. Gyppos. It fucking did me in. Me and Mikey did them all though, one by one. Slowly picked them off, good and proper.

He clenched his fist and rattled the ice cubes in the bottom of his glass.

I noticed it then, on the fleshy bit between his thumb and first finger. At first I thought it was just some ink mark, from a leaking pen or something. I waited for him to look away so I could have a good gawp.

He saw me and laid his hand out, fingers spread.

It was a tiny black spade from a deck of cards.

I wanted to touch it. He sniggered and pulled his hand away. It dawned on me then: there was more than just alcohol in him.

— It's nice, Barry.

— And what would you do, Lily? If you had money? Loads, I mean. You wouldn't buy a house with second-hand carpets?

He clasped my forearm with his fingers, squeezed.

— You wouldn't keep going to the fucking arcade every day? You could go to college. Buy that flat of yours. Get the fuck out of here. Live somewhere warm in the sun. Travel the fucking world.

— I don't know. I've never thought about it.

His eyes slitted.

34

— Just imagine it: thirty, forty grand. Maybe more.

— I can't. I've never imagined.

— Well, now you don't have to.

He wiped the table with his sleeve and put a large brown envelope down. He smiled that smug smile of his, winked, and went to the bar. I watched him talking to the barmaid and thought he's fucking crazy. I opened the envelope and took out the letter, the form. I read. Then I read it again. Then I read it again.

He sat back down and plonked the drinks on the table.

— Is this why you're back in my life? You want to sell the house?

— No to the first, yes to the second.

— But it's the council's, you can't.

— She bought it, years back.

— Bought it?

— Aye.

— But what about Don?

A dark look.

— What about him?

— Doesn't he have any say?

— Hasn't been on the scene for donkey's. Jesus, you haven't a clue, have you? He moved down to London years back. Works on the Tube or something, sad fuck. Anyway, they never got wed.

He lifted his glass and took a mouthful.

— The house is ours, Lily. She left no will. We're her next of kin.

I looked at the letter and the form. On the front it said HOW TO OBTAIN PROBATE. A GUIDE FOR THE APPLICANT ACTING WITHOUT A SOLICITOR.

Inside, Barry had coloured bits in with an orange high-lighter pen.

> three types of Grant of Representation

> *Letters of Administration*

> a grant will **always** be required to sell or transfer a property held in the deceased's sole name

He said he'd been doing his homework; I told him I could see that.

— So I just want to check, Lily. Check with you that it's OK. Me sorting it out. Selling the house. Paying her debts off. The funeral and stuff. It'll cost me a bit to start with, but it doesn't matter. It's all ours and I reckon she owes us.

I breathed through my sleeve and nodded yes. Then he was going on about an interview he had in Middlesbrough with a solicitor, and I could come if I wanted? I shook my head.

— I'll set up three accounts: one for me, one for you, and one for our Mikey.

A niggle of: I don't know you.

— I'll hold Mikey's share on trust for him.

I stared into his eyes and pointed my finger at his face,

— You fucking better. Don't touch a fucking penny of it. I don't like any of this. I know it's got to be done, but I'm not sure I want anything off that bitch.

He shrugged.

— Be like that.

— Anyway, how much we on about?

Something spread over his face.

— Well?

He opened his mouth and I could see the pinkness inside.

— I've been looking at other houses on the estate. One round the corner went for quite a bit.

— How much?

— One-twenty.

I let the numbers dance in my head.

— A *hundred* and twenty?

He nodded, licking his lips like the numbers tasted good.

— But it's a fucking shit-hole.

— One-twenty.

— It's a piss-stinking shack.

— I know.

— In a fucking arsehole town in the middle of nowhere.

He bit his top lip, chubby-chuckled. He leaned into me, his cheek on my shoulder.

— One hundred and twenty thousand.

———

I remember the moon outside that night, thin like an eyelid. It winked at me like there was some big fucking joke, and then the wind bit my face.

We got a taxi out to Paradise Mansions. Barry seemed to know everyone as we walked through the tower blocks. Mean-faced kids, all street and stagger. Seen too much of life too early. They all nodded to Barry with something like fear, and I thought: there's more to you than meets the eye.

And there was. His flat was proper massive, sparse.

Everything had hard edges and the light seemed brittle, like it'd snap.

You look at every surface.
You weigh up every corner.
And you think of your head *slamming* into it.

Everything was black and white and cream colours, like he'd been watching too many episodes of *House Doctor*. A gigantic hi-fi with tall stands stood in one corner, and two pictures of Elvis in a spangly white flared suit filled a wall.

I stood in front of the large window. Outside was a balcony and below the brown river and a courtyard all lit up. Rooftops like leaning tables, and in the distance the sea.

I went over to an old-fashioned chest of drawers, looking totally out of place against the brick. My trainers squeaked on the wooden floors. I picked up one of the framed photos that sat on top. A snapshot of Barry and a woman. She was suntanned and blonde and pretty in a magazine way. All the photos on the chest of drawers were in thick metal frames. And one took pride of place: a picture of three children.

Mikey was just a little bit taller than Barry. He had his arm around Barry's shoulder and Barry had his arms around the smaller me. Barry and Mikey wore the same T-shirt and I had a large white slide in my hair. It looked like we shared some kind of joke, like someone was telling us funnies. Our faces crumpled, eyes squinting in the sunlight. Three sets of knobbly knees brought together like we were going to wet ourselves.

Barry's footsteps behind me. The three children smiled back.

— Who's the woman?

— Long story.

He sat on the enormous black leather couch, leaned over the glass-top table and crushed two tablets with the back of a spoon. He made two lines with a card, rolled up a note, and vacuumed some up his nose. He sat back and sighed,

— Here.

— No thanks. I don't do that shit.

— Come on, sis. We're rich, let's celebrate.

— Looks to me like you're already rich.

He sniffed, rubbed his nose and shook his curls.

— I'll celebrate if you tell me who you are. What's with all this fucking stuff?

He nodded at the tabletop with his eyebrows up.

— Snort first.

I walked closer.

— What is it?

— Flat Liners from Amsterdam. I thought me and you should get to know each other better.

— What happened to good old conversation?

— Come on, have a snifter and I'll tell you a story.

His open milky moon of a face – it made me feel safe. He lifted a remote from the couch and music started playing from the four corners of the room. I didn't feel so exposed. I sat down next to him and he put his warm hand in the middle of my back. Like he was steering me towards the drugs.

— I'm sorry. My fits.

He sniffed again and said too loud,

— I thought you'd have grown out of them by now?

— I grew into a new kind. Worse. I won't bore you.

— Bore me.

— No. It stresses me out.

I made another sweep across the room.

— I think *you* should bore *me*.

He coughed, rubbed his face and leaned forward. He picked up a pair of glasses off the table, rectangular with purple lenses. He slid them down to the end of his nose.

— I started playing poker for keepsies when I was in borstal.

— Poker?

— A few of the lads here in the Mansions were in with me. I'm generous with my winnings. I've found it's best to keep the money rolling. Money breeds, you see. And I profit most of the time. They make sure no one fucks with me, or my stuff.

— Protection?

I couldn't help shaking my head.

— Been in the same boat. Dealt the same shitty hand.

He told me how he liked gambling in all of its many forms. How he was banned from every betting shop in the North of England.

— I just love gambling. It's my life, my vision of the world. It's how I experience things. I take one look at people, Lily, and I know them. They don't even have to open their mouths. I can read their weaknesses. I can gauge how aggressive they're liable to be. And you see, once you realize you've got this talent, you can bluff your way around any situation. Around anyone.

And I'm thinking: does that include me?

He had something of a reputation. Some people wouldn't play him at the casinos any more, he said.

I wasn't impressed. Wasn't surprised either. It fitted some memory I had of him. He could see I was bored. He poked me in the ribs and started talking about kids that we grew up with on the council estate. We bounced names around, laughing our heads off. Poor bastards, we kept saying. Wonder what they're doing now? Banged up. A dozen kids. I thought about our Mikey again.

— They took you both to the same place, didn't they?

— I don't want to talk about it.

— I remember I was at school, afternoon playtime it was, and rumours spreading about the police at ours.

— I really don't.

— About you and Mikey kicking fuck out of some coppers.

— Lily.

— How old were you? Thirteen, fourteen?

He looked miffed. He slid the glasses up his nose, hid his eyes.

— I thought: This Is It, we're all going to get shipped off, split up, locked up, throw away the fucking key. I was so fucking upset when I realized That Wasn't It. I was left with that fucking bitch and Don. All on my own.

— Please.

— All on my fucking own, Barry. No one to stick up for me. You've no idea.

I almost blurted it all out, but we said it at the same time: sorry.

We talked all night. Rubbish mostly. He kept getting more and more wasted and I had a few goes on a spliff and the conversation just got silly. Then he began dozing and we sat in silence. Private thoughts hanging in the smoke.

I went over to his CD rack on the wall and saw one that sobered me up. I pulled it out and stared at it. The yellow sun with the blue face and big black eyes. I took the disc out and slipped it into the machine.

I used the arrow button until I got to 'Damaged' then I pressed play.

I took a deep breath, turned it up a bit.

I looked over at him: a dirty cherub.

And then the drums came in and a funny feeling crept inside me. I hugged myself and went over to him, brushed his hair away from his face and put my cheek against his. The scent of him howled through my brain.

But it wasn't Barry; it was Alex.

I was back there, parked up on the cliff edge in his car. It was dark outside and *Screamadelica* was playing and Alex said it for the first time.

— I love you, Lil.

All I could do was smile for the gushing inside. I knew it was only a matter of time. And it was. The bastard saw me having a fit in the bathroom one night and I never saw him again. I came round, and when I could speak I called his name. But he'd gone. And I lost those four months like change from my pocket.

No letter, no postcard, no nothing.

Daylight coming into the room. It woke Barry up and drew us to the window. He opened it wide and we looked out at the town and sea. Two people shouted to each other as they made their way home. Howls and hoots of goodbyes echoing through the high-rises. We watched the sea change its colours from a blacky green, all murk, to a shimmery blue. Silver in places like tinfoil.

I shivered. Barry put his arm around me to keep me warm.

I wasn't alone any more.

21

You know winter's gone because of the smells on the wind, that seaweedy pong. An eggy smell that clings to your hair and clothes. It comes seeping into the flat off the sea. People are smiling and they look like they mean it. They walk with straight backs, heads up. People you don't know start saying hello to you on the street. Boards are coming off the shopfronts. Clothes hanging out, colours billowing and they remind me of being a kid, playing between the washing lines, the smell of soap powder and sunshine. Bus-loads of pensioners with carrier bags full of small change – they've been saving their coins all winter, wetting their frilly knickerbockers at the thought of all the slot machines and bingo halls. Jim becoming even grumpier because he hates working hard, but he loves the dosh that comes flooding in.

And the best thing is, you can go out without your coat on.

I like lists, so I wrote all of these things down that mean it's spring. I get carried away. Once I start I can't stop. I put the date at the top and skimmed over the last time I'd put anything in. It was that day after she died. There was a funny picture of me eating little children. I hadn't written anything for months. That was a good and a bad thing, because I'd been with Barry most of the time. I wrote it in black ink because it was a dead cert.

I wanted it to be true in other words. There was no going back.

I was stood by the big bay window in my bedroom, watching it happen all over again. I could see tiny figures moving up and down the beach. An old couple stood arm in arm in matching long brown macs. They stood for ages at the sea's edge. Staring out at it, like they were waiting for it to answer. A couple of teenagers cycled all wobbly across the sands. The girl – her hair was like a long brown wave behind her, clinging like a limpet to the boy pedalling, his body tilted forward.

Barry rang the bell then let himself in. I'd had a key done for him at Finders Keypers, and he'd done the same for me. We hugged and he asked me as per if I was all right, meaning had I had a fit today? He told me about some game he'd played at the casino the night before. I sat and watched him talking as he rolled a joint.

— I haven't been to bed yet. I'm still buzzing.

I was never to call him before three in the afternoon, in case he'd been up all night gambling. We were learning about each other all over again. It was like we were ironing out all the ruffled edges. Shared and unshared pasts. Mam dying like that – it gave us a second chance. Get to know each other. We weren't going to pass it up. He meant everything to me. I doted on him, I know I did. We ate together and partied together and I loved the way his plans always involved me. He swaggered when he presented me to people, like I was some prize he'd won. And he'd be like this is our lass. My not-so-little sister.

He passed me the joint and I choked on it. He laughed and went,

— So our little nest egg, what you going to do when yours hatches?

I was hoping he'd tell me.

— Still don't know whether I want it.

— Oh, come on. Don't just live a little, live a lotto.

He was right, I'd fuck all, really. I tried not to look at the flat. Money had never meant jack to me before because I never really wanted anything before. I thought that I was happy, but the money was screaming, NO YOU'RE FUCKING NOT. And it wasn't until Barry came back into my life that I realized how fucking lonely I was, and how bored with things. As long as I'd enough money in my pocket for a few gins in the Locker, then I was happy. So what the fuck did I know?

— What about you?

— Going to sit on it a while. Let it incubate. Then go somewhere hot. Smoke a lot of good-quality weed. Fuck some beautiful women.

— Blow it on cards, you mean?

— Ye of little faith.

A silence being dug between us. I pictured my money in a hole in the ground and a shovel in my hands. The house was on the market for a stupid amount. I tried not to think about it. I didn't want my mind taking me back there. And it could, if it wanted. I'd be back there and it would be more real than Barry sitting in the chair, watching me.

I could sense a storm brewing out at sea.

Summer means electrical storms. They make me nervous-as. I can feel the pulses start their beat as they make their way inland, coming to get me. I feel the storms like blind people must feel music – through my body. The throb and pulse down my veins like they're full of rust, clicking and sparkling. And then the winds come, coughing away against the front like some old tramp.

That's when I climb under my bedsheets and hide from the buzzing in my body.

— You know why me and Mikey did it, don't you?

— Did what?

He tutted.

— We'd been skiving off school. We were over at old Albert's opposite when we saw the police cars pull up in front of the house. They were trying to arrest Mam. She was screaming blue murder. There were four of them, dragging her out of the house. We thought they were hurting her bad. We were just sticking up for her.

It was like a challenge. His eyes got wide and he said who wouldn't?

It had always bothered me that: Mikey sticking up for her. It was me he protected – *me*, not her. And Barry knew it.

I wanted to say they should have locked her up and thrown away the fucking key, but I was having to learn to back down, swallow my words. We felt differently about her, but I wanted him to feel like I did.

— Here. I don't want any more.

He came across and took the spliff off me and re-lit it.

I stretched out on the bed and massaged my temples. The pounding was soft but nagging – a storm rumbling around my brain somewhere.

— You caned or something?

— Just stressed. The doc said I should avoid getting het up.

— I'll roll us another one, then.

— I'm not sure he meant getting off my face. You're a bad influence.

— Then why *do* you?

He pushed a button.

— Because I don't want to be fucking controlled by it. No more than I have to. I want to be fucking normal.

— You *are* fucking normal.

— Pah.

I spoke to the ceiling, looking at the stars, yellow against the white.

— You've no idea, Barry. You've seen nothing. Sometimes I can have seven or eight fits in a day. The drugs change me. Make me feel like a ghost. I'm covered in cuts and bruises and scars. You wouldn't believe. Most of the time, I can tell when it's coming. But not always. I can be in the middle of a conversation and it just comes on so sudden that I just drop in the middle of a word. My brain takes a detour. My blood runs cold and suddenly the world is full of sharp corners, edges out to get me. You wouldn't know.

I could sense him shrugging.

— Then I come round to ambulances, folk crowding in on me. Half an hour later, I'm ready to finish whatever I was saying. But during those few seconds I could have broken my bones. You've no idea. I'll probably have pissed myself, and I'll have been twitching like a complete spaz. You call that fucking normal?

My eyes, they switched on. Sparks and zags dancing. It was talking about it.

I sat up and tried to control my breathing. When I was a kid, I'd do it on purpose – make myself fit. I'd start breathing deep and fast and rocking backwards and forwards. Hyperventilate, just to get that feeling, that bliss-feeling before you go, before the darkness. Get the breath, the breeze, the shimmer. The teachers in the special school used to go fucking spare. But I loved it. I couldn't get enough of it. That lush feeling.

Barry looked all flustered, but I was revved up.

— And the worst thing is, I haven't a fucking clue what I look like, or what the fuck I'm doing, or what anyone else is doing to me. I've just got to put up with the broken ribs and the black eyes. Like being married to some psycho I can't ever divorce.

When I picture myself chucking a fit, I see myself from behind. I stiffen up like a shop dummy, scream like an animal being shot, then topple. I see myself in slow motion, like in a film. I look unhinged, and when I hit the floor, I begin my hurly-burly. My arms and legs twist like rope. Body thrashing – it curdles my blood. It's like when you're watching a film and the film jumps from one moment to the next, but that's all right, your head can handle that. But this is my life and I'm missing bits. You're not meant to miss so many bits. My life's all chopped up to fuck because my stupid fucking brain keeps flipping off and on. When I was a kid, I used to think I turned invisible during a fit. Like Houdini.

But you cope.

Thrash, get up, get on with it.

I stared at the ceiling, listening to him breathing. I tried to breathe in time with him, and the sparks stopped flying and my eyes dimmed back to normal.

— It's a miracle I'm still here. I've chucked them crossing the road, on top of the cliffs, in the middle of winter coming back from the pub. I once threw one in front of a tram in Blackpool. I woke up in hospital surrounded by strangers all worried. They all thought I'd been a hit-and-run. It's OK, you can laugh.

— You're so normal, Lily, it's fucking daft.

I sat up. We eyed each other across the room and I smiled.

That did it – the metal band squeezing my head, tight, tighter. My temples caving in. Noise, a purple and brown and black noise. I had to cover my ears. It tugs at your guts like a hand. Fingers scratching around in there, zigzags like fat tattoos slice into your eyes, still there when you blink. You're in a car going a hundred miles an hour and you see sparks out the window. The machine's broken. The wiring's fucked. Edges, surfaces, corners. You're going to crash and there's fuck all you can do about it. Crumpled metal and blood everywhere, wheels spinning, you're on your back.

I kicked him out.

He said he wanted to stay to look after me but I told him PLEASE GO.

He looked hurt. I just needed to lock the door.

I didn't know which one was coming. You never know. It depends. It's never just one thing. My taste goes. Or my mouth is full of horrible shit. No saliva at all or it's gushing out like spew. I can hear myself mumbling. I can see my hands tugging and pulling at things and my legs twitching, kicking. I start my rocking. I start my chewing and smacking my lips like mwa mwa. Pulses getting bigger. Temples pumping like balloons. Music inside my body.

I feel the static coughing down my veins.

ERRRRmmmmg
MMMMMg
MMMMMMM
mmmmm greeeee heeeeey aaaaa
NEEEEE MMMMM greegreegree gree heeeeeeeey
aaaaa ERRRGH ERRRGH hernyerrrGGGHHH
hergh HERRR hergh mmmmm
greegreehee yaaaaa
NEEEEE MMMMMM greegreegree gree
heeeeeyaaaa ERRRGHERRRGH
MMMMMMg ERRRR mmmmg
mmmmm greeeee heeeeey aaaaa NEEEEEEE
MMMMMM gree gree gree gree
heeeeeeeey aaaaa ERRRGH ERRRGH
hernyerrrGGGHHH hergh HERRR
mmmmmgreeeee
heeeee yaaaaa NEEEEE MMMMM gree
greegree heeeeyaaaaa ERRRGH ERRRGH
MMMMMMg ERRRR mmmmg
mmmm greeeee heeeeey aaaaa NEEEEE
MMMMMgreegreegree gree heeeeeeeey
aaaaa ERRRGH ERRRGH hernyerrrGGG
HHH hergh HERRR hergh mmmmm
greeeeeheeeee
yaaaaa NEEEEE
greegree gree
gree
heeeeeey aaaaa ERRRGHERRRGH
MMMMMg ERRRR mmmmg mmmmm
greeeee heeeeey aaaaa NEEEEEE
MMMMMgreegree gree gree
heeeeeeeey aaaaa ERRRGH ERRRGH hernyerrr
GGGHHH hergh HERRR hergh mmmmm
mmgreeeeheeeee yaaaaa NEEEEEEEE
MMM greegreegree gree heeeeeyaaaaa
ERRRGH ERRRGH mmmmg mmmmmmm

ERRRRmmmmg
MMMMMg
mmmmmm greeeee heeeeey aaaaa
NEEEEE MMMMMgreegreegree gree heeeeeeeey
aaaaa ERRRGH ERRRGH hernyerrrGGGHHH
hergh HERRR hergh mmmmm
greeeeeheeeee yaaaaa
NEEEEE MMMMM greegreegree gree
heeeeeeyaaaaa ERRRGHERRRGH
MMMMMg ERRRR mmmmg
NEEEEEEE
mmmmm greeeee heeeeey aaaaa NEEEEEEE
MMMMM gree gree gree gree
heeeeeeeey aaaaa ERRRGHERRRGH
hernyerrrGGGHHH hergh HERRR
mmmmmgreeeee
heeeee yaaaaa NEEEEE MMMMM gree
greegree heeeeyaaaaa ERRRGH ERRRGH
MMMMMg ERRRR mmmmg
mmmm greeeee heeeeey aaaaa NEEEEE
MMMMMgreegreegree gree heeeeeeeey
aaaaa ERRRGH ERRRGH hernyerrrGGG
HHH hergh HERRR hergh mmmmm
greeeeeheeeee yaaaaa NEEEEE
greegree gree
MMMMMg heeeeeyaaaaa ERRRGHERRRGH
ERRRR mmmmg mmmmm
greeee heeeee NEEEEE
MMMMMgreegree gree gree
heeeeeeeey aaaaa ERRRGH ERRRGH hernyerrr
GGGHHH hergh HERRR hergh mmmm-
mmmgreeeeeheeeee yaaaaa NEEEEEEEE
MMM greegreegree gree heeeeeyaaaaa
ERRRGHERRRGH mmmmg mmmmmmm

20

I remember the lift doors opening onto a dark corridor. I could smell weed and hear a loud bump of music coming from somewhere. We hadn't travelled that far – just the top floor of Barry's block. He'd tried to warn me about the game, what to expect with the rudeness and language and that it might last into the early hours, but I was free to leave whenever.

— Just keep yourself to yourself. Don't interfere.

I said thanks, it sounds great.

He filled me in on the players. Lamb was one of Barry's oldest mates. He was called Lamb because when he was younger he got nicked for hustling lambs up on the moors. Some deal he had with the kebab shop in town. Ted was another lad from borstal. He was caught shagging his teddy bear – I said I didn't want to know any more. Carrot was Carrot because of his hair and Dos was Dos because he was a bone-idle twat.

— And by the way, don't laugh if they call me Slick.

— Slick?

He stopped and leaned against the door, riffling through his pockets. He pulled out his purple glasses and slid them on, to the end of his nose. Then he pulled out a large wad of notes and sniffed them. He put them to my face.

— Kiss for me, my good-luck charm.

I gave the notes a big smackeroo and then I kissed his cheek.

— That dress really suits you, by the way.

— Cheers, Slick.

We entered the fug and dirty laughter. They all shut up when they saw me. One of them said something under his breath. It was just like I'd seen in plenty of films. Five men sat around a table holding someone's lucky pack of cards. Cigarettes, whisky, vodka, beers, spliffs. Bloke talk, bloke smells, bloke laughs. Some lines of coke chopped up on the kitchen table, help yourself.

I remember what Lamb looked like, because he actually did have lamb-chop sideboards, like chinstraps on the side of his blowsy head. And Carrot's hair shining orange under the bare bulb hanging above. It made their shadows hard, eyes dark. I watched their fingertips holding cards fanned out. I stood unsure in the quiet. Their hands shaking just a little bit, if you looked close. I could hear someone's guts rumbling. Cold looks passing from eyeball to eyeball. Nervousness – you could see it twitching in the smoke.

They all slipped on sunglasses at the same time. Hiding their tells.

The walls were covered floor to ceiling with photographs. Hundreds of smiling faces in clubs and pubs, on beaches. Lamb's life decorating the walls like This Is My Life Wallpaper. I tried not to look. I played with the dog and made drinks and badly rolled spliffs to order. I looked out of the window wanting the clouds to clear, so I could see the view from up there. But it was all murk. After a while I think they forgot I was there. The conversation got rude, personal. They began farting a lot.

I sat in the corner, watching.

— Am I right?

Barry was giving them the spiel. He told me he could gain advantage just with his talk. Cards flat on the table and the Stare.

— Am I right?

Leaning on one arm, eyebrow up, looking at them sideways. One beady eye on them, his glasses perched on the end of his nose. His free hand moving backwards and forwards. They were talking about folding, flopping, calling, blinds up, heads up. Hands like spiders crawling across the table.

Then they were off again. The banter. I sat behind Barry but couldn't see his hand. I was surprised he never stopped talking – just a lean-down to look at the corner of the cards, quick flick, money moving forward in easy moves.

He'd told me about tells. The little signs people give off, like coughing because the throat gets tight when you're nervous. The little scratches and strokes people do on their faces, their neck. He told me he could read them all, and that he could mimic them.

I felt like he could read my mind.

He'd tried to teach me about the rules. He told me about his game theory in a quiet voice. Selective aggression, that's what he called it. No respect for money and a fearsome table image. He said that poker told a story, that it was like putting a jigsaw together. He taught me that people who pay with their electricity bill money – they're *high stakes*; and people that are loaded – they're called *wild cards*. He tried to show me how to shuffle and deal all fancy, sleights of hand. But the cards flew from my fingers like birds trying to escape. He told me about strategies, about raising and calling, folding. He talked about art and impulse. I felt the shutters in my mind come down.

I can't remember how long I'd been there or at what

point I switched on. I think it was maybe Barry's tone of voice. The way he was talking and looking at Lamb over his glasses. I'm sat in the comfy chair with the dog asleep in my lap and I zone in.

— Yeah, I took beatings. But nowt could've been worse than the beatings I was giving myself.

Barry tapped the side of his head.

— In here, last thing at night. When you lie there in the silence and you get to thinking, mulling stuff over. And in the morning, when you're all bleary for a few seconds, that's the worst. When that room comes into focus and you realize where the fuck you are. You're not at home. It was bleak. We'd all done some bad shit, some worse than others.

He smiled and winked at Lamb.

— I kept my nose clean. Never fought back. Perfected my hospital corners. You knew who to avoid. Who was sound. You had to. You didn't want anyone holding a grudge against you in there. They backed you into a corner and there was no getting out.

There were nods and groans and ayes. Then Lamb said it,

— Nowt's been the same since your Mikey vamoosed.

Barry kicked Lamb under the table and rolled his eyes.

— I still think it had fuck all to do with his reptile house. More likely that Sylvia bitch.

One of the others chipped in,

— She was a rum fucker.

Barry slunk down in his chair.

— And a lying cunt. Only interested in one thing. Soon as he got shut down, she lost fucking interest. Playing games with his fucking head.

54

— Typical fucking bird.

— And she was about as pregnant as I was.

— Hard to fucking tell, you fat cunt.

I pushed the dog off my lap and went over to Lamb. They all hid their cards from me like I could give a fuck. I put my hand on Lamb's shoulder.

— You know where our Mikey is?

Barry showed his palms to shush them.

— Lily. They know as much as I do: nowt.

— But you know where he is, though?

They all looked from me to Barry.

— It's just fucking rumour.

— Fucking TELL ME.

My memory's been bent by what was said. It's the image of myself I see – the tears pooling, the men staring, and I left that one word dangling.

London.

I walked out of there like a ghost, Barry saying my name behind me.

— Lily?

— Lily?

— *Lily?*

———————

He found me on his bed. I wasn't crying, just numb. I made him tell me everything he knew and told him that if he didn't, I could never trust him again.

— Fuck sake, Lily. No one knows. I just didn't want to get your hopes up.

— This money's going to drive a fucking wedge between us. You promise me you're keeping his money for him? Promise you won't fucking touch it?

He looked beaten.

— I put *both* our names to it, so that I can't. I'll show you.

He went to get up, but I stopped him.

— Hold me.

He sighed and put his arms around me.

— Tighter.

I woke up alone on the bed. I found him in the living room, staring out the window and listening to the radio turned low. I sat down on the couch and rubbed my face. He started talking.

— What you heard last night, it's all I know. He was engaged to this mad bitch called Sylvia. Sylvia Smith. All bleach-blonde hair and fake tits and orange skin. They looked a right pair. None of us liked her. She was into her mind games and Mikey was too fucking soft to notice.

He folded his arms. You could see his breath fogging the window.

— When they shut the reptile house down, all of a sudden she's saying she's up the duff. I suppose she thought he had some money stashed away and would propose to her, some shit like that. But he didn't. He totally went into one. She soon got fed up of him not talking to her.

He put a finger up to the glass, drew shapes in his breath.

— She realized he was broke. Next thing we know, she's gone down to London to live with her mother or sister or something. It was her body and she'd do what the fuck she'd like. That he'd never see their kid. Ever.

He turned around with his face hard and mean. He stabbed his finger at me.

— *I* got the police involved. *I* phoned the helplines.

I did the running around. *I* was the one that got in touch with her. But nowt. She'd seen hide nor hair, and no, she wasn't fucking pregnant. He'd gone. He just fucking disappeared, and that's that.

— I didn't mean . . .

— It doesn't matter.

He walked into the bathroom and locked the door behind him.

19

It was the end of July and just another same old same old. Watching the doughy-faced kids coming in and out, making their way from one machine to the next. Spending other people's money. From my booth, I could see clear into the bingo room and I watched the same old rigmarole begin. The shell-suited fat-as family began their toing and froing.

Car-loads of them from Preston, Burnley, Middlesbrough, Gateshead. Places I've never seen. Places I never want to see, not if they're full of people like that. They come to the resort with one thing on their minds: money that isn't theirs.

I watched the mam and dad and the two scruffy kids working the busy seafront as Nana Sour-face sat and played the bingo, chain-smoking her way through two packs of cigarettes. They were out there pickpocketing daft holidaymakers and stealing from the shops. Mam and Dad and the scruffy kids appeared at Nana's side, a cocky smile as they emptied their hands inside Nana's shopping bags. Stopping to take a drag off Nana's cigarette. By the end of the day, she'd leave with bags fit to burst.

Summer fun, start the kids young.

Then I saw him – peering at me from the side of the Derby machine.

The little plastic horses galloped behind the glass and his smile bowed away. He stepped forwards, head to foot in shiny black leather, jet-black hair all slicked and quiffed up. Clean-shaven, cowboy-booted, thumbs in pockets, Barry strutted towards me and we both laughed at the same time. He stepped into the booth and kissed me on the cheek.

— Oh . . .

— What do you think?

— My . . .

— Good, eh?

— God.

I pushed him away to get a good look.

— What is it with the men in my life and fucking Elvis?

— I've a present. Hold out your hands.

— Have you robbed Al's wardrobe or something?

He fumbled in his inside pocket. I saw his ruffled silk shirt and then the tiny mobile as it went from his hand to mine.

— What's this?

He took the phone and unfolded it. His fingers – he'd had a fucking manicure, you could tell. I watched the screen flick-flicker and Elvis's face appeared to the twinkles of 'Heartbreak Hotel'. He showed me the name in the phone book: BAZ.

— It isn't nicked, is it?

He tutted and looked at his watch.

— And what happened to the bombsite in your gob?

— Caps and clean. You like it? Dentist went fucking berserk. Said he'd never seen owt like it.

He smoothed his hair back even more.

— I was long overdue a makeover.

He checked his watch again.

— I'm leaving, Lily. Flying from Manchester in a few hours.

I tried to open my mouth.

— For kicks.

I swallowed hard.

— You can't.

— The Horseshoe and Gold Strike Casino.

I think I said fuck.

— Tunica, Mississippi.

— *Mississippi?*

I held up my hands.

— You can't, Barry.

— The Jack Binion Poker Open. One of the biggest games in the world, Lily. And do you know what?

My sigh tasted of vomit.

— I'm going to win the lot.

He squeezed my arms. He looked more alive than I'd ever seen anyone look.

— In at ten thousand and I'm going to burn those Yank fucking stockbrokers. They won't know what's hit them.

He hooked his thumbs in his pockets, nodded and grinned. I noticed his teeth again: glinting white like an advert.

— Then after that to Vegas, more spoils. The Bellagio, a million up for grabs.

Something took over me as I shouted,

— YOU FUCKING CAN'T.

And though I didn't want to, the tears started burning my cheeks.

He nudged me.

— Might even meet Elvis.

He strutted his hips, curled his lip.

— A-huh-huh.

I tried to laugh for him, but I felt far away. America. I used to dream about being adopted by an American family. I had it all planned out: my Disney life, my Disney house. But that's all America was, wasn't it? A fucking cartoon.

A car horn pipped like crazy outside, making me jump. I looked at him all leaky-eyed.

— Go on then, fuck off. Leave me alone again. You know what you are?

But it was Mam's voice I heard.

He leaned down and hugged me and said into my hair,

— Come join me if you want. Anytime.

The voice inside me was shouting FUCK OFF FUCK YOU but then he said something that made me feel like

— I love you.

like he'd bitten a chunk right out of me.

And with that, he was gone.

I sat in the booth and wilted. I wanted to run after him, get in the car with him. I wanted to beat his brains out, fling my arms around his legs and never let go. I put my head in my hands, closed my eyes and tried to remember his words. Bellagio. Vegas.

He'd left me again, and I wanted to feel something other than anger. Why wasn't I surprised? He said I could go anytime. I could. I knew I could. But I didn't know how to, and he knew that.

He'd been in my life a few months. Felt like years. Felt like five minutes.

Something like a cold wind blew around inside me, and I heard two words in my head: alone again.

————————

I pretended women's problems, holding my stomach. Jim tutted and said go on then. I went straight to the Mansions and let myself into Barry's flat.

I didn't move for ages. I sat on his couch like a shop dummy with my coat on and felt hollow inside. I realized that until Barry came back I was just an empty room. I'd gotten used to the sound of my own voice echoing off the walls.

I walked around a bit, looking in drawers.

I ran my hands over his T-shirts, jumpers, tatty socks.

In his bedside cabinet I found a little brown book. An address book.

I looked under M. I looked under S.

And in the pocket bit at the back, that's where I found the photo of Mikey. I stared at it for a long time and I tried hard not to cry in the quiet of the room. To hear my sobs coming off the walls.

I put the book in my pocket and locked the door behind me.

I got a bus back into town.

I remember wandering around the fairground. All the rides were covered with awning. Striped colours over the Kiddies Carousel, Swing Chairs, the remote-control boats, Twisters, the Star Rider machine, Go Carts, the Crazy River Ride and the front of the Amaze 'N' Mirrors building. The dark shapes of the carousel horses in the middle of a leap, silhouettes against the red and yellow and blue. Awning snapping. The horses looked wild, like they were alive.

I wandered down onto the beach, headed for the water. The large pebbles got smaller and turned into hard sand that looked like tiny waves. Down near the break the sand got fine and my trainers sank. The sea was the colour of a puddle. Seagulls arguing, flying low over the water. The sea looked like it was swelling, rising upwards away from me.

I turned around. Twisted arcade lights like long neck-laces. Shopfront neon spread for over a mile and disappeared into the hills that were black-looking. Shapes of fishing boats, a tractor with a trailer in the harbour. I could see the Golden Nugget where I should've been working, the white shutters in the Clarendon's guest rooms. Distant beats of a band playing somewhere.

I remembered the night of my thirty-first, just a month before. Barry took me to a club dancing and afterwards we wandered along the beach. The sun had just come up and we were arm in arm and snuggling into each other for warmth. He was off his head on pills, but I didn't mind. I liked him hugging me and talking about our lives. The place didn't seem too bad any more. The sun was making the prettiest colours and we were together. Our shadows looked like one person and, like a dozy cow, I thought it meant something.

I looked up and could make out a few pinpricks, the brightest the Dog Star. And heading for it, I saw an aeroplane. A tiny silver bird, moving but making no sound.

It was him up there, I knew it was.

I raised my hand and waved. I took my mobile out of my pocket and thumbed my first message. LUV YOU 2.

I picked up a tiny pink shell – the colour of that sky the morning we walked along the beach. I put it in my pocket and began to run.

I ran across the wet sand as fast as I could. I ran till there was a blood taste in my throat, till the burn in my lungs was like a rip. And I remember buckling over and there was a laugh coming out of my gob and tears wetting my face because he'd gone.

He'd really gone.

18

WHO'S LOOKING OVER YOUR SHOULDER?
KEEP YOUR PIN SAFE

I looked. No one. I slid my card into the machine.

PROCESSING CARD DETAILS
flashing it said PLEASE WAIT
PLEASE ENTER YOUR PERSONAL NUMBER
then it went beep beep beep beep
WOULD YOU LIKE TO CHECK YOUR ACCOUNT
BALANCE?
press the button next to YES
YOUR REQUEST IS BEING PROCESSED
flashing again PLEASE WAIT

THE AMOUNT IN YOUR ACCOUNT IS: £42,785

Green numbers on a black screen, that's all it was. A
four. A two. Then three more. I just couldn't make anything of it.

WOULD YOU LIKE TO CARRY OUT ANOTHER
TRANSACTION?

I pressed YES and took out a twenty.

I got a cab to the address under M. A long ride along the coast road to a massive white house overlooking the sea. I spoke to a woman at the door while her children screamed in a room somewhere.

She knew nothing.

I gave her my mobile number and told her to phone me if she heard anything.

I noticed the For Sale sign when I walked back to the cab.

————————

The Locker was dead. A few old fogies sat round the bar smoking, sipping their pints. A black Labrador lying on its side in the middle of the floor, snoring loudly. They were watching a *Countdown* re-run on the big screen, that twat Richard Whiteley's face as he tried to be funny. I had to cough to get their attention.

— Gin and tonic no ice please.

It was the numbers game. The contestant asked for one big one and the rest small. Everyone at the bar said the numbers out loud as Carol stuck them up. One. Two. Seven. Five. Ten. Fifty. Carol hit the button and they said together:

— Seven hundred and five.

I shouted,

— Fifty times two times seven plus five. Piece of piss.

They all looked at me. The barmaid tutted and shook her head.

I went and sat at the far end of the pub next to the door. I took off my coat and stared at the pink carpet, the green on the snooker table, the sign for the women's toilet saying Ladies Astern and the wooden walls that were stained red.

— She's bloody right, you know.

A creak and gust from the door. A man came in, lolloping walk like a monkey, paint-splattered jeans and baggy top. The fuck-wit had bleached half of his hair yellow, the other black. He looked ridiculous.

It was Ridge Racer.

The jukey started blasting out a record. With the slidy guitar bit, I knew it right off. That one off *The Joshua Tree*. Bono's voice sounding gruff and sexy-as, the low bum-bum of piano and the chug-chug of guitar.

I watched Ridge Racer sitting at the bar. There was something of the kid about him. Maybe it was the baggy jumper making him look smaller, big body and short legs. In the background the tick-tick of the *Countdown* clock. And I was thinking that if he turned around with a nice smile, then I'd talk to him. I'd ask him to join me and I'd explain why I never turned up that day.

Wasn't because of you. It's me.

I watched the back of his two-coloured head and thought it might be nice: having some arms around me tonight.

And it was something in the music made me gush. But it was coming to an end too quick and he still hadn't turned around. Then he stood up and began scratching himself. The harmonica getting quieter. Carol and Richard's voices wishing us all well, saying goodbye. Then silence.

His hands digging between his arse cheeks and I thought oh well.

I downed the gin and went home.

☬☬☬☬

I had a dream that night. I was back at home in my old bedroom, all grown-up and living there on my own. I had it decorated nice. Nice furniture, pricey stuff everywhere. And I was asleep in my dream. But then in the dream something woke me up. Somebody was throwing stones at the window.

I opened the curtains and down below, waving and smiling up at me – it was our Mikey. He was still a kid, and had that canny smile of his, smeared all over his face. So real. I could even make out his freckles and the scar in the corner of his eye that made him look like he was always squinting. He waved; I waved back. Then he just turned and walked away with his hand in the air. And then I saw them: thousands of kids in the street with him, and they were all smiling and waving, moving away.

I woke up and rushed to the window.

Just the black sea out there, and litter blustering about.

☙ ☙

When I gave Jim the bottle of whisky he just shook his head.

— Your job's here anytime you want it.

— Thanks, Jim. You never know.

There were no customers in Mr Santa. I locked the door behind me and turned the sign around to CLOSED. Al took his present but didn't take it out of the bag. It was a small karaoke machine I got from Argos.

I told him. He started crying and pulled his wig off and

threw it across the room. I saw the tufts of white hair on his head.

I was going to break his heart, he said. We hugged for a long time. He made me promise that I would spend Christmas with him. I crossed my heart and hoped to die.

— Why London, lass? It's a filthy, stinking place.

I felt the leap inside me. Something like a risk.

— I'm going to find our Mikey. I need to know he's all right.

I promised I would phone every week. I gave him two months' rent and told him to throw out anything that I'd left behind. He managed a smile for me.

I bought a small tin of yellow paint and went over my graffiti on the walls. The writing that'd kept me safe for so long.

My wits, that's all I had now, and it scared the shit out of me.

My Special Events book, my Headache Book, the plastic sheet from off my bed – I put them in the bin liners with the rest of the rubbish and tied the top.

Goodbye, Golden Nugget.

Goodbye, Locker.

Goodbye, flat.

Goodbye, everything.

I felt myself shake. I looked out at the sea and imagined myself out there, a white shape in the blackness. I was doing what I could never do and a tiny light started to glow inside me. I wanted it to flare. Wanted it to blister. Wanted it to blind.

I sat down on the stripped bed and stared at my suitcase, waiting. The taxi was due any minute. I knew that soon I'd be getting on a train to London. Where I'd find Mikey, and then . . . I had no idea.

His little face and his wave. Find me. Join me.

Or was it goodbye?

ERRRRmmmmmg
MMMMMMg greeeee heeeeey aaaaag
mmmmmm greeeee heeeeey aaaaa
NEEEEE MMMMMgreegreegree gree heeeeeeey
aaaaa ERRRGH ERRRGH hernyerrrGGGHHH
hergh HERRR hergh mmmmm
greegheeeee yaaaaa
NEEEEE MMMMMM greegreegree gree
heeeeeey aaaa ERRRGHHERRRGH
MMMMMMg ERRRR mmmg
mmmmm greeeee heeeeey aaaaa NEEEEEEE
MMMMM gree gree gree gree
ERRRGHHERRRGH
hernyerrrGGGHHH hergh HERRR
mmmmmmgreeeee
heeeee yaaaaa NEEEEE MMMMM gree
greegree heeeeeyaaaaa ERRRGH ERRRGH
MMMMMMg ERRRR mmmmg
mmmm greeeee heeeeey aaaaa NEEEEE
MMMMMgreegreegree gree heeeeeeey
aaaaa ERRRGH ERRRGH hernyerrrGGG
HHH hergh HERRR hergh mmmmm
greeeeeheeeee yaaaaa NEEEEE
gree greegree gree
gree aaaaa heeeeeyaaaaa ERRRGHHERRRGH
MMMMMMg ERRRR mmmmg mmmm
greeeee heeeeey aaaaa
MMMMMMgreegree gree gree
heeeeeeeey aaaaa ERRRGHERRRGH hernyerrr
GGGHHH hergh HERRR hergh mmm-
mmmgreeeeheeee yaaaaa NEEEEEEEE
MMM greegreegree gree heeeeeyaaaaa
ERRRGHERRRGH mmmmg mmmmmmmm

the room cracks and shatters, the colours wrapping their arms around me but I can't hold them back, it's like rain running down windows, the air's melting in front of me, colours like feelings inside, suffocating but nice

like storm clouds up there

like bullies, black lightning off and on in their fat bellies and I need to pull at everything, need to touch and tug and twist and poke and push because it's all slipping away from me

and I know

— Mel?

I know she's here in the room, but I can't let go of the chair, my fingers crack-cracking the corners and I

can't catch my
can't catch my

ERRRRmmmmg
MMMMMg
mmmmm greeeee heeeeey aaaaa
NEEEEE MMMMM greegreegree gree heeeeeeeey
aaaaa ERRRGH ERRRGH hernyerrrGGGHHHH
hergh HERRR hergh mmmmm
greegeheeeee yaaaaa
NEEEEE MMMMM greegreegree gree
heeeneyaaaaa ERRRGH HERRRGH
MMMMMMg ERRRR mmmg
mmmmm greeeee heeeeey aaaaa NEEEEEEE
MMMMM gree gree gree gree
heeeeeeey aaaaa ERRRGH HERRRGH
hernyerrrGGGHHHH hergh HERRR
hergh mmmmmgreeeee
heeeee yaaaaa NEEEEE MMMMMM gree
greegree heeeeyaaaaa ERRRGH ERRRGH
MMMMMg ERRRR mmmmg
mmmm greeeee heeeeey aaaaa NEEEEE
MMMMMgreegreegree gree heeeeeeeey
aaaaa ERRRGH ERRRGH hernyerrrGGG
HHH hergh HERRR hergh mmmmm
greeeeeheeeee
yaaaaa NEEEEE
gree greegree gree
MMMMMg ERRRR mmmmg mmmmm
greeeee heeeeey
MMMMMgreegree gree gree
heeeeeeeey aaaaa ERRRGH ERRRGH hernyerrr
GGGHHH hergh HERRR hergh mmm-
mmmgreeeeheeeee yaaaaa NEEEEEEEE
MMM greegreegree gree heeeeeyaaaaa
ERRRGH ERRRGH mmmmg mmmmmmmm

MMMMMMg ERRRRmmmmmg
mmmmm greeeee heeeeey aaaaa
NEEEEE MMMMMgreegreegree gree heeeeeeey
aaaaa ERRRGH ERRRGH hernyerrrGGGHHH
hergh HERRR hergh mmmmm
greeeheeee yaaaaa
NEEEEE MMMMMM greegreegree gree
heeeeeyaaaa ERRRGHERRRGH
MMMMMg ERRRR mmmmg
mmmmm greeeee heeeeey aaaaa NEEEEEEE
MMMMMM gree gree gree gree
heeeeeeeey aaaaa ERRRGH ERRRGH
hernyerrrGGGHHH hergh HERRR
mmmmmgreeeee
heeeee yaaaaa NEEEEE MMMMMM gree
greegree heeeeeyaaaa ERRRGH ERRRGH
MMMMMg ERRRR mmmmg
mmmm greeeee heeeeey aaaaa NEEEEE
MMMMMMgreegreegree gree heeeeeeeey
aaaaa ERRRGH ERRRGH hernyerrrGGG
HHH hergh HERRR hergh mmmmm
greeeeeheeee yaaaaa NEEEEE
greegree gree
gree
MMMMMg
MMMMMg ERRRR mmmmg mmmmm
greeee heeeeey aaaaa
MMMMMgreegree gree gree
heeeeeeeey aaaaa ERRRGH ERRRGH hernyerrr
GGGHHH hergh HERRR hergh mmmm-
mmgreeeeheeeee yaaaaa NEEEEEEEE
MMM greegreegree gree heeeeeyaaaaa
ERRRGHERRRGH mmmmg mmmmmmm

17

It was the too-closeness of bodies. The pandemonium. The stink. The noise. The heat of the place. I stood outside King's Cross and couldn't move. Elbows and knees and shoulders jabbing and hitting me and I screamed,

— I'M NOT INVISIBLE.

Stood like a statue, I wouldn't budge. But they slammed into me no apologies.

— Don't fucking TOUCH ME.

I wanted to punch them all, giving me snarly looks like animals. Horn blasts and sirens and sudden cars, red double-deckers big as dinosaurs. Everything moving so fast and vicious and panicky. There was no air, just fumes so hot they stung your eyes. Like the air was made of vinegar and oil. The air so hot it was sweating. I coughed and gipped. A runnel of sweat ran between my breasts.

I had to get out of this.

I looked around. I couldn't work out how to get over the railings, how to get across the road and out of the bodies. The neon of the shops over there. Names all dazzly in the nearly dark street. Incredible Edibles. McDonald's. Phone City. Northumberland Hotel. Access. Storage Solutions. The Carlton Hotel. Ladbrokes. Chop Chop Noodle Bar.

And then I saw the Subway sign. I moved down the steps and people were kicking my suitcase. No one was speaking English around me. All these faces and voices and different colours, I couldn't stop gawping. I came out at McDonald's and saw the Play 2 Win amusement arcade on the corner, the lights whirring inside. Past the Bureau de Change and into Birkenhead Street and I saw the No One Hotel, the hotel for nobodies.

The street throbbing like the inside of a machine working. I could see it with my eyes and taste it metallic on my tongue, the cars in my throat.

Then I was out of the madness. The building in front was the loveliest blue colour and above it some clouds, bright orange fluffs like candyfloss. The sky was like copper all beaten. Then a sudden car in front of me, massive with tinted windows. A man inside wearing sunglasses in the darkness, the car boom boom with the music. He turned to look at me, showed me his teeth. I legged it straight into the Carlton Hotel. A fat baldy man behind the desk smiled at me good evening madam and I nearly screamed.

⊖⊖

I got some chips from Incredible Edibles and sneaked them back into the hotel. The tiny room had a smell about it. Musty like old men and the heat made it worse. The room had a window but it wouldn't open. Outside was the only tree I could see in the long street. I sat on the bed and ate the chips and watched the clouds come in. The dirty glare all purple and orange – it hid the stars.

I tried to sleep. It was too sticky to get under the covers but I had to put my head between the bed and the pillow like a sandwich with the bloody racket of traffic noise. Even birds twittered away in the tree outside. The sky never went out. And a man in the next room cough-coughing, hacks of snot like dog barks. I pictured myself lying inside the machine of the city and my arm started its slow wave.

I knew something would happen. All that fuss and heat and madness – it scared the shit out of me. My arm and then my leg moving like I was a puppet.

I got off the bed and wobbled around the room, waving hello to the walls. I took my tablets out of my suitcase and tried to down them, spilling water all over. I threw myself back onto the bed and rolled onto my side. My whole body moved in a big wave. And I'm like so this is London, this is what it does to me – makes me jerk, waving to people who aren't there. I watched the red numbers on the alarm clock move, watched them until gone three in the morning.

The numbers moving, the hacking in the next room, cars revving up, slowing down, horn blasts and sirens. Fucking mad-as. But I think the noise stopped at some point and I fell asleep, but it wasn't for long. The clock was saying it was nearly five and the din seemed louder than ever. The jerking had stopped. Just the insects moving in my arms – dirty streets crawling under my skin.

☙❧

I showered and watched morning telly. I turned it up really loud to drown out the sound of cars but the cougher was knocking on the wall. When I went downstairs, the breakfast room was empty. Music playing somewhere. I sat and had runny jam on cold toast. I went back up, got my suitcase and went to pay, thinking I'd complain. Fifty quid – I might as well have slept in the middle of a fucking motorway. But I was too tired. My eyes felt dry and dirty. I paid and said thank you and I was back at King's Cross.

I asked the woman in WHSmiths if she had a map of London and she was like you're better off buying an A–Z. So I bought a little notepad as well – it'd be my London Book.

I couldn't believe all the pages of streets. I used the index and found King's Cross Station and said: so here I am. I got Barry's address book out of my bag and looked up Sylvia's street. Then I studied the Tube map on the back of the book. It looked like a diagram in a biology book. Veins and nerves. All the straight lines, the straight tunnels underground. I wondered if the tunnels were painted the same colours? The District and Circle lines – it'd be like being inside a stick of rock. Then it reminded me of the sky charts in my Night Sky book. Constellations in colour. Names like magnitude and brightness and the distance of stars, but instead they were names like Notting Hill Gate and Willesden Junction and Bethnal Green. Some stops were double and treble stars, Hammersmith, Mile End, and the blue line of the River Thames – it was the Milky Way.

Then I found it: South Acton. I went back into the WHSmiths and asked the woman behind the counter how to get the train and she tutted. That's the Silverlink. You're better off getting the Tube. She told me some names and I wrote them down in my London Book and found them on the map, but I couldn't tell if they were miles away or not. She was just lying to get rid of me. I'd been in London nearly fourteen hours and I'd hardly fucking moved. I got some money out of the machine in the station.

I pressed the OTHER AMOUNT key. 2 then 0 then 0.

I decided to walk for a bit. See what happened. So I joined the din, dragging my suitcase behind me. I was tired and wanted to lie down, but I walked past St Pancras Library and kept going. There was a crossing and on the other side was a red building that looked like a multi-storey car park. It had a sign saying British Library and next to the British Library was a big white building with a blue Novotel sign on. It was the one I could see from the hotel window the night before. It had so much glass and was so shiny you could see clouds reflected in it all blue and grey.

I stood and watched the see-through lift on the side of the building going up and down. Some of the people inside waved down at me.

The revolving doors moved when you stepped on the carpet. The foyer was enormous and busy-as. I sat down and looked around. It was the poshest place ever.

I asked for a room away from the traffic noise. The woman behind the counter smiled, her lipstick and mascara too heavy. She looked like Crystal Carrington with her bouffant hair and shoulder pads. She eyed me up and down and said: are you a business customer? Plummy, like the Queen.

— Yes. I'm in London on very serious business.

Gunky eyelashes like a hair clasp, blinking at me.

— I'll put you on the sixth floor. Check-in isn't until two. You're a bit early but I'll see what I can do. Health club, sauna, steam room, solarium and gym are on the fifth floor. The Mirrors Restaurant and Bar will be open this evening with an international menu. Can I see your credit card to guarantee your booking, please?

I took the two hundred pounds out of my purse and slapped it on the counter.

— Will this do?

She looked around.

— You better put that away.

She took my purse and pulled out my card and waved it in my face.

— This will do fine.

Then she was rummaging around under the desk and hitting some keys on a computer.

— There's a little safe in your room, in the wardrobe. Here's the combination for the lock. Just type it in, like you're dialling a phone. And I really *do* recommend that you *don't* carry such large amounts of money in London, madam.

Snooty bitch.

There were three lifts. The middle one had a sign on.

THIS LIFT HAS PANORAMIC VIEWS

It went up so quick, the street disappearing, making my stomach light like I was floating. It proper shit me up. I moved to the back, afraid I'd fit and fall out through the glass and down into the street below. I couldn't get out of there fast enough.

The room was number 1603. It was proper gorgeous. I ran over and jumped on the massive double bed, running my hands over the sheets. They were cold and crisp and smelt of washing powder. There was a nice coolness in the room coming from somewhere. I propped myself up on the big suede cushions and looked around. There was a little desk with a brown leather chair and a lamp. A glass-top table with a bouquet of flowers making the room smell sweet. A big television and radio alarm clock and minibar and a big rectangular thing that said Trouser Press on it. There were two remotes on the table next to the bed. One was for the telly but the other only had two buttons on and they had arrows going < > and when I pressed one the curtains began to move. It was tops – you didn't even have to get out of bed to open the fucking curtains in the morning.

I peered out the window, and there it was: the whole mess of London.

I could see down Euston Road to King's Cross and the Carlton Hotel. I thought I'd seen it all, but I hadn't seen fuck all. Not an inch. It went on and on as far as you could see. I couldn't believe the size of the place. London stretching out like a mess of Lego. It looked ridiculous, like something a kid would draw.

I let out a little laugh and went into the bathroom, white and sparkly with loads of posh toiletries, Molton Brown shampoos and shower gels, body wash and little soaps. I thought I'll be having those.

I found the little metal safe in the bottom of the wardrobe. I put my purse and mobile in and pushed the door to. I pressed the numbers and heard it click shut. Sometimes I forget numbers but I always remember shapes.

It was easy: a back-to-front Z: 3 1 9 7.

I flushed the combination away and opened a window. The sound outside was just a swish with a distant beeping like electric birds.

I couldn't remember lying down, but when I woke up the clock said it was just after four. I felt brand new. I walked around the room massaging my arms, shaking my legs. I used the phone and got room service to bring me a sandwich and Coke and then I showered and put on my jeans and a T-shirt. I took two tens from my purse and put the purse back in the safe. I took the photo of Mikey and slid it into the back of my London Book. I got the lift and I was Alice in Wonderland going down down down.

ळळ

A pong of tramps in a doorway. Booze and piss. Five or six men and a youngish girl sitting on bits of cardboard with raggedy clothes and woolly hats in the heat. The nearest one spotted me.

— Have you got any change, please?

The shock of the posh voice. I looked at him and didn't know what to say. I was thinking, yes but what the fuck you going to spend it on? I was thinking, fuck it, what's twenty pee, a quid? Why don't you just fuck off? I want to take you home and give you a bath. How the hell did you end up like this?

I ran off.

I remember ending up sat on a bench, all the traffic just a swish in the background. The sky was a machine, making a whistling noise, revving up and slowing down. I knew it was aeroplanes up there, but I couldn't see any. I looked at the photograph of Mikey and had a few words with myself. I reminded myself who I was and why I was there. I kissed his face on the photograph and said tomorrow you'll go and see her, you will. I took out my A–Z and put a cross over the stop called South Acton.

I was getting cold. I headed back past Euston and got

to that stinking doorway again and tried not to look. Most of them had gone. There was just a bundle in a sleeping bag and the girl.

She was perched on the step, hugging her legs, twisting her hands, staring up at the little bit of sky you could see through the tall buildings, like it was talking to her.

— Are you OK?

Dirty little fingers and scraggy hair. I wished I'd some chocolate to give her.

— You all right? You warm enough?

It sounded stupid soon as I'd said it. Of course she wasn't fucking all right. Her eyes moving slow, she looked up at me with her little heart-shaped face so white. Cold sad-eyes, but big and brown like Maltesers. She snivelled her nose with the back of her hand. Her nose red-tipped like a cherry, hair needing a damn good brush, clothes hanging off her like a rag doll.

But the eyes were a woman's eyes. She looked about forty. No, she looked sixteen. I could see all the fastness and jaggyness of her life. I shoved my hand in my pocket and dropped the notes and coins at her feet. She looked down, then up at me. She showed me her teeth, flecked brown. She made a little noise with her breath, but I rushed off before she could say anything.

⊘⊘⊘⊘

You put the ticket into the slot at the front, and then you move forward into the gate. Then you take the ticket out of the top and the gates open and you have to rush through, the gates shutting quickly behind you. You can't get it wrong because the gates'll trap you. I watched a dozen more people doing it, just to make sure. I was thinking, I'm skinny enough to squeeze through, tall enough to step over. Fat people must get stuck in them all the time.

Yep, it was The Right Thing To Do.

The escalator took us down. It was like being inside a toothpaste tube but stinky and dusty and hot as armpits. I started to sweat. Adverts everywhere, curling around the tiles. On the platform a crackly voice said there would be further delays at somewhere or other. Most of the men with briefcases slumped and sagged. Then the wind came. Nice bit of coolness on your skin. Suck and gust. The train shot into the station too fast, shiny like a metal worm from its hole, and I'm thinking if I fit down here I'm fucked. I pictured myself on the floor, people stepping over me, ignoring me and tutting.

The bowels of London. It smelt of humans and sweat, coffee and fags, of hot crotches and nasty perfume. It was weird, sat facing people like that. I took in their no-looks. You're not meant to look at people in London: it's The Wrong Thing To Do.

Like smiling or saying hello.

Like being polite and saying thank you.

Like talking to people you don't know. No one wants to talk, they think you're fucking mad. Shut your face. Watch where you're walking. Never apologize. Stick out your pointy fucking elbows. Don't fucking scare anyone by talking to them, it's not natural. Everyone gets so close to you. Kiss goodbye to your personal space.

A dark wavy voice came from somewhere. We began to move fast, the walls of the black tunnel outside the window all wires and soot. The sway and fro and din of the carriage. I tried not looking at people, but couldn't help it. People jabbering loud above the noise. I stared at an advertisement for a cheap day trip to Cambridge. I read it over and over again until I knew all the words.

It was The Right Thing To Do.

The Tube map was wrong – I could feel we weren't going in a straight line.

The Tube map was a fucking lie.

At the next stop a bloke sat down opposite me. I tried not to, but I caught his eye and I was sure he gave me a sex-look. I looked back at the advert thinking he could reach over and place his hands on me if he wanted. No one would stop him. They would just ignore him and pretend it wasn't happening. He could pin me to the floor and spread my legs and everyone would pretend to be asleep or reading a book or playing a game on their mobile. But when I slyed another look at him, it wasn't me – it was the girl next to me he wanted.

I looked at her sideways. She had her head lowered and was writing into a diary thing. If she knew he was staring, she wasn't letting on. She nibbled on her pen and tapped it between her teeth. Then she started sucking it up and down and I thought: don't do that.

I turned away. I became one of them. A sameshit face behind the magazine I'm not reading, fingernails I'm not chewing, eyelids I'm not rubbing, compact I'm not checking my lippy in. Anything but play eyeball ping-pong. We all look away. It starts and stops, starts and stops. They come in, get on, sit down if they can. And then they hide behind their books and magazines and fingernails. It starts and stops, starts and stops. The man gets off and then the young woman. I watch my journey on the long thin map above the doors, the lie of the straight lines. And then it's me bustling and racing up the escalators. I got to the gates and London was proving me stupid again. No one said. There were no signs anywhere. Everybody but me knew that that was The Wrong Thing To Do. I told the guard I'd chucked my ticket away and he looked really tired and let me through.

I was out at Goldhawk Road.

It took me an hour to walk a few centimetres in the A–Z. I stopped folk and asked them the way and they looked at me unsure. I found the street eventually, though. I took a deep breath and walked up the path and knocked on the door. Heart in my gob and I knew it was stupid but I thought he'd answer the fucking door. I did. Hello, Mikey.

Keys in the lock. Noise like a hasp being dragged then big glasses and frizzy hair staring up at me. Her mouth an arsehole puckered up.

— Sorry to bother you. I'm after a Sylvia Smith.

I could hear the television going somewhere. She pulled the door to a bit, looking me up and down.

— Who's asking?

— I'm Lily. Lily O'Connor. Mikey's sister.

But her face didn't change.

— Well there's no Sylvia here. What address do you have?

I told her and looked up and down the street.

— Well I'm sorry but there's no Sylvia here.

— Maybe she lived here before you?

— I'm sorry, I can't help.

She closed the door sharp in front of me. I still had my mouth open and my hand in the air. I knocked on the door again. I could hear her moving about. I thought she was just old and deaf and maybe a bit daft.

— Hello? Hello missus?

I prized the letter box open with my fingers and put my mouth to it.

— I just wanted to ask you how long you been living here?

Nothing.

— Missus? Hello? Hello missus?

I walked back down the path, the net curtain twitching.

⊘⊘

I showered and changed and went to that doorway where I'd seen the tramps. The girl was there on her own. When she saw me, there was something like surprise on her face. It was the first friendly face I'd seen in London.

— Howay, I'm taking you for some chips.

She looked at me for a long time, then stood up slowly. She was tiny next to me. She had a Safeway carrier bag that she pressed to her chest. We began to walk and she kept lagging behind like she was going to run off and I kept saying come on, it's all right, I just want to buy you some food. Her little feet shuffled. We got to the pub and went inside to the loud music and busyness and warmth.

— What do you want to drink?

The surprise of her voice, deep and crackly and fast,

— Vodka and Coke.

— Go find us a seat.

She sat twizzling her matted hair round her fingers. I'd ordered us both fish and chips off the Not So Light Dishes menu. The barman came with the two plates and gave her a funny look. I went: you want a photograph? He left. She wolfed her chips down with tons of tomato sauce and necked the vodka in two gulps. She was jiggling her legs and bouncing her head. I didn't mean to, but when she'd finished polishing off her plate, I went how come you're living in that doorway?

Her face said I'm scared, fuck you, mind your neb, thank you – all at once.

— My father kicked me out.

She drew circles with her grubby fingers in the ketchup on the plate. I went,

— I never knew my dad.

She peeped up at me and I realized who she looked like.

— He left before I was born. I never met him.

Me, as a bairn.

— You're lucky.

I shrugged.

— You a religious nut or something? Doing your good deed for the day?

— What?

She leaned back and sucked her fingers. She caught a bloke's eye on the next table and flicked the Vs, staring a hole right through him like acid. He turned away.

— I'm staying at the Novotel over there. Do you want to come back? You can have a shower. I've some clothes you can have.

Her eyes slitted.

———

She spent a long time in the shower with the Molton Brown stuff. I told her there was complementary tooth-brush and paste, to help herself to anything. I could hear her humming a tune in there. I poured two drinks from the minibar and flicked through the music channels. When she came out, she was red from the heat, fresh-looking. I noticed for the first time she was really pretty.

Even with the bruise on her cheek.

Even with the tiredness under her eyes like black thumb smudges.

She smelt of my perfume and her face was shiny from moisturizer. I'd given her a pair of jeans that she'd rolled up and up at the bottom. And she had one of my T-shirts on. It looked like a tent on her. She bundled her dirty clothes into her carrier bag.

— Thanks for that. I hate it when I can't wash my hair. Sounds stupid, doesn't it?

— You in a hostel or something, then?

— They chucked me out.

She rummaged in her bag and pulled out some papers and tobacco. She picked up the drink and sat by the opened window and lit her rollie and blew the smoke out.

I went where you from then? She looked at me like she was weighing me up.

— Middle of nowhere. Near Falmouth. You been?

— No.

— You don't want to. It's a shit-hole.

— Worse than London?

She laughed.

— I don't even know your name.

— Lily.

— Rachel.

We looked at each other across the room.

— So why did your dad kick you out, then?

— Because he's a cunt.

I noticed how skinny her ankles were. I wanted to hold

them in my hands, to warm her up. I moved my chair over to the window and showed her the photograph.

— It's my brother Mikey. Mikey O'Connor. That's why I'm down here.

— Does he think he's lord of the jungle or something?

— He owned a reptile house, but it got shut down, and well . . . he disappeared.

She moved the picture closer to her face and then handed it back.

— Do you know him?

She shook her head, no.

— He'll be my height and well built, and talk like me.

— Never seen him before in my life.

— Take another look.

She looked with a smile on her face.

— I'd recognize him, fit geezer like that.

— I'm down here to find him. I don't know where to start.

She just shrugged and went good luck. I felt like the air had gone out of me.

I poured us more drinks. Rachel went over to the telly and started swinging her hips to one of the songs, singing along. I could picture her at a disco making boys blush and cross their legs. We drank more drinks and watched MTV. She spread herself out on the bed and things felt easy. Then she just came out with it,

— My mother died when I was eight.

A noise filling the room, coming through the window from outside. A helicopter chugging – it sounded like it was right above the hotel. She shouted it out,

— My uncle raped me.

I moved to the window and shut it.

— Rachel.

— My father's the local vicar. Said I was a disgrace. Found my stash of blow and said it was the final straw. Kicked me out he did. Said I was no daughter of his. If I wanted to walk that path I could do it alone. Said my mother would be spinning in her grave.

She got on the bed, put her face in the pillow and heaved. I put out my hand, but I couldn't touch her.

— I'll take you shopping tomorrow. I'll buy you some new clothes and stuff. You needn't hang around with those men any more.

I wanted to see her smile, that's all, but she turned and looked at me hard, her hair stuck to her face.

— You a lezzer? You want to touch me, is that it?

— No.

She turned her back and hugged her legs.

I stood in the middle of the room and listened until she began rattling and I knew she was fast asleep. I turned off the TV and went to the window and looked out at the streets: a thousand headlights and windows and neon signs. I pictured the people in the bowels down there, whooshing along the sooty tubes, and I wondered where Mikey was.

I felt like I'd stepped out of myself and couldn't get back in.

I crept across the room and put the little lamp on. She was making little moaning noises, moving her legs with little kicks.

I went back over to the chair and crouched down and lifted the side of her carrier bag. I moved her clothes around inside. There was a hairbrush and some of the Molton Brown stuff from out the bathroom, and in the bottom there was the corner of a small photograph.

I wanted to pull it out. I wanted to look at her life.

But I didn't.

I climbed onto the bed next to her and stroked the tips of her hair.

Then I closed my eyes and listened to her sounds.

16

I called her name. Nothing. I knocked on the bathroom door.

— Rachel?

She'd gone. And so had most of my clothes and the money from my jeans. She'd even taken my fucking tampons. The only thing to say that she'd been there was the wet towel on the bathroom floor.

Then I saw that my pills had gone.

I ran to the window and looked down. But of course she wasn't there, in the street below, her arms a bundle of clothes. I checked the safe and it was still locked. I stopped crying and told myself it was OK, don't panic don't panic.

Aeroplanes, helicopters, car alarms, horns blasting, telephones, postcards, curved adverts, foreign faces, MTV, violins in the lift, thousands of no-looks – right then it seemed these things were trying to get inside of me, forcing their way in, and all I wanted was to be back home with my writing on the walls, Elvis playing below and the sea lushing against the beach outside the window.

I put my hand on her dent in the pillow and wondered what I'd done wrong.

My tampon was full so I flushed it away. Then I had to put tissue paper down my knickers.

It reminded me of what my nana used to call it: being on the rag.

I went to the St Pancras Library over the road, careful how I walked. I went up to the woman behind the counter.

— Where's nearest doctor's surgery please?

The woman sighed and pointed over my shoulder.

— Yellow Pages are over there.

— And do you know where's the best place to get clothes?

Her face beamed.

— Best place for shopping is Oxford Street, without a doubt.

She put her hands on the counter and leaned over.

— What are you after? Anything particular?

— Just, you know, clothes and stuff.

— Well, you'll find *everything* you need on Oxford Street: Selfridge's, John Lewis, House of Fraser, Karen Millen, whatever takes your fancy.

I thought she was going to ask to come with me.

I thanked her and sat down. I flicked through the thick Yellow Pages to find D.

I thought they might've only existed in films. American films.

EMPLOYEE AND MATRIMONIAL OBSERVATIONS.

LIBEL AND SLANDER MATTERS. PHOTOGRAPHIC EVIDENCE.

STALKING AND HARASSMENT. TELEPHONE BUGGING AND DE-BUGGING.

SATELLITE VEHICLE TRACKING.

Then I saw the words.

TRACING MISSING PERSONS

I tore the page out of the book and left.

London in the summer, the heat's too much. It's like being in bed with all your clothes on, two duvets on top and the radiator on full whack. A double-decker goes past, moving the air about and it's like a hairdryer in your face. I found a shop and it was even warmer in there, like being inside a mouth. I paid the rip-off price for a box of thirty-two Super Plus and when I got to the doctor's I went straight into the Ladies and put a new tampon in, the tissue sopping already. I'm always heaviest on the second day. Rachel couldn't have timed her spree worse.

I went to the front desk and told the woman what'd happened with my pills. She gave me a form to fill in and said she wasn't sure how long I'd have to wait.

I said I'd wait all day if need be.

I felt clumsier than usual, half-asleep. My lanky legs full of sweat. I was too tall and too skinny, too pale. My hair was too frizzy. That room stank of new carpets and paint.

Fucking waiting rooms – it's where the real examination begins.

Chairs lined up so everyone faces you. The magazines are on a table in the centre of the room – they put them there on purpose because they know you have to pick one up. It's the only way you can hide from THE EYES quizzing you. I walked into the middle of the room feeling on show and picked up a year-old *Cosmopolitan*. I sat down and pretended to read, but I could feel them on me. What's wrong with her? She looks normal. Isn't coughing or snivelling. Must be a sex thing. It was an hour and a bloody half before they called Lily O'Connor to room six please.

He looked up at me with that calm look all bright sparks have.

— So how can I help you?

He was younger than me. Longish hair, smart clothes, nice teeth.

— I got robbed of my pills this morning. I've temporal-lobe epilepsy.

— Have you been injured at all?

— No. Nothing like that.

— Have you been to the police?

— Yes.

— OK. So which anti-epileptics do you usually take?

I reeled it off. My type and how long and how often, the name of the doctor back home. The bright spark was writing and nodding slow, like *he* was on medication. I told him the name of my pills and how many I take each day and then he said something about levels, when I last had them checked?

— Can't remember. Sorry.

— How long are you planning on being down here . . . erm, Lily?

— Don't know. Few months maybe?

— Well, I think it would be a good idea to set you up with a specialist.

I pictured my hands around his neck, throttling. I thought I was going to have to turn on the waterworks. Get on my knees. Beg the fucker.

— But I'm all right with my dose. I just want a repeat.

— I'll have to contact your GP.

But praise the lordy lord he started scribbling.

— I'll give you these for now. Come back on this date and we can discuss things further. I'd like you to get your levels checked, to look at some of the newer treatments available. The chemist is out the front door, second on the left.

I left with a big thank you.

⊘⊘

I went to that doorway. I didn't know what I was going to say to her. Something like she didn't need to do that because I was only trying to help, that I wasn't bullshitting. And that I knew. I knew what men do. I just wanted her to be safe. Something like that.

One of the men was there. He had a scabby dog. You could see its ribs.

— Have you seen Rachel?

A hard look. Pink tongue moving in brown beard.

— Who?

— The young lass. Rachel.

He rubbed his face, making a scratchy noise.

— Have you seen her?

He tried to tap me for some money. I tore a page from my notebook, wrote down my mobile number.

— When you see her, give her this. And tell her it's OK. Everything's OK.

He looked at the paper and muttered something.

———————

The first name on the torn-out page was on Harley Street. I remember loads of flash cars, Ferraris and Porsches and a massive Roller with darkish windows. I stopped and peered in: there was a man inside wearing a cap and I waved but he pretended not to see.

I was thinking Madonna. I was thinking Kate Moss.

I found the number and went up the steps. It had a doorbell but nothing to say it was a detective's agency or not. The hallway through the glass – it was plush-as, with shiny brass doorknobs and white carpets. I couldn't think what I was going to say. I pictured a handsome man in a chair, looking at me, twiddling his thumbs, eyes in shadow under a big lamp.

I rang the bell four, five times. I rang it for fucking ages, but nobody came.

I knew I was getting towards the centre of the city, that I'd hardly seen any of it. I knew the busyness of Euston Road would just be trickle compared. But fuck me, I'd never seen so many people in all my life.

Oxford Street – it sucks you in, and if you don't keep moving they'll trample you to death. I stuck my hands out in case I tripped, and joined the conga of people with their shopping bags and saw a megaphone sticking up above the thousand heads,

KEEP TO THE RIGHT, LADIES AND GENTLEMEN, PLEASE KEEP . . .

I felt children running between my legs. There were horns going mental, people running between the traffic. In the shops it was all grabbing and queuing and get your bloody card out and we're off again.

For a while I was in high-street heaven, but then it just became music changing, and watching my hand signing my name over and over like it was someone else's. Perfume being sprayed in my face. Lipsticked gobs shouting about facials. Hands leading me by the elbow. All the shoppers looked like they could've pissed themselves with joy.

But I got muddled. I can't remember which shop I was in, but I walked out of the changing room wearing just my knickers and bra. I spoiled the party. I got told off and hustled into the cubicle and the security guy looked like he wanted to slap me. I ended up in a ladies' toilet somewhere, shopping bags around my ankles, using the toilet roll to wipe the sweat running between my breasts and the tears from crying.

I was so fucking confused.

I was used to shopping in the market back home, the indoor one on Thursdays, the covered one next to the Town Hall on Saturdays. I knew the stallholders' names and we always had a laugh. But it was nothing like this. London was a running battle. It was a pile of bodies writhing like fat worms in a fisherman's box.

I looked at the bags, all the names on them. It was so fucking exciting but I knew I'd spent a fortune and it made me feel like shit. I got a taxi back to the hotel and closed the curtains and left the bags on the floor and got into bed. Outside, the sun was shining and people were laughing and cars were vrooming. The day was still happening but it meant fuck all. I cried myself to sleep because I was so useless, I was so fucking selfish, and Mikey felt further away than ever.

❧❧❧❧

A man knocked and came in with breakfast on a tray. I sat up in bed and watched him serve me like I was in hospital.

I ate and dressed and was about to leave when my mobile went. A text from Barry. My belly flip-flopped. It started with a howdy doody sis and then how crazy America was and that I'd love it there, it was just like a big Blackpool. He texted that his big poker game was in two weeks, and that I could call him if I needed to, but he was playing all the time and that he'd call soon anyway. He signed off El Slicko and put three Xs for kisses. I wanted to send a reply but I didn't know what to say. I didn't want him to know where I was, and I didn't want to lie.

———

I got the Silverlink train to South Acton. It's like a proper train and you can look out of the window at the walls of graffiti and all the tower blocks and forest of cranes in the distance. In places you get right up to people's houses and flats and you can see the people inside, frozen like snapshots. It took about half an hour to get there, and the old woman's house was only three streets from the station.

A small boy opened the door. He looked up at me and said are you the nosy parker?

A hand dragged him away, making him scream. I heard a slap. Then she came out onto the doorstep. She closed the door behind her and folded her arms.

— Sorry about that. What can I do for you?

— I came the other day. I spoke to the older woman. Your mother?

— What do you want?

— I'm trying to find Sylvia Smith.

I could hear her breathing through her mouth. She had a blonde bob, lines around her mouth, crow's feet round her eyes like she was too keen on sunbeds. Her hairline was really low and uneven, fluffy and white. She put her hand behind her and fumbled with the door handle.

— I'm Mikey's sister. I'm trying to find him, that's all.

She looked at the floor. I could see the brown roots of her hair.

— Our mam's died.

She squinted up at me.

— I need to find him, to tell him.

— Look, I haven't the foggiest where he is.

I put out my hand, touched her elbow.

— Can we just talk? Five minutes, that's all.

She sagged a bit. I went,

— You've no idea how much it'd mean to me.

She walked past me, down the garden path, and started walking along the street. I caught up with her and she said did you come on the overland train?

— Yes.

— I'll walk you there. I don't want to see your face round here ever again.

She had her arms crossed, marching fast. I grabbed her shoulder and yanked it back. I was thinking she can be as arsy as she likes, I'll fucking knock it out of her. She looked at me shocked. I pointed my finger near to her face.

— If you know where he is, you fucking tell me, or I'll come here every fucking day until you do. I'll camp on your doorstep. I'll put banners up. Just tell me what the big fucking secret is?

— There ain't no fucking secret.

— You tell me, woman, or I'll go to the fucking police.

She started looking around and showed me her hands.

— Just calm down. I've got to live here, you know.

— Tell me.

— Please keep your . . .

— TELL ME.

She turned this way, then that.

— I saw him just the once. After I left. That's all. He came to the house and we had a few choice words and that's it. Haven't you talked to your Barry? What's he said?

— Barry? Nowt. Just that he tried finding him and got nowhere.

— He *would* say that.

— Eh?

She huffed a massive sigh. I went,

— And what about that lad? The kid that answered the door.

— Simon?

— Is that his name?

— Simon *has* a dad. Knows no different. Loves him to bits. Want to ruin that?

— No.

— Listen, it's Barry you need to be talking to, not me. Barry was the last one to see Mikey. Not me, all right.

— Barry?

— I've told you everything I know. Now please, leave me alone.

My gob open, my hand in the air, I watched her walk away.

☙☙

I slept so badly that night. I was sick with the agony of it all, the not-knowing. But Sylvia knew something, I could feel it. I had to go back there. I had to find out.

I got up when I heard the foreign maids jabbering along the corridor, and as I showered, I thought about Rachel in a doorway somewhere, a needle in her arm. Spare some change please? I saw men going at her and the smell they left, like wet soil. I thought about all the things she'd said and what I'd done so wrong.

No sleep and the heat of the shower – it proper wiped me out. I thought I was going to faint just putting my knickers on. I had the Feeling, and I was only making it worse by fretting. This little voice inside my head was saying Lily, do yourself a favour, and get yourself back to fucking bed. I told it to shut up.

I knew if I took the tube that I'd lose it down there, like burying myself alive, so I got a taxi to Highbury Station to take the Silverlink train, but I got on the wrong platform and I ended up going east instead of west. By the time I realized what I'd done the train had stopped and the sign on the platform said . . .

But I don't know what it said.

There's nothing there.

When I squeeze my eyes tight and think back to that day, the colour drains out of my mind. The memory is dead, empty, nothing but black.

I lost a whole day. I was on the train going the wrong way and then, sudden-as, the sunlight's slapping my eyeballs, piling through the open curtains in the hotel room.

Chop it up. Chop it out of my life. All these fucking outtakes. I wonder what they'd look like, if you'd put them all together?

I rang reception and asked them what day it was. Wednesday, the woman said, like I was some kind of spaz.

I got into the shower and thought fucking *Groundhog Day*. Then something came back to me, a whisper in the hish of the shower noise. I rushed into the bedroom, dripping water everywhere, and looked at my mobile. But there was only one name there: BAZ. It made me queasy. Then I looked in my jacket pocket and found it: a piece of scrunched-up paper. A name and telephone number.

I necked my pills and got dressed, repeating the name in my head. I took the lift down and wandered along the Euston Road, stomping the name out with each step, screaming it into the traffic whirr: Mel. Mel. Mel. Mel. Mel. Mel. Mel . . .

Hoping it would tell me something.

15

— Mel?

It took me till Saturday. Three whole days, but I slept for most of that, having to fend off the maids in the afternoons, telling them I was sick. The telly kept me company, kept my mind off it all because I had this awful feeling someone had done something to me, something proper bad. I couldn't feel anything inside of me, but I kept on showering anyway, scrubbing my skin sore.

So I did it, I pressed the number with that high feeling in my stomach.

— Yes?

I was surprised by the woman's voice. I'd been thinking Mel was a bloke.

— Is that Mel?

— Speaking?

— I found your number.

— Sorry?

— Your number. In my pocket. The other day, Tuesday. I don't . . .

— Oh wait. Yes. It's Lily, isn't it?

She sounded youngish, friendly, but her voice did nothing for me. It didn't magic me back there. I closed my eyes, listening to her breathing on the other end.

— I don't know what happened.

— You don't know what happened?

I tried to explain about my memory going and she went,

— I was coming back from the shops and I heard a car breaking hard. I looked up the road and I could see you lying there. The car didn't stop, it just swerved around you and sped away. I thought it'd hit you.

— I know. That's happened before.

— I ran over to you and you had your eyes open. You looked up at me and blinked. I could see blood coming out of your mouth. I started to call an ambulance but . . .

— I kicked off.

— You started shouting and trying to get up off the road.

— Sorry. You must've thought I was drunk or something.

— I was a bit confused, yes, but you said the word epilepsy and I kind of knew.

She said she helped me to the side of the road and we'd sat on a wall together and I'd tried talking to her about Sylvia but I was slurring my words bad.

— Then you asked me to call a cab for you, to get back to the hotel. You seemed totally with it, just a bit shaken.

I wanted to say I was sorry. Wanted to sob. Wanted a new life where I wasn't me. To disappear into the blackness forever. To be in bed back at home, looking at the Big Dipper with Elvis rumbling away downstairs.

— Where was I, when you found me I mean?

— The road just outside my house. Canonbury.

— The train station?

— No. It's nowhere near the train station.

The thought of me traipsing through the streets like that – you've no idea. I've done it before, wandered around all day on autopilot, had conversations with people, gone and sat in the pub even, had a drink and a laugh. But the next day I can't remember a fucking thing. It's like sleepwalking but you're totally awake. It was a proper reality check, doing this in London.

I decided there and then that I needed to see her face.

— Are you all right now, Lily?

— Yes. And thank you for looking after me. Really. Thanks.

— That's OK.

— I'd like to meet you, if that's all right? I'd like to thank you, properly like.

— Oh.

— We could meet for a drink, a coffee or something?

She wasn't saying anything on the other end and I thought fuck, I've proper freaked her out.

— Yes. Of course. That'll be great.

— You sure?

We arranged to meet on Monday night after she'd finished work. She named a pub near Euston and I thanked her twice and hung up.

I wasn't expecting to see her again.

☙☙☙☙☙☙

Sunday morning I was feeling tons better. I got room service and stuffed myself silly, stocking up for my big stomp. I needed to walk. Needed to look around the streets, searching in all the dark places. I put on my new Nike CityKnife trainers and felt buoyed up, fizzing with the idea of finding Mikey by walking the streets of London and staring into tramps' faces. But when I think back now, those days are just a smudge of dirty faces, bottles in grubby hands. Down every London street there's gangs of them, off their faces, shouting at you for looking, lunging at you with their fists for not making them invisible. And the thought that Mikey was like that – it really fucking scared me.

∂∂

— Nowhere To Hide, how can I help?
— How much does it cost to hire a private detective?
The man cleared his throat and sighed.
— That rather depends on the assignment.
— I'm trying to trace my brother.
— Well, traces can vary from anywhere around three hundred pounds to an unlimited amount.
I'm sure he could hear me swallow.
— Fine.
There was the sound of paper rustling.
— OK madam, why don't you give me a few more details and we can discuss . . .
— How long will it take? On average?
— There is no such thing as *average* because the length depends on too many variables. Such as the complexity of the investigation.
This is a bad idea. The man sounds like a total knob.
— It's like asking how long a piece of string is.
What a prick.
— How much can I get involved? I want to help with it.
He laughed.
— Only as a point of reference, madam. Listen . . .

— How do you do it? I mean, what do you do exactly?

— We cannot share our methods with outsiders.

— Can we meet up? I'd rather we met.

— I charge one-two-five an hour off peak, one-seven-five on peak.

— Jesus.

— That's standard, madam. My name is Mr Morris.

— I better meet you off peak then, Mr Morris.

— That's after seven. You can come to my office on . . .

— I know where it is.

— OK. Thursday night at seven thirty. We can discuss my terms and conditions. If you can't make it, then I'd appreciate it if you'd let me know. Thank you for calling Nowhere To Hide. There's no hiding from know-how.

⊖⊖⊖⊖

It'd just gone three by the time I got to Sylvia's. I thought I'd time it so's I'd be there for when Simon came back from school. I wanted to see him again and look into his eyes. Wanted to speak to Sylvia one last time before getting anyone else involved. And I wanted her to tell me the truth – whatever that was.

I knocked on the door but no one came. I opened the letter box and shouted hello. I put my ear to it: no telly blaring away, no nothing. I sat on the step and stared down the path. I closed my eyes and listened to the birds in the trees, the cars vrooming by at the end of the street, and I was just about nodding off when I heard his voice.

— Mummy.

He was stood at the gate, pointing.

The eyes, blue like a summer's sky. And the shape of his face: it was Mikey staring back at me. I wanted to hold him.

She opened the gate and gave Simon some keys, telling him to go through the back door.

— I'm not here to make trouble, Sylvia.

He ran past me without looking. She folded her arms on top of her breasts and came up close to me.

— His dad'll be back *any* minute.

— It's his dad I'm trying to find.

She looked away with a big huff, then she spoke low,

— Please let this go. I've told you *everything*.

— Hasn't Mikey tried keeping in touch? He must know about Simon?

— Please, keep your voice down.

— I'll shout all I fucking like.

She stood on her tiptoes, her face close to mine. I could see the patterns in her eyes, flashes of orange in blue like flowers.

— I won't tell you again: leave – my family – alone.

I opened my mouth and she punched me in the gut, winding me good and proper. She started dragging me back down the path, her fingernails cutting into my arms. She pulled me up the street. I knocked her hand away and clung onto a fence until I could breathe properly.

— There's no need for that.

My heart was jiggered but I was ready for a fight.

— I don't care how big you are girl. You fuck with me and I'll drop you. You mess with my family and you'll wish you'd never been born.

I took a step back, straightened out and rubbed my belly.

— You O'Connors are nothing but fucking trouble.

We stood looking at each other and I couldn't help it – big fat tears started plopping down my cheeks. I turned away and tried to even myself out.

— Why do you think Mikey fucked off, eh? It's your Barry you should be talking to. It's your Barry that was last to see him. It's your Barry that knows where he is.

Then she touched my arm and it made me flinch.

— If I knew where he was, I'd tell you. I really would.

She squeezed my arm and went,

— But I don't.

Then she walked away, the feeling of her fist still in my gut.

She didn't look back, and I realized how stupid I was, thinking I could just come down here and speak to her, find him like that. Like it'd be that easy.

I felt so stupid. So lost. And so fucking clueless.

⊘⊘

Mel was late and I thought she wasn't coming. I'd finished my drink and was about to leave when I saw a woman stood in the middle of the pub, looking from face to face. Our eyes met and she smiled. I waved, trying to remember.

I stood up and we shook hands and she gave me that quick up-and-down look: fuck me, you're tall. She looked pleased to see me. She took her coat off all gaspy, like she'd been running or something. She was pretty and looked about my age and had a smart suit on. She had a nice figure and I pictured her in a gym on a treadmill, sweating on her lunch break.

— So sorry I'm late. The tube was cram-packed.

— It's a bloody nightmare down there. Can I get you a drink?

— Ooh, I could murder a gin and tonic. Cheers.

It was nice to put some space between us. I ordered two gins and leaned against the bar and she caught me peeking a look at her. I felt my cheeks flush.

I'd thrashed, I'd got up. Now I just had to bloody well get on with it.

I took the drinks back over and she took a big gulp.

— I've had a nightmare day.

— What do you do?

— I work for an investment bank in the City, supporting a global electronic trading system.

She must've seen my face.

— Trust me, it's pretty geeky. I execute worked orders and resolve any client issues like execution prices, queries on fills, FIX connections, discrepancies. I have four bloody screens on my desk.

— Jesus.

Her hair was cut short at the back with a longish fringe at the front and dyed a chestnut colour, sleek-as. She really did look like she'd just stepped out of a salon. She had a small mole on her cheek, dark coloured eyes with smoky kohl making them darker, and she had that glow about her: well off. I looked down at my new clothes and they seemed cheap.

— Where you from, by the way?

I felt an urge to lie, strong like a punch to the back of my head. But I stopped myself. She was successful and pretty and had been nice to me, and compared to that, who the hell was I? Anyway, I knew where lying got you – it got you into shit because you have to remember each and every little lie, and one day you trip up and people see the truth, and that truth is that you have holes in you. For some reason, I didn't want Mel to see the holes in me. I wanted her to see me properly.

— Yorkshire.

— Thought so. Your accent's lovely.

— What about you?

— Wales.

— You don't sound it.

— Boarding school.

— Ah.

— I can speak some Welsh though.

She said a few words and my laughter was like lids banging off the walls. The air turned light and I felt a tiny fizz between us.

— So anyway, thanks for meeting me like this. It means a lot. I suppose I'm just scared about what I was doing and saying and wanted to make sure, you know, that I was all right and that.

— You were fine. Honest. Just a bit dazed, I'd say.

There was something babyish about her face when she smiled, the soft shape of her cheeks, the curve of her jaw. Her skin was tanned and bright and firm. It said toning Clinique creams.

There was a moment of silence before she went,

— So how did it go with Sylvia?

— Jesus.

I took a swig of my drink and leaned back against my chair.

— You know what this is like, don't you? It's like blabbing on about something when you're pissed and you have no memory of it the next day.

— I didn't realize epilepsy was like that.

— Most folk don't. They think it's just falling on the floor and thrashing.

So I told her everything, warts and all. I opened up to her and surprised myself. All the shit about me and Barry and Mikey and Sylvia – the lot. She was almost a complete stranger, but it felt like we'd shared something special, secret, important. And as I was talking, things kept sliding into place inside my head.

I realized her eyes were welling up. She sat on her hands, looked down at the table and took a deep breath.

— Have you been to the police? I mean surely.

— Barry did all of that.

She shook her head, coughed. Her neck was patched with red.

— And so what did this Sylvia woman say?

— She just fobbed me off.

— You think she's lying? You think she's hiding something?

— Someone's lying, I just don't know who.

She downed the rest of her drink and then looked at me like the answer was written in my eyes. It felt like I'd cleaned myself, like she'd breathed new air into me and suddenly I wanted to be off, raking the streets for Mikey, knocking the truth out of that Sylvia bitch.

She looked sad and I felt the weight of what I'd just said.

— Can I get you another drink?

☙☙

I got into bed and clicked to Messages. All the empty places in the night, all the gaps where Mel went to the toilet or to the bar and I was left on my own, I'd get this niggle at the back of my head and feel angry-as. So I thought fuck it, I'd let him know. I went to Write Messages.

I MET A WOMAN TODAY. SYLVIA. RING ANY BELLS?

Then deleted it.

HELLO BROTHER. NEVER GUESS WHERE I AM? LONDON. YES REALLY. YOU ARE SUCH A CUNT!

Delete.

WHERE THE FUCKS OUR MIKEY? IF YOU EVER WANT TO SEE ME AGAIN YOU TELL ME!!!

Delete.

CUNT!

I looked at the word for a long time. The way it comes out of your mouth, explodes in your head. The way it hits you in the face with that tut at the end. CUNT. It was nowhere near bad enough for how I felt. TWAT. BASTARD. CUNT. It didn't make me feel any better. I needed a new word, something proper evil. I flung the mobile across the hotel room and wanted it to smash. But the fucking thing didn't. CUNT.

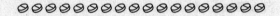

111

I sat on the steps in Harley Street and took my mobile out. I pressed one to listen to the new message. There was loud music in the background and then Barry shouting.

He said something about having the best time of his life, he'd met the most amazing people, it was a different world over there, and he said would you Adam and Eve it he was into the next round. I was to wish him luck, and that he loved me. That's what he said: love you, sis. Then he ended the message with the weirdest thing:

— I'm climbing a mountain on roller skates but I'm getting near the top.

Twat. I pressed three to delete.

I went up the steps and rang the buzzer. An old woman let me in.

— Miss O'Connor?

She showed me up some stairs and knocked on a door and I nearly changed my mind there and then, nearly bolted. It felt just like going to see a bright spark.

I'd imagined him being really tall, handsome, moody. But Mr Morris was a titchy man with a baldy head and jowly bits on the side of his face. I thought he looked like a bloodhound and I could imagine him sniffing things out. I thought that was a good sign.

He stood up, buttoning his jacket. I remember his hand was large and puffy and warm. I got a picture in my head of a loaf of bread. He spoke all breathy like he had the hiccups. I was surprised the room smelled of fresh flowers – I'd imagined him sitting in a reek of smoke.

He asked me to take a seat and would I like a tea, coffee?

— No. Thank you.

He nodded at the old woman and she left the room. He waited a second, like he was making sure she wasn't nebbing at the door. I wondered if she was his mother. Then he picked up a fat black fountain pen.

— Let's start from the beginning.

He asked some weird questions, and I told him things about my family I'd never told anyone before. Something in his eyes – I felt like I had no clothes on, like he could see right through me. Everything is evidence, he said. *Everything.* I gave him Mikey's last known address and told him I didn't want him to bother Sylvia yet, that he'd scare her off completely and I wanted to talk to her myself. His face was: we'll see.

— So do you have any other information? Any photographs?

I gave him the photo. I saw a flicker of something go across his face. A twitch in his cheek.

— I want it back mind. It's the only one I've got.

— No problem.

He got up and went over to a machine on his desk. He pressed some buttons and it hummed and whirred and spat out a large colour copy of the photo. He stood looking at it, frowning. I went,

— Can you make me some copies?

He took a deep breath in.

— Please? You can add it to my bill or whatever.

He shook his head and pressed some buttons and the machine began whirring, spitting out pages. He handed them to me and they were warm.

— How recent is this picture?

— Don't know. Ten years ago maybe?

He passed my photo back and made a noise in his throat.

— So he's a strong man. And you say he owned this reptile house?

— Yep.

It was like he'd worked something out, something that I'd missed. I was waiting for him to tell me, but he just scribbled another note, checked his watch and shuffled his papers. He coughed into his fist, looking at the clock on the wall. It'd gone half eight and I'd kept him long enough. I wanted to go with him, looking for our Mikey. I wanted us to sit in a parked car, eating hotdogs together, keeping an eye on some house or other.

I stood up and said it as quickly as I could,

— There's someone else. Donald Blackman. I was told he works on the Tube. I want you to find out his address, that's all. Nothing at all to do with our Mikey. Donald Blackman.

— Your erm, mother's ex-partner?

I nodded and he sighed, leaned over his gut, scribbling.

— You understand that this is a separate case, yes?

— Just write it down. I want his address. And what hours he works. And I want you to use my mobile number to contact me day or night, OK?

I marched out of there, feeling puffed up, proud, and fucking terrified about what I'd just done.

14

Waiting for a call, wandering the streets, showing Mikey's picture to people who squinted and shook their heads. I'd written on it have you seen this man, Mikey O'Connor? And they asked me is he a rough sleeper? Have you checked the hostels? Maybe he's in a squat, have you thought about that?

I found the nearest hostel and showed the manager the picture and he shook his head and said thousands of men pass through here every year, but yes, he'd stick the picture up and took my mobile number just in case. Then he told me the address of some other hostels but said there were hundreds of them in London.

At the next hostel the woman said she couldn't share information about guests and I lost it with her and shouted how the fuck am I meant to find him then? She closed the door in my face.

Always feeling like he was just around the next corner, imagining seeing him and what he'd look like now – it kept me slogging on.

I met Mel again for a drink that week. It was a proper relief having someone to talk to, knowing I wasn't going totally off my rocker. But I kidded myself she just felt sorry for me, and when she went goodbye, I thought I'd never hear from her again.

I tried to stick to nine to fives, tried to get enough sleep, take it easy on myself, making sure I wasn't overdoing it because a fit would only set me back. But one morning I woke to the coldness up my back and the stinging between my legs and I knew.

I got out of bed and looked at the damage. The wet made the sheets look grey. I lifted them: a dark patch on the mattress. The ring, the sharp smell.

I showered and packed my bags and pinched the rest of the nice toiletries. I took the lift down to the foyer for the last time.

I can't remember how much the bill was exactly, but it made me gulp.

I signed my name and scuttled away.

∅∅

I moseyed around, trying to find a hotel that wasn't so close to the main fucking road as the Carlton. I wandered between the streets, wiping the tears away from my eyes and telling myself to get a grip. I wasn't sad, just empty, apart from this feeling in me like a brick, dragging me to the ground, and I knew that if I let it, I'd never get up again.

I was a car crash with no passengers inside.

I went and had dinner in a greasy spoon and it made me feel homesick. I'm going back home, back up North. That's what I kept thinking. But I knew it was a coward's trick, so I kept on walking, up and down the Euston Road.

I could see the Novotel. I could see the Carlton. I could see the Chop Chop Noodle Bar and Incredible Edibles. I could see King's Cross and the scrum of people outside.

Cranes like dinosaurs, filth and noise and panic and fucking metal everywhere. It made me sick. And I didn't know what I was waiting for until it went off in my pocket.

— Hello?

— Hi, it's me. Mel.

My lips got tight with the grin.

— I was just wondering if you're OK, you know?

— I'm fine. Thank you. Thanks for everything.

— That's great. What you up to?

— Just booked into a hotel.

— Oh right. That's good. Great.

I felt like a soggy clod of earth and Mel was this bright shiny thing on the end of the phone. She went,

— Listen, what've you got planned for this evening?

I met her at the Angel Tube station. When she saw my case she smiled and I went,

— I'm fucking useless, aren't I?

She laughed.

— Listen, you can crash at mine tonight if you want?

— No, it's all right. I can find somewhere later.

We both looked at each other.

— Come back to mine, honestly.

— I don't want to put you out.

— I've got a spare bed. Really, it's no problem at all.

The brick in my stomach turned into a flower. She took my arm,

— Come on: let's have a quick drink before the film.

I watched her at the bar. She had on some cropped trousers and a pretty camisole top that was a faded blue and yellow colour. I saw some men eyeing her. She looked so much younger out of her work get-up.

I realized I'd been hoping she'd ask me to crash, and then I realized how fucking cheeky I was.

She brought the gin and tonics over and I took a massive swig.

— I've been gasping for a proper drink all day.

— So how did it go with the detective?

I huffed a big sigh and she went,

— Only if you're comfortable.

She touched my hand and I felt safe for the first time in a long time. Having someone to listen – it was the best thing. But when I told her that I felt I was chasing my own tail, she looked proper sad.

— I don't know what to say, Lily.

I didn't want her to ask me what I was going to do next, because I didn't know. I hadn't a fucking clue. I really needed a hug.

— Have we got time for another round?

She looked at her watch and smiled.

———

We went to a pictures called Screen on the Green. I can't remember what the film was. I think it had Tom Hanks in it, or maybe Tom Cruise. Anyway, it was the same old Hollywood shite and I couldn't concentrate; my head was stuffed with images of Mikey from when we were kids. I wondered how I'd got there, sat in that dark cinema in London next to Mel, not knowing what was going to happen from one moment to the next. At one point I started crying and had to hide my face. Mel's company was like a strong pair of arms around me.

She elbowed me and I realized the credits were coming up.

— What did you think?

— Er, yeah. I don't know.

— It was absolute rubbish, wasn't it?

We stopped in a pub on the way to hers and sat in a snug. We sipped at our gins and we got onto Our Pasts.

She told me about her mum and dad in the big house in the country and how boring and normal they were. About her older sister and her sister's perfect husband and their perfect kids. She put her middle finger in her mouth like she was making herself puke and kept apologizing. It nettled me. As if she had anything to apologize about? I was starting to notice how my voice sounded compared to hers: clumsy, and thick.

— So tell me about Barry. It must've been strange, meeting him after so long?

— Weird-as. But we soon got close as anything.

— I hope you sort everything out.

I thought she was going to start bawling.

— So what about your dad, Lily? You didn't mention him.

— Because I never met him. He left before I was born.

— I'm sorry.

— Don't be. My mother said he was a useless Irish cunt anyway.

A look away; a deep swallow.

— So did she marry again?

— She was the village bike for a while. Had one fella shack up.

— I hope you don't think I'm being nosy?

— What about you? You got a fella?

She downed the rest of her drink.

— It's hard meeting people in London. Anyway, I never really get the time.

— I bet you're beating them off with a stick?

She just laughed and got another round in. When she came back she made a fuss about how tall I was, which I hate. I've heard it all a million times before. Then she said if I ever needed her during the day, that I wasn't to think twice about calling her. I noticed her lovely nails as she was thumbing her name into my mobile. French-manicured. And then the tiny earrings in her ears, twinkling like only one thing can twinkle. And the waft of her lush scent.

We walked back to hers through the posh streets. We talked and laughed, but it was just chitchat and silliness – you could tell we both had a million thoughts flapping around inside. I was thinking about the people back home, and the problem is they all know you, or think that they know you. And if they don't know you, they make stuff up. Everyone has an opinion on everyone and everything, like they're scared not to. I realized that I didn't know anything about anyone, not even myself. It felt fantastic.

And her? Well, I was just hoping she wasn't regretting inviting this freaky Long Tall Sally back to hers.

And me? Well, I was just hoping I didn't piss the bed that night.

☺☺

There's someone in the room and they're crying.

— Lily?

It's Mikey's voice, cracking. He's clambering into bed and budging me over.

— Lily?

I get out the other side and put on the light. It's bright and hurts my eyes. I can see his head. He's just had it shaved: nits. He's too big to be getting into bed with me. I must be five, sixish. And he's got to be eleven, twelve maybe. He turns around.

— I killed it.

He's struggling to breathe.

— I killed it.

His chin's going, creasing up. His face is horrible, wet and red. I need a piss and he's scaring me. It's freezing cold and I want him out of my bed before Mam catches us and gives us a good hiding.

— Killed what?

He sits up, wipes his face. He gets out of bed and takes my hand and we tiptoe across the landing into his room. The light's on and Barry's asleep in the other bed – a lump under the covers. Mikey points at his own bed, but doesn't move. I go over and look but I can't see anything. Then I pull the sheet back.

Brown fur and ears, the pink of its little feet and I want to scream.

He puts his hands over his face.

— I just wanted to cuddle it. Keep it warm. Just wanted to cuddle it.

— I won't tell.

He walks over to the bed and pulls the rabbit out by the ears. He holds it up and looks at it, turns it slowly. He squeezes the front of his pyjamas like he needs to piss. He goes to the window, opens it, and drops the rabbit into the back garden. I see his breath as he looks down at it. We go back into my bedroom and he gets in behind me.

I listened to him until he stopped crying. He put his arm over me, and it was still there when I woke up, his breath all hot on my face. The toilet cistern was whistling across the landing and I thought about the rabbit in the garden outside.

We found it that morning. Frozen into a weird shape in the grass. We dug through the hard soil and made a little cross for it with wooden clothes pegs and elastic bands. Mikey put his hands together and mumbled 'Our Father'.

———————

I was lying in Mel's spare bed, looking around the bedroom and listening to the whirr of traffic in the street outside. I knew it was Saturday morning. The walls in the spare bedroom were a beige colour, blank like skin, and I pictured my scribbles all over them in thick black pen.

I felt lost. Felt nothing was going to work any more. Like an intruder in this massive, posh flat. Thick, clumsy.

I tiptoed through the long corridor and into the kitchen. There was a long garden out the back, and houses like little palaces beyond. We were on the second or third floor. Mel said she only moved in a month before and that's why the place seemed so sparse. I realized her kitchen was bigger than the whole of my flat back home.

I could hear children making a noise below and a baby crying somewhere and a woman shouting STOP IT. I watched the planes flying in the sky. I thought of Barry and felt very far away.

I found a cup and ran some water into it and necked two tablets.

Mel started coughing in her bedroom. I hished across the shiny wooden floor back into the bedroom and shut the door behind me. I opened my suitcase and spread all my stuff out on the bed. I chose my new Nike CityKnife trainers, my zippy khaki trousers, my new spangly gold belt and the plain white top, the one I think I got from Gap. Then I lied back down on the bed and I must've gone into a proper mong of a sleep because I heard a door slam somewhere and it woke me with a fright.

A voice sang hello? I went into the hallway and there was Mel with carrier bags.

— How you doing? You looked a bit peaky when we got back last night.

— Aye, I'm fine. Cheers.

She was out of breath. I kept looking at the bags and she went,

— What's wrong?

— I need to find a hotel.

— Oh.

— I've got tons to do.

Her shoulders dropped and the bags clanked on the wooden floor.

— Do you want to stay for breakfast? I've got some nice food in from the deli.

I could've eaten a scabby donkey. Be polite, eat her food, and leave.

— OK.

— Great.

She came back to life again and picked up the bags.

— But then I'll have to be off.

She put some music on a little flash-looking stereo and began her chopping and slicing, talking to me all the time like she was scared of any quiet coming between us. The way she spoke, the way she looked, the way she moved – she was off a film with Hugh Grant.

We ate breakfast together at the kitchen table and then I made my excuses to leave. She told me to ring her any time that I wanted, and to let her know where I was staying.

— Hopefully, I'll see you soon. We can go for a drink or something?

— It was fun. Definitely. Thanks for having us.

— Good luck.

And as soon as I closed her front door behind me, I realized that leaving was the last thing I wanted to do. The loneliness – it was a knife twisting inside of me.

∞

I ended up going to the No One Hotel. The name suited my mood. It looked pretty skanky after staying at the Novotel and Mel's place. I sat on the bed in the quiet of the room and struggled not to cry.

I dialled the number. It was ringing for ages, then the loud sound of jangly guitars blurted in the background.

— Al, it's me.

He made a long noise.

— Oh it's you lass, it's really you. I've been worried *sick*.

Hearing his voice, picturing his wig flying across the shop and his little face.

— How you doing, Al?

— Ee, it's not the same without you here. How's London?

— Didn't you get my postcard?

— Aye, I did, I did. It's here on the wall next to us. Marvellous.

— Have you got someone in the flat yet?

— No. Haven't had time. Knowing my luck, I'll probably just get some druggy.

It felt like a relief.

— You've got to be careful.

— By the way, a lad's been in here asking after you.

— Who?

— Had his hair all daft. Just a minute . . .

Ridge Racer. I heard Al laughing and the till pinging and then some goodbyes. It was nice, a comfort, hearing the Northern accent again. That first real tug of home.

— Sorry about that, love.

— What did he say? Did he leave a message?

— No. Just asked me to say he'd been asking after you. Pass on the message like.

— You didn't tell him where I was?

— Said you'd won the pools and gone to Barbados.

— Cheers, Al.

— So really, how is it?

— I've made a friend.

— Champion. Won't be long until Christmas now? Still spending it with Elvis?

— Promised, didn't I?

— I've got some photos to post you. Won the Karaoke again this year. I know, I know. I've got a new outfit as well: '68 Vegas comeback. Black leather, top to toe.

— Sounds kinky.

He went quiet. I thought about Barry and the last time I saw him. I could hear commotion in the background.

— Sorry I've got to go, love. Busload of purple rinses. We'll speak soon, yeah?

— Bye, Al. Love you.

I saw the seafront in my head; I saw pensioners with carrier bags walking down the promenade and moaning about the weather; I saw Jim having a fag in his office, fidgeting with his crotch; I saw people walking dogs on the beach, staring up into the oily sky. I buried my head beneath the pillow and tried to suck sleep into my head, but it wouldn't come.

———

I don't know how many days passed, how long I was moping around the No One Hotel or wandering around the streets with his picture, waiting for a call from Mr Morris. One night I went to King's Cross with my case all packed and stood on the platform, staring at the train that'd take me back home. The guard came along, closing all the doors, and I stepped back. I heard the whistle and watched it move away. It took a piece of me with it. I'd never felt so lost in all my life.

But Mel phoned and saved me from myself.

I walked to hers through the park near her house. The sun was making patterns through the trees and people were smiling and kids were playing fifty-a-side football with jumpers for goalposts and dogs were sniffing each other's arses. It felt so good to be among people and I started to feel better, more alive, but as soon as Mel saw me and said Lily, you OK? Well, that was all it took.

It came out all wet blubbers. She led me through to the living room and we sat on the leather couch and I cried so hard it felt like something had broke.

— I'm sorry.

Mel's hand in warm circles on my back.

— Shush. You don't have to be. I understand.

— You must think I'm a loon? You must think who's this crazy woman I've met?

— I think you're so strong, do you know that?

I stood up and went to the window.

— I don't feel strong. I feel like I can't breathe. Can we go out? Please?

I was walking fast and she was struggling to keep up with her little legs. We came to the park and I stopped and looked out over the grass, at all the green cut into shapes by the paths, triangles and rectangles. She stood next to me and put her arm through mine. I don't know how long we stood there, watching the joggers, the dogs chasing balls, the kids on bikes, just saying nothing.

I felt something hard in my jacket pocket. It was the little pink shell I'd picked off the beach back home, the day Barry left. To remind me of him. I rolled it in my fingers and something settled in me. I started talking, not looking at her, just staring at all that green and the tower blocks poking above the trees.

— Something's not right. Someone's lying to me. And Barry's run off to fucking America and I'm stuck here, trying to make a jigsaw with all the fucking pieces missing.

She looked at me like I don't know what to say.

— I know this sounds mad, Mel, but I can feel he's alive. I feel him inside of me.

I coughed and tried to shake the feeling off.

— Let's do something. Let's do something exciting.

She opened her mouth.

— Howay, let's have fun. I can't *think* about this any more.

She smiled.

— I need some fucking fun.

— OK.

I chucked the pink shell away into the grass.

———

We took the number four bus and got off at St Paul's and walked down to a big white bridge. It was the first time I'd seen the Thames. It looked filthy, the colour of coffee, and I got a waft of sea on the wind. It made me close my eyes and smile.

We were heading for a big orange building and you could see the massive words written on it: TATE MODERN. Mel suddenly ran in front of me.

— Turn around.

She twisted my body and I think I even gasped.

— It's amazing, isn't it?

It was scary and beautiful and too big and I wanted to scream.

— I was just the same, the first time I saw London from the river. Takes your breath away.

She put her arm through mine and started pointing out all the buildings. The names meant nothing to me back then – apart from Shakespeare's Globe. I'd seen *Romeo and Juliet* on video but it was a load of mumbo jumbo.

I followed her finger as it waved about.

— That's Tower Bridge. London Bridge. The nearest is Southwark. Don't know what they are. That's Cannon Street. The Lloyd's Building. The green-coloured one, looks like a dick, that's the Gherkin.

— Stop. You're making me dizzy.

She hugged my arm into her.

— This is so exciting. I feel like I'm experiencing London all over again.

We walked for ages along the river and for the first time I got a proper sense of where I was and what I was doing. Mel wanted to go into galleries but I said no, I'd rather die. I wanted to take in the size of the place, the massive buildings, the buzz, the argy-bargy of the crowds.

We came to a bridge and opposite was a big orange Vienetta cake with all of its fancy bits and layers. Mel said it was the Houses of Parliament and she pointed to Big Ben and I went oh yeah. I thought about all the New Year's Eves that I'd listened to it, the music in the pub switched off, couples moving into each other shouting ten, nine, eight, seven . . . and me on my own as per.

We found a bar and it was nice and loud and smoky but the drinks cost a fucking bomb. And that was where Mel asked me.

— Lily, I wanted to ask you something.

— Ask away.

— I know this is going to sound completely mad . . .

I folded my arms and leaned on the table.

— Go on.

— I've had some ads in the local shops and at the library. All of my friends are either married with kids or have moved out of the city. I don't really know anyone that's free and single any more. And my place is too big for me. I'd get lonely, and the mortgage . . .

— Listen, Mel.

She showed me her palms.

— Just hear me out. I was dreading that whole

interview thing. Strangers in my house. Weirdos. You can never be too sure about people, can you?

She had no idea.

— I've lived on my own for years. My fits are unpredictable.

— I can cope.

— I've got habits. You'll go off me. You'll want rid of me.

— You're free to leave any time you want. Come on, it must be a better prospect than those horrible hotels? And maybe having a permanent address will help your search for Mikey?

I looked at her and she said I like you.

— I can't do the girly thing, Mel. I don't get on with women. I think I give off this thing and they can smell it on me. I've never had a woman friend before.

— Well, you can change all of that. We're friends, aren't we?

— But you don't know me.

— I know enough.

— You *really* don't know me. I'm used to being on my own. I've never done anything like this before, coming down to London, not knowing what I'm doing one minute to the next. But yes we can be friends. We can meet up and do things?

There was a long quiet. No one had ever spoken to me like that before. I got up and used the toilet and I almost left, there and then.

But the knife, it was twisting away inside of me.

When I went back into the bar I asked her: how much for rent?

Her face was a total picture.

— Only three hundred a month.

— But we've got to be honest.

— The room is quite small.

— If I do your head in, then tell me, there and then.

— Come on, it'll be fun.

— I hate things lingering.

— I hate atmospheres.

— Things going unsaid.

— You've got to respect my space.

— Mine too.

— Of course.

— Course.

We smiled at each other and I thought who am I trying to kid?

— I'll think about it.

She shrugged and looked away.

— It's up to you, Lily. But the offer still stands.

We had a few more drinks and tried talking about other stuff, but of course it was there, looming. I was relieved when we went to say goodbye and she came straight out with it,

— So will you take the room?

— I don't know.

— I know this hasn't been the most normal of introductions, but life's like that, isn't it? Call it fate.

— You forgot the most important question before.

She frowned.

— What's that?

— Are you going to spaz out and piss everywhere every so often?

A tut; a look away.

— Because the answer is yes, I will.

— Lily.
— And you don't mind? You honestly don't mind?
She grabbed my hand.
— No, Lily. I don't.

13

The phone in the living room was going all morning, waking me up, but I kept nodding back off. When I finally got up, Mel was in her bedroom with her stereo on. She was listening to Massive Attack. There were boxes and papers and books and clothes lying everywhere. She was dressed but she was in bed, reading something. I said hello and she looked up startled and folded some papers.

— You finally unpacked those boxes then?

— Yeah, sort of. It's taking longer than I thought.

I stepped over the piles of stuff and sat on the edge of the bed.

— I'd offer to help but.

She laughed.

— It started out well. Then I kind of lost track and everything ended up on the floor. I got up early to sort it out, but it's never-ending. I keep finding things I thought I'd lost years ago.

She leaned over, picked up the cordless phone. She looked at it.

— It's hot. It hasn't stopped ringing all morning.

— I heard.

— If you're not feeling too well, let me know and I'll unplug the whole thing.

— Who was it?

— First my mother wanting to come and visit. Then my

sister filling me in on the latest drama with the twins. Then an old friend of mine from Cambridge. We studied economics together. She's getting married next weekend and has only just got round to inviting me. Said she didn't know my new address which is a *total* lie.

That's when I saw the picture in the frame. Mel and another woman. They had their cheeks together and were laughing. It was taken in a pub or a club and people were in the background holding glasses. The woman had gorgeous hair, all blonde and straight, like I've always wanted mine.

— Is that her? The one that's getting married?

Mel frowned at me then looked at the picture. She held her breath before saying anything.

— No. That's not her.

She got out of bed and left the room, leaving me sitting there, wondering what I'd done.

☯☯

After breakfast she brought her laptop through to the kitchen.

— I've had a bit of a brainwave, and would you blah-di-blah me.

This was happening a lot. Sometimes she went off on one and left me standing, not knowing what she was going on about. And sometimes I was saying words or things in ways she'd never heard before. She called it the North–South Divide. She always apologized; I didn't.

I told her that I'd heard of it, of course I've fucking heard of it, but didn't really know what the Internet was. She looked flabbergasted, and told me to prepare myself, that my life was about to change forever. She gave me the mouse-thingy and pointed at the screen. To start with, it was just loads of colours and words and lines, confusing-as.

— I thought you worked in an arcade? You should be a computer whiz.

— The machines only do one thing. Even a barmpot can work one.

— Don't start that again. Put your finger there. Left click. That's it.

So we got onto the Net and she said why don't we Google epilepsy and see what comes up. There were one and a half million hits. One site said there were forty million people round the world with epilepsy. Another one was called Famous People With Epilepsy and I wrote them all down, even though I hadn't heard of most of them.

Julius Caesar. Agatha Christie. Socrates.
Edgar Allan Poe. Alexander the Great.
Napoleon Bonaparte. Sir Isaac Newton.
Charles Dickens. Feodor Dostoyevsky.
Truman Capote. George Frederick Handel.
Edward Lear. Philip K. Dick. Pythagoras.
Vincent Van Gogh. Gustave Flaubert. Saint Paul.
Heracles. Archduke Charles. Pope Pius the Ninth.
Alfred Nobel. Lord Byron. Joan of Arc.
Vladimir Lenin. Margaux Hemingway. Molière.
Danny Glover. Mohammed. Ian Curtis.

— You're in some pretty amazing company, Lily.
— Yes, well. We can't all be talented.

She gave me a worried look.

— What?

— At work this week, well, I've been doing a bit of research. I hope you don't mind? It's just that I found this site.

She typed in the address. It was the National Missing Persons Helpline. I looked at the page, then at Mel, then at the page again.

— They're a charity, so they're not there to rip you off. It's where the police go when they need help tracing people. They have this massive database of all the missing people in the UK. They use advertising, putting people's faces in magazines and on buses and on milk cartons.

— And why the fuck would I want to put Mikey's face on a milk carton?

— To find him?

— So he's *missing*, is he?

— I thought. Well. It's either this or . . .

— I don't think he's missing, Mel. I don't think he's lost. I think he's done one. I think he's somewhere where people can't hurt him any more. He's fucking dead, Mel. He fucking topped himself.

— You don't mean that?

— He'd lost everything. EVERYTHING. Why wouldn't he?

She'd nettled me. I was fuming at her and myself and the whole fucking world.

— You don't believe that?

— Don't fucking tell me what I believe.

She stormed out and slammed her bedroom door behind her. I listened past the hammering in my ears – the only sound was the hum coming from the computer.

I'd only been living with her for a week and already I'd lost it. I thought I best get out the road, before I said anything else. But when I put my hand on the door handle, I couldn't leave.

I knocked on her bedroom door.

— Mel?

I knocked again.

— Mel?

The curtains were drawn but there was a lamp on. She was sat up in bed, looking at me. I'd put a needle between us. I whispered,

— I'm sorry.

I sat on the end of the bed.

— I bet you're wondering who this mad woman is you've invited to live with you?

She shook her head like she was really tired.

— I'm sorry.

— It's OK.

— No, really. I don't think he's dead, Mel. I don't know why I said that. It's just that the more time goes by, the further he feels away from me, that's all. But I know he's alive. I can feel it in here.

I put my hand to my chest and she looked away.

— Look, there's something I need to tell you.

She picked the framed picture up off the bedside table and passed it to me. I looked at the photo.

— Two years ago, I started a new job in the City. I was meeting lots of new people, making new friends, one of which was Anna.

I could see now – it wasn't a pub or a club they were in, it was somewhere abroad. Palm trees in the background, fairy lights hanging from trees.

— We got on really well and we became really good friends. Anna was getting married and she invited me to her hen party down in Brighton.

I could see the drinks Mel and the woman had been supping: bright green cocktails with cherries and umbrellas in.

— I was dating a woman at the time.

The laugh jumped out of my gob; Mel looked at me, then away again.

— And everyone knew I was a lesbian.

I swallowed the word. It nearly choked me.

— Though they didn't like my girlfriend very much. She had a drink problem, so she didn't get invited out by my friends very often. Anyway, on the hen night . . .

I was on Pause. My face was burning up.

— We all went out and got really drunk and I ended up getting off with Anna.

I watched my finger rubbing the top of my leg.

— This caused a bit of a crisis in her. But that wasn't immediately apparent. I just put it down to drunkenness. You know, last night of freedom. Bit of a pissed-up snog.

The line I was drawing up and down my leg – it meant that I didn't have to say anything because there weren't any words there anyway. The line was rubbing out the tale as it came out of her mouth.

— Anyway, the day of the wedding came up. She rang her husband-to-be in the morning and told him she wasn't going to marry him. Because she'd realized she was . . .

I caught her eye for a second and tried to smile.

— Then she phoned me up and told me what had happened. That she was in love with me and wanted me to move in with her. So I left my girlfriend and me and Anna set up home together that very day.

Mel rubbed her hands together. I watched them move.

— And it was two of the happiest years of my life. But now it's all over and my friends hate me. They *really* hate me.

She folded her hands on her lap and looked at me.

— So now you know.

12

The sudden light feeling in my gut. The lightness was like a wave going up through my stomach, up through my lungs into my throat, right at the back there. And when it got to the back it felt proper stuck, like a lump of something meaty dangling on my tonsils. But it wasn't a sick feeling, it was nice. I could hear the fizzing, brain frying in its own lard, electricity zapping down around my heart like a ball of light. Insects creep-creeping and I scratched and scratched but I didn't black out. I wasn't going full welly.

I knew that I was sat on a bench in Clissold Park and that it was windy and there were people about, trees and grass and kids going home for their suppers. I knew where I was and all that.

Then I let out the high noise. I opened my mouth and out came the wave, warbling and high, belting out like I was an opera singer, and that's when I saw it: I could see a room in front of me.

I could feel and see that I was small, the door handle just eye level and I'm watching my hand open it, a small bony hand and the wings flapping away in my tummy. I feel the carpet under my feet and there's darkness but I can just make out a bed, I'm walking across to it and I'm so excited the wings are lifting me. I'm feeling for the warmth between the sheets, slipping my hand in. I feel the warmth there and . . .

But that was it.

And it was like the park was nothing but some reflection, like in a TV screen. But I could feel it, feel the warmth as I stuck my hand under the sheets. It flick-flickered. It lasted a second and then it was gone, and so was the feeling in my gut. Like I was going to somersault backwards, sprout wings and fly away. I felt different and I felt happy but I didn't know why, I just knew I wanted Mikey back. To look after me, to protect me. This solid feeling inside.

I didn't want to go back to the flat. I didn't want to see Mel yet. I waited until they were shutting the park gates, the wardens shooing people out, and then I sneaked back in and hid under my bedsheets.

☺☺

I stared at the photo: Al on stage at the Clarenden. Disco lights and Al in black leather, his quiff and hands in the air and the people below him – you could tell they were cheering, you could tell they were loving it.

I heard her alarm go off. Her bedroom door went, then she clattered about the house. A sneeze. A cough. Rufflings. Slap of feet on the wooden floor. The hiss of the shower. Her feet on the bottom of the bath, farty noises. Blowing her nose like an elephant. Deodorant hissing. Knockings and bangings. Her feet thomping as she went back into her bedroom. The wardrobe door creaking, hangers rattling. The hairdryer sounded. Then she was in the kitchen. Clatters of cutlery. Slurpy sips.

I half-expected her to barge in. Have a go at me for running out like that.

I rolled over and pulled the duvet up to my chin. The clock said seven-seventeen in its green numbers. I screwed up my eyes. She jingled the keys off the hook. Heels on the floor, clunk of the door. Clomps of her footsteps down the stairs and gone.

I found a note on the kitchen table. Written like she didn't even know me. It said an electrician would be round at nine to fix the dodgy light in the bathroom, would I let him in? There was no Dear Lily. No kiss goodbye. Not even her name.

I took my case down off the top of the wardrobe, put it on the bed, unzipped it and stared into it.

I pottered around, drinking tea, had a shower, stared out the windows and watched morning telly. Then the buzzer went. It was almost twelve. I looked out the front window and there was a yellow van outside.

DavELECTRICS

ELECTRICAL CONTRACTOR

"One call and I'm on my way!"

Your **Local** Electrical Servicing and Maintenance Man

ALL NORTH LONDON AREAS
MOBILE 07941 779876 ANY TIME!

I was ready to give him a bollocking for being late. But when I opened the door, I saw the tools hanging from his waist and it did something to me. Then I saw the huge Cheshire grin go across his stubbly face and my belly flip-flopped.

— You must be Dave Electrics?

— You must be Mel?

I felt myself bending a leg. My voice went low.

— No, I'm Lily. Mel's at work. I'm just staying here.

I stepped back and he came into the stairway and praise
be, he wasn't a short-arse. As tall as me and tooled up to
boot. He had a black T-shirt on and tight jeans and you
could see he had a nice body. His brown hair was long
and tied back in a ponytail. He followed me up the stairs,
talking about some crash on some ring road or other,
and that he was sorry he was late. I felt his eyes on my arse
as I climbed the stairs.

I let him go past me into the hallway. He came
close and I could smell him, some kind of deodorant
like he'd just got out the shower. I suddenly remembered
my pills.

— Bathroom's in there. Do you think you'll be long?
It's just I've got an appointment this afternoon and I'll
have to be off soon.

— Don't worry. It's my fault. I'll be out of here in two
shakes.

I can't remember what I imagined him shaking, but it
made me blush. I went into the kitchen.

— Can I get you a coffee, a tea?

— Coffee milk two sugars please.

You could tell he was from London. Cockneys sound
like seals. Ar-ar-ar-ar. I could hear him fiddling with his
toolbox. I flicked the kettle on and peered out into the
back garden. I couldn't remember the last time I'd felt
like this. I leaned against the sink, smiling. Then I took the
coffee through for him. He was down on his hunkers and
I saw the muscles twitch in his arms.

— Cheers there, darling.

143

— You're welcome.

He lifted it to his lips and took a sip and said smashing. He put it on the floor and busied himself. He wasn't wearing a ring. He looked up at me and I blushed saying sorry.

— Don't be sorry, be saucy.

Fuck me. There was a spark and it lit the air and zapped us both. I went into my bedroom and shut the door.

There was this gorgeous man on the bathroom floor and he wanted me to be *saucy*. I opened the wardrobe and ran my hands through some of the clothes that were still hanging up. He was whistling a tune out there. I put some No7 Wheatsheaf eye shadow on my top lid. Then I smudged some kohl pencil round my eyes for a smoky look. Then I put some Plum Beautiful lippy on, and bit of my new Ralph Lauren Glamorous. A dab on my wrist and a dab on my neck. Not too much. I looked at myself in the mirror again and wondered what he'd think, what he'd see?

Was I pretty? Gorgeous?

I sat on my bed listening to him whistling, humming away to himself, happy as Larry. I waited as long as I could, then I went into the hallway and he was stood looking at me, his hand up his T-shirt, rubbing his stomach.

— Sorry, did you need to use the bathroom?

— No, you're all right. But thank you.

He had a way of smiling. Mouth up at one side. Eyes crinkled, shining.

— Let me guess: Lancashire?

— Careful, Yorkshire born and bred. Thick in arm, thick in head.

I pulled a face and he laughed, putting his hands on his hips.

— How come you're down here, then? What kind of work you in?

— Haven't decided yet.

— Mysterious. I like that.

— What about you? Is being a sparky all you do, or do you have hidden talents?

— Meet me for a drink tonight and I'll tell you.

— You're not fucking shy, are you?

— Life's too short.

I snorted down my nose, making a noise like a pig. I went back into my room and closed the door. I was burning up and he was calling me again.

— Listen. This is going to be a bigger job than I thought. I'll have to get some new parts and come back some other time.

He took a small pencil from behind his ear and scribbled on a scrap of paper.

— That's my mobile number. I'll be in the pub next to the Tube at eight.

I looked at the number and nodded. I couldn't help myself – I took a quick look at the bulge in his jeans as he picked up his things. He said see you later then, but it wasn't a question. I went into the living room and peered down at him walking back to his van. He looked up, but I don't think he saw me.

It had been a long time.

⊘⊘

The bright spark stood up and went behind me, putting his fingers through my hair. I wondered if he thought the make-up was for his benefit.

— I've spoken to your GP. He's informed me of your medical history.

Then he found my lump. He prodded it all over, humming in his throat.

— It seems that although you're happy with this medication, and are relatively free from side effects, that your epilepsy is rather blah-di-blah.

— What?

— That's why I would like you to consider alternative treatments. I've written a repeat prescription for the time being.

I told him I'd moved and that I was happy with the way things were. He washed his hands and sat down again, scribbling down my new address. I felt I was lying to him.

— I recommend you see this specialist. He's a leader in the field, and considering the focal aspect of your epilepsy and the newest treatments out at the moment . . .

He saw my face; it was saying no fucking way.

— Well, it's entirely up to you of course.

— Oh really. Thank you.

— There's a *very* good chance that surgery could remove any form of medial sclerosis. There's a *very* good chance you could subsequently lead a seizure-free life.

Chance? I grabbed the card and prescription, said another thank you and did one. I didn't want to look at his stupid face any longer than I had to. Didn't even want to *think* about people opening my head up. He was talking like I'd never heard of any of this shit before. I just wanted to get on with it. They could fuck themselves.

I walked through the streets thinking there were too many people in London and I hated it, it wasn't right, and in every doorway, in every dark place, there were tramps.

I stared into every dirty face, looking for eyes the colour of summer.

————

I heard the door go downstairs. Low clomps of her feet coming up. I switched the telly off and went into my room. I shut the door and put the stereo on. The keys rattling in the lock, heels on the floorboards and she dropped the keys and swore. She didn't shout hello, didn't knock on my door. I heard her getting her tea in the kitchen. I'd made a half-arsed attempt at packing my suitcase.

I knew I had to talk to her. I just didn't know what to say.

I went into the bathroom and locked the door behind me. I stripped off and had a good look in the mirror. My scars shimmered. I looked at myself sideways and told myself to stop breathing in. The little belly. I'd really let things slide. And my tache was way overdue – dark fuzz turning bristly. And my legs felt like suede and my pubes were out of control.

It was blitz time.

I tied my hair up and spread the Jolene Cream Bleach on my top lip. While it dried, I put a new head on my razor. Then I trimmed the forest between my legs and put the trimmings down the toilet bowl. I did my legs stood in the bath, then turned the shower on.

She was in the living room, door shut, telly turned up loud.

I dropped the note on the kitchen table and sneaked out. The note said I was going on a date with the electrician and I might see her later. I put a tiny kiss.

I made myself late on purpose. I was totally dressed up, and to be honest, I was scared. Scared my new skirt made me look like a tart. Scared that I was too old for something so short. Scared of VPL and that I'd fit and my skirt'd ride up around my belly and Dave would see. I thought about my last date, with Ridge Racer. I didn't even make it. And now it was spitting on and I didn't have a brolly. My hair was frizzing like an Afro. Garnier Fructus Sleek and Shine my arse. A little bit of me was wishing he wasn't there, because if he was, then I had to go through the whole rigmarole of Do I or Don't I?

If I told him about my fits, he might run a mile. He'd pretend it wasn't a problem and that awkwardness would spread between us until he couldn't take it any longer and started making his shite excuses. And if I didn't tell him, and I threw one in front of him, then he'd probably just Do An Alex. I'd wake up alone somewhere, and that'd be goodbye Dave.

But he was there, stood leaning against the bar. I tapped him on the shoulder and he beamed. He looked totally creamy. He was wearing a suit jacket with a top underneath. He kissed me on the cheek. His stubble scratched in a nice way and I wanted to rub my palms on it. We didn't have time for a drink because, he said, he'd booked a table at this restaurant just up the road and we were a bit late. My face must've been a picture.

— Is that all right? I hoped it'd be OK?
— Yeah great. Brilliant.

We walked along the street together with him yapping away, but it just made me more nervous. Then we were there and he's taking my coat and I'm sat down and staring at the menu and shouting in my head: READ.

The words were floating away from me and sinking.

Dave went Lily, you OK?

— Huh?

— What do you fancy? Do you want a starter?

— Don't know. It all looks gorgeous. I'll have whatever you're having.

He looked disappointed and said something in his funny accent that I didn't catch. I smiled and watched him trying to get the waiter's attention. I was going to fuck it up. I just knew I was. He took his jacket off.

ALCATRAZ PSYCHO WARD
OUTPATIENT

He saw me staring and looked down. I noticed he was balding a bit on top and at the front. He stuck his chest out.

— I went to San Francisco a couple of years ago. Most people say that a day at Alcatraz will just ruin your holiday. But I loved it.

He stood up and pushed his groin towards me.

— What about this?

His belt buckle said **WORLDS GREATEST ELECTRICIAN**. I saw the bulge to one side of his fly and the room felt very hot.

The waiter appeared and I ordered what Dave was having. He asked for a bottle of something-or-other. The waiter came back and poured a bit in my glass and stared at me. Dave and the waiter smiling, Dave nodding.

— Try it first.

Fuck sake. I necked it.

— Yum.

Moby's *Play* was on. The place had loads of candles and Dave's eyes were sparkling. People were being quite loud and Dave had the Banter. He started reeling off the cheesiest chat-up lines.

— There must be something wrong with my eyes because I can't take them off you. If I said you had a beautiful body, would you hold it against me? Does God know you've escaped from heaven? Do you have a map, because I'm lost in your eyes?

— Shut up, you div.

He made me laugh and I began to relax, but I was wondering when's the best time to break the News. He had a mole on his cheek, same place as Robert de Niro, same place as Mel. And dark chocolate-coloured eyes as well. My mouth was watering.

— I have my own house. Overlooking Hackney Marshes. I live on my own. Inherited it from my parents when they died.

— I'm sorry.

— Don't be. And in answer to your question this morning, I'm not just a sparky. To be honest, the job drives me crazy at times. I blame fucking *CHANGING ROOMS*.

He shouted it and the woman on the next table smiled at us. Veins were popping out on his forehead.

— Botched DIY. It's those stupid programmes on TV. That *House Doctor* bitch. They're so irresponsible. You wouldn't believe the things people do. It beggars belief. A little knowledge is a dangerous thing.

— OK, OK. So what is it that you really want to do?

— I'm an inventor.

— Really?

— I make things. Things that make life easier for people. I'm kind like that.

I tried to look interested, but I glazed, nodding away, wondering why the hell he asked me out.

The meal arrived and he ate like he was starving. There was something sexy about it. I watched how he twisted the spaghetti with his fork onto the spoon, then wolfed it down. Red spots on the serviette hanging from his collar. The hair, the stubble, the way he munched with his mouth open – there was something animal about him. I copied what he was doing with the spoon and fork. The chunks of meat, when I prodded them with my fork, I was sure blood came out. I put a chunk in my mouth and it was just like chewing on my tongue when I have a fit, flopping in my mouth too big. I swallowed it down, hard.

— I love tall women. I'm a legs man. You've got amazing legs.

His eyes got big when he said amazing.

— I know.

— Modest as well as gorgeous.

— Flattery will get you everywhere.

He thought I was gorgeous. I *felt* fucking gorgeous. I had to tell myself to stop twizzling my hair around my fingers. He poured the last of the wine and I was fuzzy and warm and giggly. He kept reaching over, holding my hand, stroking the back of it with a finger and staring into my eyes. He had a real man's hands: nails bit to the quick and palms so hard they were smooth.

Then it goes all hazy.

I remember looking at the clock and it was gone eleven and thinking wow we'd been talking for hours and I was so glad he didn't ask me too much about myself. Though I remember lying about why I was in London. And I lied about my family and other stuff. I don't know; I just didn't want to have to explain myself all over again and have it shoved back in my face. I wanted to tell him before the night was up, about my fits. I did. But before I knew it he'd paid up and we were standing outside. He insisted I get a taxi and flagged one down straight away.

I was gutted.

He opened the cab door for me and I got the sinking feeling: I'd fucked up and he hated me. But then he pulled me to him. He took my face in his hands and when he kissed me I felt sick, like he'd stuck his hands inside me and squeezed out all the air. The kiss was awkward, not quite right. I could feel him against me and I squeezed him because I didn't want to fall. He pushed his groin into me and then he pulled away, smacking his lips.

And I knew, right there and then, that I'd end up sleeping with him.

I got in the cab, my lips burning from his stubble. We waved at each other as the cab pulled away. I crossed my legs and felt the wetness.

———

— Hi there. What you watching?

— How was your date?

She didn't turn around, she just sat facing the telly and said *date* like it burned her mouth. I wanted to say he'd changed my fuse, got me wired, fried my brains out, plugged me in and turned me on.

— Yeah, good. He's *really* nice.

— So, you going to see him again?

— Definitely. He's gorgeous.

It hung in the air like a bad stink.

— Goodnight, then.

She just stared at the screen.

———

I closed my eyes and I had that feeling, that buzzing feeling when I touched my skin.

After a while, this is what I saw.

I'm stood on sand in a black swimming costume. It's summer, and the sand's warm under my feet. I'm back up North, stood on the beach, looking out across the sea. It's rippled and green – you can see black rectangles of ships and boats out there on the horizon. Then I'm walking into the water. It's cold. Over my feet and calves, my knees, my thighs. I lie down and make a noise – my lungs tighten with the coldness. I stop and pedal the water.

I know I shouldn't be doing this.

If I fit, I die.

I swim out a bit and turn around. The pier and dark hills, lights from the arcades and shopfronts, twisted and pretty. The sun has just gone down and I'm alone. No one around. I can see the painted fishing boats in the harbour, bars and restaurants along the front. I can see the Golden Nugget and white shutters in the hotel rooms like closed eyelids. A breeze with music on. Revs of mopeds – they sound like angry bees. And the beats of pop music coming from somewhere. When I tip my head back, the water runs into my ears and I can't hear any sound, nothing but the swooshing noise and my voice in my head, humming to myself. I float on my back and look up into the sky. It's pocked with lights. I know their shapes. The darkish blue is all creamy with them. My arms flap by my sides like I'm smoothing down sheets. Cool blue sheets.

I see a bed, made then unmade, sheets thrown back, flip-flap. Then the bed's shaking, headboard banging, mattress taking the weight of a body but I can't see the body, just two heads on pillows. Long brown hair – it looks wild on the sheets. And then I see the curtain, something's pawing at it. Light falls into the room like a heavy sound. It's from the moon, blue and grey on the sheets and this heaviness on top of me. Then I see lips. My lips drinking from his. There's a swaying, a toing and froing. I can feel his heat and smell his body when it's pressing against me. I fit the water. It holds me there, rocking, swaying.

My fingers moved down over my breasts, all swollen and sensitive. Down my tummy to the hotness between my legs. It was aching. Throbbing. Two fingers over the spot in circles. I rolled over onto my front, on all fours thinking it's him doing it. I felt what he'd feel and it was lush. I folded the pillow tight, put it between my legs and rocked my hips. My body up and down the bed. I heard distant music playing in the living room and my deep breaths. Up and down, grinding. I got the spot and my feet curled and I juddered. Like I could feel him against me. I pinned him down and I knew I was getting close.

I imagined I came with three high noises. I made a splash.

I spread out like a starfish and kissed my hand. I could smell him there, could smell his aftershave and taste myself as I sucked, as I licked my fingers and thumb and prayed that he was the one.

That he would be the one to make me come.

MMMMMg ERRRRmmmmmg
mmmmm greeeee heeeeey aaaaa
NEEEEE MMMMMgreegreegree gree heeeeeeeey
aaaaa ERRRGH ERRRGH hernyerrrGGGHHH
hergh HERRR hergh mmmmmm
greeeeheeeee yaaaaa
NEEEEE MMMMM greegreegree gree
heeeeeyaaaaa ERRRGHERRRGH
MMMMMg ERRRR mmmmg
mmmmm greeeee heeeeey aaaaa NEEEEEEE
MMMMM gree gree gree gree
ERRRGHERRRGH
hernyerrrGGGHHH hergh HERRR
hergh mmmmmmgreeeee
heeeee yaaaaa NEEEEE MMMMM gree
greegree heeeeyaaaaa ERRRGH ERRRGH
MMMMMg ERRRR mmmmg
mmmmm greeeee heeeeey aaaaa NEEEEE
MMMMMgreegreegree gree heeeeeeey
aaaaa ERRRGH ERRRGH hernyerrrGGG
HHH hergh HERRR hergh mmmmm
greeeeheeeee
gree yaaaaa NEEEE
greegree gree
MMMMMg ERRRR mmmmg mmmmm
greeeee heeeee
aaaaa NEEEEE
MMMMMgreegree gree gree
heeeeeeeey aaaaa ERRRGHERRRGH hernyerrr
GGGHHH hergh HERRR hergh mmmm-
mmgreeeeheeeee yaaaaa NEEEEEEEE
MMM greegreegree gree heeeeeyaaaaaa
ERRRGHERRRGH mmmmg mmmmmmm

11

She was weeping. Proper sobbing. Wiping her face all panda eyes with the mascara smudge. Something had to give, to break. The tears meant everything was going to be OK, that the needle had gone.

— Do you want me to go on?

I could talk properly now, thinking in straight lines. But I felt low. All the life and light wrung out of me. But I wanted to know.

She'd stayed. She hadn't legged it.

I watched her talking on the other side of the room. I'd told her to go sit over there because I was still buzzing with it. I thought I might electrocute her.

I nodded.

— Please, Mel.

— It went on for about ten minutes. Then you said you were going to have a fit. You went and sat on the sofa. You were rocking. The rocking got worse and you had to lie on the floor to stop it.

I looked at the floor but I couldn't remember a thing. Just the before, the after. At least I hadn't wet myself. Small mercy.

— I was talking to you, and you were talking back to me, but smacking your lips all the time, like this.

She did the noise. It was horrible.

— Your legs were going, and your foot was banging

against the coffee table, so I moved it out of the way. Your body was twitching and your head started banging on the floor. I put a cushion under your head.

I closed my eyes. I tried and tried to get a picture. One image, that's all. I looked up to the ceiling and imagined the light spinning, me scuttling across the floor below, like a beetle on its back.

— Keep going.

Mel stood up and I nodded. She came and sat down next to me. I saw her move this time – her body coming across the room.

— Then you couldn't speak. Your eyes were darting around the room. Your breathing was difficult. I was kneeling next to you, holding your hand. Then your body started shaking really hard.

I put my face in my hands, closed my eyes.

— Your breathing became more and more difficult, but you managed to tell me not to call an ambulance. Then you couldn't speak at all. It didn't seem like you any more.

I put my hands in hers. I tried a smile.

— Then you were in a seizure for about ten minutes. I felt so helpless. I wanted to make it stop, but I didn't know what to do. I tried talking to you, calmly, like you said. But it didn't seem like you were there. I tried. I really did.

She stroked and squeezed my hands.

— Your body was all twisted and your eyes, they were staring wildly. You looked like you were in such pain. I thought you were going to stop breathing. I thought you were going to die.

She started sobbing, tears coming in a gush. Something had to give, to break. I hugged her really tight and went,

— I'm really sorry.

— Don't be, please. It really doesn't matter. It just

scared me, that's all. I'm the one that should be sorry. I'm such a crybaby.

She rubbed her face. Her lips went pale over her teeth when she smiled.

— But you came back to me. You seemed really confused for a while. I asked you if you knew your name and where you were. You didn't know. But then you said Mel.

The room felt loose.

— I want us to be good friends, Lily.

— Yeah.

— You've no idea what that means to me. I know you're a loyal person.

— Just give me a minute.

I went outside and sat on the steps in the back garden. Some birds were going mental in the trees. The sky looked fucking weird, like bits of orange peel floating in blood. I could just make out the Dog Star. I followed it north and I felt like a piece of elastic. Some of the leaves on the trees were starting to turn brown and rippled like they were underwater. Grey balls of squirrels dashed about between the branches. I could hear the swish of cars going by the road out front and I felt fried. Frazzled. Shattered.

Mel was in her bedroom when I went back in. She'd transformed the place. There were pictures on the walls and it was all spick and span. She was sat on her bed looking at the photo in the frame.

— I'm sorry for avoiding you this week.

You could tell she didn't believe me.

— I'm not like that, though. You know that, don't you?

— Yes, Lily.

— I just haven't known anyone that's gay. My aunty back home was meant to be, but she had a kid though, my cousin Spug. I don't suppose she could have been, but. Though some lesbians have children, don't they?

She huffed a laugh. I was making a knob of myself.

— Things are never what they seem to be, are they?

— I'm not making *any* apologies, Lily. I am who I am. But I respect your thoughts, and if you want to . . .

She didn't finish. I felt like a total bitch. I wanted to spew it all out. All the thoughts she'd started stirring in my head. I went,

— About this wedding, you still want to go?

— I really do. Yes.

— Well not all of your mates have abandoned you?

She started picking imaginary bits of fluff off the duvet.

— These are people I haven't seen for a long time. But there'll be people there who have serious issues with me. I mean, it'll be a wedding, won't it?

I wanted to say the bride'll have to watch herself.

— What about Anna? You still friends?

— My emotional Waterloo. She went back to him.

— Well, listen, about this wedding, I'll be there to stick up for you. If you want?

Her face was a picture.

— Are you serious? You'll come?

— Yeah. I might even spaz out during the ceremony to top it all off.

— We're not invited to the ceremony. The bride's Jewish, but the man she's marrying isn't. They're having an Embarrassed Small Family Do. We're invited to the reception afterwards.

— Free booze and grub. Fantastic.

She got a serious look.

— You mean it? You'll really come? You're not bothered they'll think you're my girlfriend?

— As long as *you* don't get any ideas, I don't give a shit. She smiled with a shake of her head. I went,

— We're a right fucking pair, aren't we?

— Thank you, Lily. I mean that.

❂❂❂❂❂❂❂

I listened to the water pump in Dave's fish tank. Blue fish zapping in and out of the bubbles. I stared at them until my eyes fogged. My head was woolly, my guts smarting from the wine and the gin and the glass of whisky he'd just shoved in my hand. I knew I shouldn't be drinking this much. I knew it was making it worse. That I'd have to pay the price: me chucking a fit in front of him. My legs were two Zs as I tried to sit on the floor lady-like as I could, and my hands were in my lap holding my skirt down. The whisky had a soil taste about it. Dave came back into the room out of breath.

I watched him move about the room, change the CD. Watched him bending over, his arse so grabbable in his jeans. Watched the muscles in his legs, his arms, the way his broad shoulders and his hips moved and turned.

It's not like me, feeling like that. My pills mess with me. I could feel my cheeks and throat flushing with the thoughts. I bet I looked totally pink with it.

He kneeled down beside me. I thought fuck: he can read my mind. He put his head on my knee, his eyes closed and a smile on his face. I put my hand on his head and stroked his hair. He made noises like a dog and I froze. He looked up at me and said should we go upstairs?

He took my hand and led me up. The house was

massive. We passed a door with a load of chains and locks on it. I was nervous and the air was heavy and I said bring out the gimp but he ignored me. We climbed another flight until we were right at the top of the house. I could feel my pulse throb in my temples.

His room had a sloped ceiling with a big window in it. There was a lamp on and some candles and music playing. I think it was Sade. He must've come up here when he went to the toilet, got it ready for us.

We stood in the middle of the room and clung to each other. I loved the way he kissed now. Gentle. We seemed to fit. His mouth not too wide, not trying to stick his tongue down my throat. And he kept licking my lips. Chewing on them a bit. It was sexy-as. He watched me unbutton his shirt, his arms down his sides. I did it slowly. He was strong but didn't have any hair there. I kissed down the middle and then I licked his nipple. His legs buckled, he groaned.

— Come on.

There were shadows in the room from the candles and I was pleased. I didn't want him to see my scars. I waited for him to be totally naked before I took my dress off. He looked different to how I'd imagined him, but I was thinking maybe it's the light. The little bump of his stomach. The flab of his pecs.

I put my arms behind me, to unhook my bra.

But I couldn't.

His eyes shining with the candlelight. The stubble on his face looked reddish. It made his face look scrubbed. His nipples were two bullet holes shot through his chest. There was scribble-hair down from his sticky-out belly button to his cock. The end looked like a fruit, split and purple. It looked like it was pointing at me. So I pointed back. I lifted my arm and straightened my finger at it. He smiled and moved towards me and his cock flicked like it was alive. I reached out and took it in my hand and it was red hot. He flinched and held me tight. The smell from his crotch, like soil.

— Are you on the Pill?

— Yes.

The lie was a ballerina spinning in my head. He pulled me onto the bed and licked my neck, then he went straight to my bra, trying to get at me. He pushed his fingers up under the wire and I felt something like fire in my breast.

— Don't, Dave.

He turned away from me; I put my hand on his shoulder.

— Do you know what'd be really nice?

He looked at me like a little boy, like he'd just been told off.

— Sleeping next to you. Cuddling. Lying with you. That's all I want.

He tried to smile. We got under the sheets.

My skin felt like it was ready to jump off my bones. I snuggled into him and he said sorry and I shushed him and we kissed for a long time. I rolled over and he spooned me. He held my breast in one hand and it made me feel safe. Then after a bit he started rubbing his palm over. It tickled in my brain somewhere and I made a noise. I felt him hard in the small of my back. He kissed my shoulder. I rolled over and we kissed really wild.

But I held him back.

I looked up through the skylight, listening to him breathing. I had his warmth on me, his smell in my nose, his taste in my mouth, his skin on mine. It was everything I wanted, but I felt if I gave myself to him, that I'd be lying to him. I turned my head so I had his breath on my face. It reminded me of Mikey, waking up with him that morning we found the rabbit frozen in the snow.

I pictured him in a doorway. A lump of rags. An empty crisp packet. A fresh pile of dogshit. A two-pence coin in acky black fingers and a white plastic cup. I wondered if he thought about me, about the special thing we had between us when we were kids, and if it made him warm inside, like it did me.

I'd tell Dave about my fits in the morning, that's what I told myself. And just hoped I didn't piss on him in the night.

☙☙

When I got home next morning, Mel said where the hell have you been? I thought you weren't coming. She was almost ready and I hadn't even decided what to wear. Mel showed me her outfit. It was a sexy-as black cocktail dress she said had been handmade by someone she used to know. And she had this pair of Jimmy Choo shoes she said only cost her two hundred quid, but I could tell she was fibbing. She had the Happy Mondays blasting away on her stereo and it was like getting ready for a Friday night at the Locker.

I showered quickly then showed Mel a couple of the nice dresses I'd bought.

— I can't decide. Help me, please.

— The greenish one. Definitely. You got any heels to match?

— As if.

She started going on about fads and clothes and how bad high heels are anyway.

— It's nothing to do with being a dyke. I just see things clearly, that's all.

— See?

— I see long-term damage. I see years of suffering.

— From what?

— Arthritis. Knee damage. Ankle damage. Claw toes. It's one of the first things I noticed about you: you always wear flat shoes.

— I'd just be making the space between my head and the ground even bigger.

— And push-up bras. I like to goggle at a bit of cleavage as much as the next girl, but all I see is restricted breathing, crushed diaphragm, back problems. Nail varnish: I see contact dermatitis. Skin-tight trousers: I see nerve damage. Pierced tongues and eyebrows: I see shattered teeth and hepatitis. As well as just looking *absolutely* stupid.

— Where do you get all of this shit from?

— *Elle. Cosmo.*

— That why you dress so old-persony?

— Ouch.

— I'm messing. I'm so glad you're not one of those, you know, with bog-brush hair and dungarees, Doctor Martens and that.

— Not all lesbians are bull dykes, Lily. Zip me up.

☙☙

Cambridge. It looked even more foreign than London. Mel showed me where she'd stayed, the places she used to drink, the library she used to study in. She'd lived in another world to me.

———

I remember the sky was mostly blue, except for a tiny bunch of clouds and half a rainbow hanging down from behind them, like a hippy curtain. I remember the throng of toffs walking about in the massive garden with the high walls. Folk chatting and laughing like horses. The whine of some orchestra playing classical shite under a little tent thing. Men in penguin outfits and uncomfortable-looking shoes. Teenage boys and girls wandering around holding silver trays of champagne, dressed like they were in a museum. By the time we were asked to go inside, my champagne had turned warm in my hand and there was a coldish breeze goosefleshing my arms and legs.

———

— So how's it going? Are you OK? It's not doing your head in, is it?

— It's fun. I can't understand half of what the people are saying like. But it's great. It's the poshest thing I've ever been to in my life.

— Good. But it's started already.

— What has?

— The looks. *Snide*, as you'd put it. I've had a few that could kill.

— Pay no notice. Anyone says anything to you, I'll knock their block off.

— Let's just do this for Lizzie, OK, and then we're off.

Mel said I was a trooper, a true friend, and was so pleased I'd come with her.

— We can go as soon as the speeches are over.

— They're not finished yet?

— No, sorry, it's a Jewish thing – goes on for hours.

— Jesus.

It was getting parky so we went back inside and she was right: the eyes were on us. People talking. Leaning close. Snide-as.

I put my arm through Mel's and smiled until my face ached.

———————

Casualties poured out of the pubs. I saw a man slumped in a corner of a building.

— You can tell they're posh here: they puke in the drains.

Mel tottered and grabbed my shoulder.

— So what did you think?

— I'm not even that pissed. I thought Russians knew how to party. The fucking bar shut at one. We only had time for a couple of drinks.

— I know. But what did you think about it? The whole kaboodle.

— It was a right spectacle. Bits of it were amazing. The hall, the women's dresses, the food, the crap breakdancing the men were doing. And hearing the bride's brother singing in what was it?

— Hebrew.

— I almost started bawling. His voice was amazing. But

165

I was looking around and some people were asleep. I felt he was singing just for me.

We walked back to the hotel not saying much after that. She was more pissed than I thought. She staggered and I had to help her up the stairs in the hotel. She must have had a rough night of it. She managed to get her dress off and got into bed. The last thing she said was do you know what I love about you, Lily? – you're straightforward and honest. And then she started snoring.

I sat on the floor, watching the small television with the sound turned down and drinking booze from the minibar, thinking about Dave. Where he was, what he was up to. And I was like please don't let him be a wanker. I wanted him to be at home, on his own, working, and thinking about me. Not in the pub pulling birds, flirting. Proper missing me. Thinking about me when he's touching himself.

I slept on top of the covers, and even though the sheets were separating us, I realized I'd never felt so close to a woman before.

And it felt good, it felt right.

It felt special.

10

I met Mr Morris at the Starbucks the top end of Upper Street. He was sat at the back wearing a baseball cap and shellsuit. He looked like a proper charver. Like a fat middle-aged man trying to look young but failing. He got me a coffee and sat back down and handed me an envelope.

— Mr Blackman's address. He no longer works for London Underground. Early retirement, left last year. That's his last known address. I suspect illness of some kind.

He smiled, nodded, blew the top of his coffee and took a big gulp. It left a little froth tache. I went to open the envelope but he put his hand up to stop me.

— There's an invoice for my hours in there too. As you'll see, I've left the other case until last. It's a much bigger job.

— So you haven't started looking for our Mikey yet?

— I've been very busy. But let me assure you, there's no hiding from know how.

— So you keep saying.

I got this picture in my head of Mr Morris at school, curled up on the playground, a gang of lads kicking the shit out of him. He kept peering over my shoulder and then looking away. I went to turn around, but he put a hand on my arm.

— Don't. Please.

He pushed a fiver across the table and nodded at the coffee cups.

— I'll be in touch *very* soon, Miss O'Connor.

Then he weaselled out of there.

I went into the toilet and locked the door behind me. I sat and looked at the envelope, but I couldn't open it.

I put it back in my pocket and left.

The shoehorn on the mantelpiece. That was the sign: she had a man home. Next to her money for the pools, for the milkman. Don't you even *think* of fucking touching it.

I could always sense them though, before I saw the shoehorn. The house would be full of their grunts, their signs, their shady morning-looks.

But Don was different.

First time I met him, he picked us up in his car. It was the first car I'd ever been in. I thought he must be proper rich. It was white and had cream seats inside that stuck to your skin in summer.

Me and Mam, we were stood outside the house and she was in a right temper. She kept prodding and poking me. She'd washed my hair in the kitchen sink that morning with Fairy Liquid and then brushed it red raw until I thought my scalp was bleeding. She said Donald wanted to take us out for the day, but she said it was *his* idea and she *hated* it. So we waited outside the house next to the gate, and she kept clouting me round the head for fidgeting, for humming, for breathing, for being alive. She told me that I wasn't to go embarrassing her that day. That I wasn't to fuck it all up by chucking a fit. She'd made a show of packing some clean knickers for me into her bag. Just in case.

He pulled up in the car and she pinched me really hard.

— Don't go showing us up, young lady.

He had his window down and his arm hanging out. Mam started acting like a right daft bitch. She pushed me into the back seat. Don was smoking a fag and there was pop music on the radio. His hair was slicked back in a duck's arse. Mam gave him a kiss while Don looked at me in the mirror, and he winked at me when he was kissing her. He fucking winked at me.

I moved behind his seat, so that he couldn't see me, and I stared out the window all the way to the seaside, practising winking back.

I knew it was him, in the room in the park. My tiny hand between the warm sheets. I knew what it was. Of course I did. The fucking memory of him.

I just didn't know why now.

Mel was in when I got back. I told her what had happened with Mr Morris and she sat there listening, but she was looking at her arm the whole time. Doing her Picking Invisible Bits Off thing. I knew what it meant now: she didn't approve.

— So you don't trust this Mr Morris?

— No. Suppose I don't.

She'd done her make-up in a new way. I thought my God, she's so beautiful she doesn't even have to try. I could just stare at her for hours. But her face was full of fret.

— I've a confession to make.

Here we go.

She lifted her hand and showed me her palm. Then she put her hands together. Her hands were always telling me things.

— I phoned the Missing Persons Helpline. Don't get upset, please. I told them that I have a friend involved in a search and that she was unsure whether to use a private detective or not.

She watched me trying to put the look on my face that said that's so *good* of you.

— So?

— The lady I talked to, she said there was *nothing* a private detective could do that they couldn't.

I went to the window and stared out at the pissing rain. Summer had gone, like putting the lid back on a steaming pan. You could breathe again and sleep at night. Didn't wake up in sweaty sheets. Didn't feel like you needed a shower all the time, like the air was sweating on you. The street was turning to mush outside, the fallen leaves sopping.

— Two hundred thousand people go missing in this country every year.

— But that's like a city. Every year?

— And they're all on a database. If Barry had started the search, then they'll still have Mikey's records. They may still be searching for him, or may even have some results by now. The lady said they could tell you there and then.

It felt like a promise. Like he was in the next room. I could hear him moving about, coughing.

— Get me the number, come on.

— There are a few things you need to know first.

A finger up on each hand, like bull's horns.

— The lady told me something that you need to consider.

— And what's that when it's at home?

— There's a chance that Mikey might not want to be found.

— Eh?

— I'm sorry, Lil.

— Shite and like. He'll find out I'm looking for him and be over the fucking moon.

— The woman said that they have to respect the missing person's wishes. They'll pass on your details, but it would be entirely up to Mikey to get in touch with you. They'd have to respect his confidentiality.

— Well, maybe I need to be more, what's-the-word? Mr Morris is on his case.

Mel was saying yes but shaking her head. It was the first time I'd thought about Rachel for a while. I imagined her uncle trying to find her.

— You need to imagine what it would be like if *you* found out someone had been stalking and following you. How would *you* like it?

I wanted to shout and stamp my feet. I wanted to smash something up.

— Look, just give us the number.

I looked out the window again, listening to her open and shut a drawer. She came back through with some stuff she'd printed off the Net. She nodded at me: go on.

I dialled, took a deep breath, answered the voice.

— My brother, Barry O'Connor, he started the search. It would've been about six years ago, just after our Mikey went missing. He's our brother: Michael O'Connor, but we called him Mikey. And I'm Lily. I'm wondering if you're still looking for him? How's the search going and that?

— OK, Lily, do you have his case number?

— Sorry?

— If your brother started a search, Michael would have a case number.

— I don't know. Barry's abroad.

— That's OK. Do you have Michael's date of birth and full name please?

I reeled it off and I could hear her typing.

— Our mother's died. I want him to know. He'll want to know.

I looked at Mel. She put her hand on me and I shrugged it off.

— Can you tell me of Michael's last whereabouts, Lily?

I told her about the reptile house, his address back home, and about him coming to London to see Sylvia.

— Right. We do have a search for Michael matching those details on our database. But it was only set up last week. By your uncle.

— *Uncle?*

— A Mr . . . Morris?

I think I took the phone away from my ear. I think I might have put my head on Mel's shoulder.

— Hello?

— Sorry. That man isn't our uncle. He's a detective I hired.

She made a little snort, like it'd happened before. I wondered what Mr Morris was playing at.

— We'll have to verify this.

I told her the name of his agency and gave her the phone number for his office.

— And then I'd like you to remove him from the search.

I could hear pages being turned.

— OK, Lily. I have some further questions that will be essential to our search, so if you can be as honest as possible that will be a great help.

I could hear her breathing.

— Have you any reason to believe Michael is, or was, vulnerable in any way?

I just said it: no.

— Do you think there may be drugs involved, or that he may be suffering from any mental health problems, such as depression?

— Nothing like that. He's just missing, that's all.

She told me what Mel had said, about them having to respect Mikey's wishes if he didn't want to be found. Then she said I should write a letter to pass on to him.

— Do you have any photographs of Michael? Any at all? We have an identification department that can manipulate photographs to age images from childhood. We can also use his image on advertising.

— Just the one. I'll send it, but I want it back.

— Of course.

She took my contact stuff and then gave me his case number.

25920/CM.

———

I went back to Clissold Park where I saw the room. Mel wanted to come – she said I was upset and she should come with me. I told her I was right as rain and needed to be on my own. I've never done so much thinking in my life. Mel said some women had been stabbed while they were out jogging in the park, to be careful. So I put my hoody on and tucked my hair inside the hood. I looked like one of the kids off the estate there. I put my keys through my fingers. If anyone tried anything, I'd stab them in the face.

I found the same bench, next to the high cages with the fancy birds and the enclosure thing with the deer. I shut my eyes and tried to remember it. Trying to make it happen again, to see the room. I could hear the budgies and those parrot things tweeting away, a dog barking far off, a digger or something rumbling. Sounds, plenty of sounds, but no room. No being small and warm. No flying away. No wave screaming up out of my gob like an opera singer.

I went to the Silverlink. Mel called it the Smacklink and said I had to be careful using it. I kicked the shit out of leaves along the road.

———

His hands were all over me, my breasts, between my legs, rubbing hard-as. He licked my nipple and bit it and I gasped. He pushed my shoulders down, moaning, writhing. His stubble and teeth were jaggy.

— Slow down.

He stopped right sudden. He sat up and put his face in his hands.

— It was nice, Dave. Sorry. I just . . .

I thought he was crying. I rubbed his back. We were both breathing hard.

— They're just really sensitive. You've got to be gentle with them.

I tried to kiss him, but he pulled away. Then I felt the wetness on my hip and saw the come on his legs.

— It doesn't matter.

———————

I noticed something weird was happening to my period. Something not right. It wasn't that I was pregnant or anything. I owned up and told him I wasn't on the Pill. I said I thought it was evil. But that was a lie too. It's just the pills I take for my fits, they mess with the Pill big time. Make it not reliable. Something to do with the liver. I didn't tell Dave. Three weeks and I still hadn't told him. I said he better get used to wearing johnnies. *Doesn't feel right. Stops the feeling.* Moan moan. I thought you *need* to stop the feeling, Mr Spunk-up.

Third week of my period's always a funny one. Getting all mushy and weepy, my breasts swollen and sensitive, feeling like I just want to be hugged all the time. Hear someone say I love you. Sad-as. And it was during that third week that I told him. I can't believe it now, but I did. I caved in. We were both drunk and in the middle of having sex when it just blurted out.

— I love you.

He froze. Stared down at me between my legs.

— I'm sorry, Dave. But I do.

He got onto the bed next to me and stared up at the ceiling, not saying anything. I thought I'd messed it up, but then he rolled over and hugged me. He kissed my neck and then he looked at me, looked at my mouth when he went,

— Let's take it easy, eh?

He made light of it, but I knew it wasn't a fob-off. It

175

was an: I feel the same but daren't say it. One of those. After that, each time I got the mad urge to say anything, I had to swallow it. It was whenever we were naked and touching – I'd just feel so close to him, so special. So loved and excited. Bubbling up with it. Fizzing. It was hard not saying it, but harder not hearing it.

Then fourth week all hell broke loose – the tears, walking in circles, feeling like my spine's made of metal, that girly need to be hugged all the time. Drives me mental. I turned into a dog on heat. I decided it was time.

I told Dave to get his coat.

We went to the Three Sisters at the end of his road. I met some of his mates. Maybe I was rude? Maybe I flirted with them? I think they could smell it on me – I remember their looks: roving. I drank and drank. I followed Dave into the toilet and bought some johnnies from the machine. I kept whispering all the things I wanted to do to him. I licked his ears, wanting him to shove his hand down my knickers right there. He looked fit to burst.

I was like fuck this, let's do one.

I ran up the street ahead of him, laughing.

———————

He had me pinned against the wall in the hallway, thrusting like a mad bastard, grunting, pulling my top off over my head and licking my breasts like lollipops. We were the perfect height to do it stood up. We hobbled through to the kitchen, him still in me. The two of us laughing and licking and biting. He had me against the fridge. My arse cheeks made slapping noises and the cutlery rattled in the drawers. He came dead quick and it was like he lifted me into the air, twitching. A pulse inside me.

He pulled out and plopped the johnny on the lino. I went after him into the living room. He flopped on the sofa, hand over his eyes, breathing deep.

I was totally rampant.

I wanted to get on top of him and ride him. I wanted him to fuck my brains loose. He put his hands down his jeans and rubbed himself. It was soft, I could tell. I went to the upstairs loo and tried to bring myself off, but as per I couldn't.

I felt a proper mess.

When I went back down he was snoring, mouth gawping wide.

Next day I came on, and felt like a total fool. It wasn't meant to be like that. It was meant to be romantic. It was meant to be like we'd shed our skin and mixed together, like we were made of light. Hormones running rampant like that. The hot-water bottle came out – one pain over another. Someone puts the plug back in and it starts all over again. Men haven't a fucking clue.

But I wasn't meant to come on that day.

I was having my fourth week stuff in the third. Early-as.

I was all confused inside.

When I was in the care home, my periods were all over the shop. The bright sparks had to mess around with my pills a lot, and that made my periods go doolally. In the end, though, they got it sorted and I'd been regular for years. But now it was all skew-whiff again. My body was a mess.

I remember the first time I heard the word. I thought of science at school. I thought of maths. I couldn't tell the difference between menstruation and protractors or compass. Big words like that just made me feel sad.

I was at this girl's house. She was a proper brainbox and I remember this one Christmas she got a chemistry set off her mam and dad. We used to try and make explosions and bad smells, and we soon used up all of the chemicals and shit. Nothing was left that stunk or fizzed, changed colour or set fire. We didn't know what to do with ourselves. And we were sat on the bonnet of her dad's car when she turned a funny colour. She ran to the toilet and when she came back she had this queer look on her face. She said there was blood when she'd done her toilet.

— I think I'm having a menstruation. That's when your egg comes out.

It was better than a fucking chemistry set. I had this picture in my head: a little hard-boiled egg on some toilet paper with a drop of blood on it.

But when I asked to see, she said she'd flushed it away.

⊘⊘⊘⊘

There was his name. An address in a place called Camberwell. It didn't seem real. I'd come here to find Mikey but instead I'd found Don. I A–Zeded it. South London. I looked at his name one last time: Donald Blackman.

I remembered the day I started bleeding and he pushed me away.

I felt nothing. Blank.

I put the address in a drawer, and then I put the bill in my pocket.

———

We had a bit of argy-bargy at the front door. The old woman wasn't having any of it. I was surprised how strong she was. I had my foot in, then my leg, then my arm. I grabbed her cardy and told her I didn't care how old she was, I was going to slap her if she didn't get out of my way.

She laughed. She looked up at me shaking her head, and let me in.

— He got client. They be long time.

I glared at her again. She shrugged and pointed at his door then hobbled off. I knocked and went in.

They both looked at me through the reek: Mr Morris and some woman done up to the nines, a tissue in one hand and a fag in the other. Her raccoon face said divorce, said cheating bastard husband. I gave her a quick smile and Mr Morris stood up.

— I'm sorry, Miss O'Connor, but . . .

He made a move to come towards me. The woman tutted, muttered. I put my hand up. We all looked at each other. Blood whooshed in my ears.

— The deal's off. Give me the picture of Mikey and my files and I'm gone.

— I really don't advise that, Miss O'Connor. I've made some great advances.

His face: you just had to look at it to know he was lying.

— Come on, then. *Convince* me. *What* have you found out, eh?

Gobbing fresh air.

— Just give me my fucking file.

He looked at the woman; she looked at me, she looked at him. Looks in circles. He turned around, bent down, and opened a drawer. I could see his arse crack, all hairy and brown. It made me gip. He kept talking, saying how *irregular* this was and that I was making a mistake. The woman was smiling at me. She had big hair like the receptionist at the Novotel. Her fingers sparkled when she dabbed her eyes. Dripping money.

Mr Morris stood up and handed me an envelope. I snatched it off him.

— So, may I ask, *who* are you using? Are you using the agency down the street, is that it? I can better *any* deal they've offered.

— I'm using the Missing Persons Helpline. Heard of it?

A look to the woman; his mouth going but no words.

— As you said: there's no hiding from know how, is there?

I slammed the door behind me.

Outside, I put my hand in my pocket, and realized I hadn't given him his cheque.

———

Dear Mikey. The tip of the pen touching the paper. The pen in my hand. Then my eyes on the two words again. I put the pen in my mouth and held the paper up. Dear Mikey. I couldn't get the next bit in my head. I stared for a good couple of minutes and then I thought fuck it.

Dear Mikey, it's Lily here.

I told him I was trying to find him because Mam died and I thought you should know. I told him that we got the house left to us and you have your share of the money waiting for you. I told him I knew about Barry and Sylvia and the reptile house and how much it must have hurt. But I want you to know I'm on your side. I'll always be on your side. Then I went on about getting put into care after him and Barry got taken away. It was for the best.

Then I took that bit out. And so we lost touch. But now I'm trying to find you and want to get to know you again. I really do.

I said I was living in London and was happy, but finding him and just knowing he was safe was the most important thing in my life.

So please reply to this letter, Mikey. As long as I know you're OK, that's enough.

Please please get in touch. I miss you so much. Lily x

The photo. Mikey smiling, sprawled on some kind of table. Sunshine making him squint. Though he always did have a bit of a squint eye, where Mam backhanded him one time and cut him with her ring. The table's made of metal or something, and he's leaning back on it, on one elbow. His black hair's long and slicked back – he looks like a gangster. All he's wearing is that Tarzan loincloth and a massive smile and that fucking fat snake around his neck. I pictured the freckles on his nose spreading into one. His muscles look fit to burst, shining in the light, he's so oiled up.

And I wondered who was behind the camera? Who was he smiling at?

He was out there somewhere, and I just wanted him to know that I loved him. That somebody cared. That I've never forgotten the way he looked after me when I was a girl. Protected me from her.

The anger filled me. I grabbed my mobile and I pressed Barry's number. I was doing it, I was ringing the bastard. But it went straight to voicemail.

I took a deep breath, but didn't leave a message.

I gave the envelope a kiss before sticking it in the post box, and now the waiting game began, and I knew it'd drive me spare.

It hurt in itself, all that fretting, not knowing, fighting the bad thoughts.

It was proper agony.

I needed Dave's arms around me. I wanted to tell him. I wanted to tell him everything. But I was scared I wouldn't stop. I was scared of myself and what was in there, of what would come out. He stood at the front door with his blue overalls on. I think he was pissed off I'd disturbed him. But he saw I was upset and took me in.

I remember the early days with Dave, how he'd take my hand whenever we walked down the street together, how he kept kissing me and hugging me and saying sweet things. I remember lying in bed breathing hard, listening to music from the eighties. The Cure. The Smiths. Depeche Mode. New Order. Human League. But he was a metalhead at heart. I remember standing on the landing listening to him in his lab, tinkering about, listening to AC/DC really loud. I remember how excited he was about his inventions, even though I never got to see any. Did I mind him going into the lab for a couple of hours? Always after we had sex, like it proper fired him. His eyes shone, and he would squeeze me so tight when I said no I didn't mind.

And I remember him saying sorry he came too quick, just the once, and asking all the time: was that nice? And me going yes, it was lovely. Top ten, I'd say. Perfect timing. You hit my ON button.

It was a proper turn-off.

And I remember him watching me from the bed when I got dressed. How he wanted me to bend down for him so he could lick my nipples goodbye before I put my bra back on. He called them Pinky and Perky. Goodbye Pinky, lick. Goodbye Perky, lick. There was something not right about it, but it made him happy.

I remember him holding my breast as we did spoons, my arse in his lap. It made me feel soft inside. Safe. Him learning how to touch me. Taking his hand and showing him how. He used to do it before sex. I think he thought it made it OK, you know, if I pretended to come before he went inside.

But I never came. I faked it every time. Mind you, it drove him proper crazy, made him happy. Sometimes, if he was hurting me, all I'd have to do is pant a bit, moan that I was going to come, and he'd explode. Hair-trigger Dave. He was already every position in my top one hundred, I told him. Top five, I'd say. My number one.

And I remember being so shocked how hard he liked me to hold him, wank him so hard my arm totally knacked. I thought his cock would drop off.

And I remember that little speech he gave me, when I thought he was going to say I love you. He said most women are gushers.

— They tell you everything about themselves, about their lives, as soon as you meet them. Like they have to get it all out as soon as they can.

He said they come across as neurotic, desperate, and there's nothing to know about them after that.

— But you're different. There's a mystery to you.

And I was thinking you haven't got a fucking clue, mate.

— I've been with a lot of crazy women. Shouters. Always throwing things. Cutting themselves. Stealing stuff. I'm not kidding.

And I thought well, at least I'm not like that.

I remember him saying I was his perfect woman. Ideal, that's what he said. He used to have fantasies about women like me when he was a teenager. Women *like me*. And I thought is that all he wants me for, my looks, my body, like I was meant to be made up by that? Or was he saying that because he thought I needed to hear it, like I needed reassurance or something? Maybe he said it so that I'd start asking him all the time: How do I look? Does this look good on me? Do you think I've put on weight? Do you fancy *her* more than *me*? That old fucking rigmarole.

But he was learning about my body. Not chewing on me, nipping, prodding me all the time. Being gentle with me.

I started feeling so close to him.

But there was always the three of us in bed: Dave, me, and epilepsy. The shadow figures in the room, watching, waiting with their long fingers, ready to slide them into my head and take me into the dark.

He'd light candles and I tried not to look into the shadows, in case they were there. He'd kiss me all over. He'd tell me he thought my scars were beautiful. He never pried. Never asked. Never nebbed where he wasn't supposed.

He was nothing like Alex. Nothing like Don.

But then I remember the ambulance. And Dave's face.

And even though he was holding my hand, I was thinking it was over.

It was over.

————

I'd been sleeping at Dave's every night for ages. I was going back to Mel's during the day to get changed because I was scared about leaving make-up or anything at his, in case it scared him off, thinking I was getting too settled, making my way in.

And I'd spend my days travelling on buses, walking the streets, looking for that squint, the blue sky in the dirty face, the angry frown.

Me and Mel went to some more of the shelters and hostels together, handing out photocopies of Mikey's photo. And I remember those places were proper mean. The people inside, they all looked so gone. And after raking the streets I'd go home, get dolled up, put a new face on. Convince myself that Mikey would never be in one of those places. Convince myself I still had a life. I buried over all the pain and worry with lippy and mascara and perfume.

Mel kept leaving little notes out for me. One of them asking if I was OK, was anything wrong? One asking me to be around to meet her mum.

I guess I got carried away with it all, the Dave thing, the Love thing. Hiding it all away, the not-knowing of it all. Our Mikey gone, disappeared into thin fucking air, and there I was picking away at the scab of his life.

One of Mel's notes said that Al had phoned, so I rang the shop and got through and we said our hellos and caught up. I told him about Dave and he said he was pleased someone was looking after me. Then he said how all of this stuff had arrived for me at the flat.

— Loads of presents. Wrapped up all fancy. Must've cost a bomb.

I was thinking it was Ridge Racer. Or some daft mistake. Then Al said some big bruiser had dropped them off in a black BMW, and I knew.

— He said his name was . . .

— Lamb?

— Aye, you know him, then? Looked a bit shady if you ask me. Don't worry, I just said you were out for the day.

— Open them, Al. And sell whatever you want in the shop.

— Eh?

— Or drop them off at Help the Aged. I want nothing to do with them.

He said he was flabbergasted, but didn't ask any more.

— You get anyone in the flat yet, Al?

He didn't say anything.

— Al?

— I'm hoping you're coming back, lass. I'm keeping it free for you. Won't be long until Christmas now.

— Jesus, mate. You don't have to do that.

— It's no bother. I'm getting it redecorated anyway. New bed and that. Be ready for you staying at Christmas.

I was choked.

— Nowt's too much bother for you, lass.

My days had become this toing and froing between Mel and Dave and I did – I almost packed up that day. Almost ran back home to Al and the seafront.

But then there was the message on my mobile.

There was a lot of screaming in the background, music and noise like metal clanging. Then his voice saying I fucking won, sis. But he wasn't shouting or screaming, just said it dead flat, like it was no big deal. He said he was going to Las Vegas next and then there was some woman with an American voice speaking down the phone and then the phone went dead.

That bastard wasn't allowed to win. He wasn't allowed to be happy. I felt the anger, let it fill my body like black water – it was heavy and cold but it kept me going.

It was the next morning. Me and Dave had just got out

of bed and his moby went. He took it out of the room and when he came back in he said he had to go out to some woman having problems with her wiring.

I was dressed, ready to go back to Mel's. Thank fuck I was dressed and had my keys on me. It could have been so much worse. Me in my pissing wet knickers and nothing else. Doesn't bear thinking about.

I was stood next to his bed and all I remember is feeling someone behind me

and that one word in my head

NO

and that was it. Next thing I know, I'm in the back of an ambulance. And his face – Jesus. The *fear* there. He was bawling like a bairn, like he thought I was going to die.

— STOP THIS FUCKING THING.

The paramedics gave me a look and I thought they were going to strap me down. I jumped up and banged on the window at the driver.

— LET ME OUT YOU BASTARDS.

I think I said I'd sue them – something stupid. I felt the ambulance slowing, pulling over. One of them started having a go, whining at me.

— We're out here now, you've got to come with us.

I went to slap the bloke round his face, but I missed. Shocked looks, then the woman shook her head and opened the door. I jumped out the back and fell, my hands and knees cut to ribbons. I ran off, all wobbly down side streets and fell again because I couldn't see straight. I got up and kept on going.

Thrash, get up, get on with it.

But I can't remember what happened. Not really. That was me doing my dot to dot, filling in the colouring book of my life.

I must've hailed a cab down to get home, and I can imagine the driver looking at me in his mirror as I stared at my hands and the blood there. He'd have thought I'd been beaten up, that my boyfriend had twatted me. Well it wasn't any bloke, it was me and my brain, my electricity slamming me into the ground. The stuff that turns that lump of meat in your skull into something alive – it was trying to fucking *kill* me.

I would've touched my face, would've smelt the sharp stink of piss from my jeans. I would've crossed my legs and pictured Dave in the back of the ambulance, crying, thinking I was dying. Thinking I'm a psycho.

I'd fucked it up big style.

Goodbye, Dave.

9

Wednesday morning, I peeled my face off the pillow. It tore the scab off my nose and I screamed blue murder. My bedsheets and pillowcase, they were brown with blood. It looked like shit. The scabs on my knees, they cracked and stang like fuck as I clambered out of bed. I checked my teeth with my tongue: all there. I went into the loo. I dreaded it. Scared what I'd find looking back at me.

I looked proper fierce.

I took my clothes off and turned this way and that. My scars shone in the light. Flickered like broken glass. It's who I am. Writing all over me in special ink. The long yellow and purple bruise running down under my arm, down my ribs, onto my hip. A battered banana. It proper knacked when I breathed, but nothing was broken. I told myself nothing was broken, like I could count my fucking ribs. The knee bone's connected to the.

I'd landed on my face.

I opened my gob and looked inside. Black bits on the cheeks. Scabs that weren't scabs because they never got hard. Chewing my face from the inside, like my fit wants me to eat my face off.

I tried to smile at myself, tried to make light of it. I must have whacked something proper hard when I dropped. Dave's bedside cabinet. There was a cut under my eye.

Not too big, but you couldn't see the eyeball underneath. Just mush. Skin black and yellow and green. Swollen shut. It looked like polished wood. Varnished. There was blood dried under it and a big itchy chunk up my nose. Fire in my eyes when I blinked.

But I was fine. It'd happened before. Broken fingers and hands, feet and legs and arms and nose. I'm hijacked, slammed into the ground. That time Mam chucked me down the stairs, repeating it like a stuck record, over and over again. All my life having to repeat that smack, that flight down there.

Thrash, get up, get on with it.

I climbed into the shower and stood there, feeling the water bite.

I found the letter from Mel in the kitchen. I had trouble reading it with just the one eye. She thought we needed to talk. She was busy as hell at work and wouldn't be back until really late, but would I meet her for dinner? She'd put tea-time in brackets with a number six and a smiley face. There was a little map and two kisses at the end, so's I could tell she wasn't pissed off.

I ran a tea bag under the tap and stuck it on my eye. I tried hard not to pick at the scabs on my knees.

It's hard walking with just the one eye – it's like half your brain's missing. You have to keep swinging your head from side to side to make sure you're not walking into things. It was cloudy outside, but the sunglasses weren't totally black. I'd checked in the mirror: you could see the shiner plain-as. Good thing about London is no one bothers you. They might catch your eye, but they always look away. Back home, folk'd make a right fuss. Some old woman would've come sat next to me on the bus and asked was it my bastard husband that'd done it? Domestic violence – makes it sound clean. Brushed under the carpet. Hoovered out of the way. One of those women with wired jaws, tired-looking. I wish some bloke *had* done it – at least I could fucking leave him.

I've noticed how women look at you different. They see your bruises and cut lips and it's pity they give you, that's what it is. Sisters together. They look at you and shiver while the men look away, ashamed or something. Guilty maybe, because they've all thought about it. Men can't help it though – their mothers raise them like that.

Sisters together – my fucking arse.

————

— Jesus.

I tried to smile.

— My God.

I put my hand out to feel for the chair and sat down. I one-eyed her in her work get-up. Dark-blue trouser suit with a white top underneath, hair tied back and her little glasses on, sensible black shoes with black sheer tights. She looked like a headmistress, like she was going to give me a proper telling-off. You, girl, yes you with the chimney on – detention *for a week*.

She shook her head, sat down opposite. Then she

looked around, like she was checking who was looking, so I said it really loud,

— Epilepsy, eh?

She still had her hand to her face. I could see the blood in her cheeks.

— My God.

She leaned closer, her eyes getting wet.

— Have you been to the hospital? That looks *really* serious, Lil.

— Don't worry, I'm tough as old boots. I've had worse than this.

She held my arm and squeezed gently. A waitress appeared.

— Howay, let's order.

The waitress winced when she saw me. I ordered the same fancy salad as Mel and some water. My head was splitting. Mel looked like she was going to start bawling so I put the shades back on.

— It's no big deal, Mel. And I don't like fuss. What is it you want to talk about?

She put her hand on mine, fingers in mine.

— What happened?

— I was in Dave's bedroom. I think I've scared the poor bastard off. But come on, help take my mind off it. Tell me what I'm here for?

She took a deep breath, eyes narrowing.

— Are you sure he didn't . . . ?

— Batter me? Yes. Now, come on.

She sighed and hummed for ages.

— You're not making me feel any better doing that. Talk to me.

— Well, it's nothing really. I just want to know why

haven't you been around? I've missed you not being in the house. I just want to know, are you avoiding me?

— Don't be daft.

— I've hardly seen you since the wedding. Did I do something to upset you?

— I've just been with Dave. You know, doing stuff. That's all.

She ruffled her red serviette; cleared her throat.

— Don't you think you might be spending too much time with him?

— What's *that* meant to mean?

— I'm sure he's nice and everything. I just think people should take it slowly at the beginning. Not rush things.

Her and Anna again.

— Well, thank you, Oprah, but I think I'm in love with him.

Her face went soft; eyes creased up.

— Oh, Lil. I'm absolutely over the moon for you. I am.

I leaned over and we had a little hug.

— He's really nice, Mel. He wouldn't lay a finger on me. I'm looking forward to you meeting him. That's if I haven't totally scared him off.

The waitress brought the drinks and Mel took a long gulp of her orange juice. Then she wiped her mouth with a serviette, taking her time about it. I could see her picking words off the washing line in her head.

— Why didn't you want to meet my mother? She was *so* looking forward to it.

— Parents and me, we don't get on. I'm sure she's lovely and everything. I just, I don't know. I was busy with Dave.

The salad came. I had to chew on one side. The food

didn't really taste of anything. I fry the bit of my brain where taste is made.

— I'd like to see you a bit more, Lil. That's all. It was like we were getting so close and then you disappeared.

— There's nothing behind it. I've not been conniving to avoid you or anything. I've been having fun. Actually, we've been shagging like rabbits.

I said it loud and she nearly spat her lettuce out. She put her hand to her mouth and gulped.

— Lucky you. I've forgotten what it's like.

Music was playing but you could hear cars and buses in the street outside. I finished off my plate and drank the rest of my water and popped the orange ☺ ☺ out of their foil.

— So have you ever been with a bloke, then?

She leaned back in her chair. She seemed to forget about the mess of a woman sat in front of her.

— I think most dykes have. I think that's what makes our minds up.

— But you didn't like it? You don't miss it?

— I'm sorry, Lil, but I think most men are pricks. My father included.

— But you're definitely gay?

— One hundred per cent.

— So you're not bisexual, then? You've been with women and men and you say you're not bisexual?

— No. The act itself doesn't define you. It's a decision, or a state of mind. Or something deeper. I don't know. I just haven't thought about sex with a man in years. Haven't wanted it. I don't even *think* like that any more. I don't find them attractive.

— Not even Robert de Niro? Not even George Clooney?

— De Niro's a pensioner. George Clooney has no lips.

— But don't you miss it?

It looked funny, her blushing in her fancy suit.

— Men are such a regular disappointment. I don't like the way they smell, or taste, or touch me.

— Well why the hell aren't you out there, getting some lezzy action?

She looked down at her plate like it was miles away.

— It's taking me longer than I thought. I spent two weeks sleeping on the couch, eating chocolate, pizza. Four months on and I'm still hurting.

— You know what the best cure for that is, don't you?

— It still feels raw. I'm still hurting inside.

— You know what you need?

— Please, enlighten me.

I leaned over.

— A right good seeing to.

— Thank you for that insight.

— Howay, when was the last time you went on the pull?

— I don't *pull*, Lily.

— Get down off that high horse. You'll be growing a scab over it if you don't treat it nice.

She pulled a face like she was going to puke.

— Let's go to a gay bar this weekend, get you a woman.

It was out, running out of my gob like water. Her look. What are you like? *You.*

— I hate gay bars. They're so predatory.

— I'll protect you. I'll be your Uma Thurman. Come on, it'll be a giggle.

— Well, I hope your eye looks better by then. They'll think you're my bitch.

— I'm bitching, but I'm no bitch.

— *Sex and the City?*

195

— *Donnie Darko*. You need to watch more movies, brainbox.

She went back to work and I moseyed round the shops. I found one selling cards, so I bought one with a picture of a beach and blue sea and sky on it. I got the number four bus back and when I rang Dave's mobile he wasn't answering. I thought I'd messed up big time, but then I saw he'd left a message saying he hoped I was all right?

He put LOVE DAVE XXX on the end of it.

It was just something folk say. Throwaway. But I rolled around in bed excited, fretting, making up conversations between us. About what he'd say. Was he going to dump me? Was he in love with me? He'd seen me having a fit, and I saw his face afterwards, the pain there. Proper horror. Maybe I'll try calling him again. No, I'll leave it. Then in my head we're getting married on a beach. Stupid. What would our kids look like? Lily Levine. Nice ring to it. I'd never find anyone to love me. I texted him to say I'd be round the next evening. I put I LOVE YOU at the end. I didn't care, I did love him. It was the truth and I had to tell him.

I pressed Send and regretted it straight away.

⊘⊘⊘⊘

Early Thursday morning, we were staring at her laptop. It broke me in two. The faces kept flashing up in little boxes. The missing men, they looked so young and healthy. Some were beautiful like film stars. Then Mel clicked on it: Unidentified. There was a sign on the page in red saying

CAUTION. Even though the faces were sketches or recon-structions, you might find them disturbing.

— Go on.

I looked at each of the photographs, drawings, read the descriptions slow. Four on each page. Waiting for that bell to ring in my body that said that was him – the right dates, height, age, hair colour. There were descriptions of tattoos, of scars, of shoe size. Some of the drawings looked like kids had done them.

> Case 0004: A police-issued artist's impression shows a man whose body was found in the Thames, London, on July 2nd 1993. He was around 30 years old, 5' 8" tall and slim with brown eyes and dark brown collar-length hair. His teeth were in poor condition. The man was wearing a navy anorak with purple buttons, a black short-sleeved shirt, blue jeans and black shoes with Royal Mail written on the outside of them.

I was choked with it: no one was missing them. Bodies with no names. It wasn't Mikey, though. Wrong height, wrong year. We kept looking.

> Case 0057. No picture. The body of a man was found in the Thames, London, on 29th May 1997. It had been there for one week. The man was white, aged in his twenties and about 5' 10" tall. He had brown shoulder-length straight hair and was wearing an extra-large long-sleeved T-shirt with a short-sleeved cotton 'Pantera' shirt underneath. He was also wearing black jeans and Reebok Classic trainers.

Just for a minute: a dip in my gut. But no, it didn't fit. I squeezed Mel's hand.

— Go on.

Pictures of watches, jackets, boots. Some seemed so

close to Mikey, found around the right time, but they were too old or too young, too short or had the wrong eye and hair colour. Something just not right. A kid chopped up in some ritual and chucked in the Thames. So many people in that stinking river. People washed up on beaches, found hanging in trees, in ditches on the moors, in lochs in Scotland, even a baby in a concrete block. All these stories and no names. And I didn't know whether he had fillings or not. What colour his underpants were. If he had scars. How many moles or tattoos he had. I didn't know any of that stuff.

— It's OK.

We were on the fifteenth or sixteenth page and I'd had enough. I let go of her hand and rubbed my wet palm on my legs. I put my head on her shoulder and she put her arm around me and I let myself sob for a bit. I'd pushed these thoughts so much that I couldn't go any further with them. But I could feel him. It made no sense but I could feel he was still alive. There was this spark inside me and it was our Mikey, I knew it was. The only one that ever cared for me, and I had to find him. Had to. Just to thank him, if nothing else. For being there. For protecting me from her.

— This is proper morbid. I've seen enough. He's not dead.

— You're so brave, Lil.

She closed the site then looked at her watch.

— Shit *shit*. I'm *really* sorry.

— Go on, don't be late.

She kissed me on the cheek and rushed into the bathroom.

I tried to put it out of my head.

I clicked on Google and typed in his name. There were

so many hits it made me sick. Replacing one pain with another.

Place	Player and Hometown	Prize Money
1	Barry "Slick" O'Connor (Yorkshire, UK)	$589,995

Buy-In: $10,000
Number of Entries: 160
Total Prize Money: $1,552,000

The *Cincinnati Enquirer*: BRITISHER SLICK O'CONNOR TAKES HOME HALF A MILLION. The *Indianapolis Star*: SLICK MAKES HIS BIGGEST KILLING YET. The *Tennessee Tribune*, the *Casino City Times*, CasinoWire, Tenessean. com, *Jackpot Magazine*, even the *Yorkshire Post* and the *Darlington and Stockton* fucking *Times*. His name was all over the shop.

World Poker Open draws record number of hopefuls.

He's known as SLICK – and once again his opponents are spinning in circles.

One report said that his form at poker tables had caused more than one weary heart to miss a beat. Slick O'Connor, from Yorkshire, England, took over 500,000 dollars in one of the world's most celebrated poker contests, in what has been hailed as the most dominant performance ever recorded.

He'd won a bracelet of gold and diamonds and said it would be a welcome addition to all the other trophies he was going to win. Flying to Las Vegas tomorrow and then back to Europe for the next stage of the World

Poker Tour. One said he was a former bricklayer. One said he'd been barred from every betting shop in Britain and Ireland.

The air went out of me. I phoned Al straight away, but no one answered.

Oh well – some old granny would be getting more than she bargained for when she made her weekly visit to Help the Aged.

Fucking diamonds. He wouldn't?

And what's all that shite about him being a bricklayer? He's never done a hard day's graft in his life and he's proud of it. Probably said it to make him sound tough or something. Twat.

Mel came in to say goodbye. I was too flabbergasted to tell her what I'd just seen. When she left, I got that card I'd bought out of my bag and wrote the message that'd been swimming round my head.

Dear Sylvia.

I said I was sorry for the trouble I'd caused her, but I was Simon's auntie after all, and was there any chance I could see him some time? She could tell the lad anything she wanted, I would go along with it. I left my address and number and said I'd respect her wishes if she didn't reply.

❧❧

Thursday evening, I got dressed up. The eye made me feel like a total minger. I washed my face as well as I could. I put moisturizer on my eyelids, both of them. Then metallic Gold Shimmering liquid. Then dark blue eyeliner to the bottom eyelid of my good eye. Then some lip-gloss. It made me feel awake, like it usually does, but I looked a proper state. Like something off the *Rocky Horror*. I messed around for ages, different colours, different shades, then I just thought fuck it: he'd seen me. He'd seen me having a fit. Like there was any mystery left.

But he was funny about body stuff. We could never go to the toilet in front of each other – not that I'd want to. One of the nights I stayed over, I asked if I could borrow his toothbrush because I'd forgotten mine. You should've seen his face. I thought he was going to gip. No way, he said. And I thought: you've just had your tongue between my legs and I can't share your fucking *toothbrush*?

Fuck it. I went without a face and stuck some shades on.

———

— You should have told me. I didn't know what was going on.

— I'm sorry.

— I didn't know what to do. I called an ambulance because you had blood coming out of your mouth. Gushing.

— I bite my tongue sometimes.

— I tried to stick my finger in to stop you.

He stuck out his hand and pulled the plaster off. There was a nasty gash. It'd leave a scar. I could've fucking slapped him.

— Never stick *anything* in my gob. OK. I could've fucking choked to death. I could've bit your fucking finger off the bone. No shit, Dave. Never ever do that to anyone having a fit. Ever.

— I thought you were going to die. The noises you made. The paramedics said you were out of order. They couldn't believe you hadn't told me. I felt so stupid.

— Jumped-up fucking van drivers. They know *fuck all*.

I knew it was Make-or-Break. I knew I had to get it all out, and if he freaked, he freaked.

— It's called a tonic–clonic seizure. The tonic bit is when you relax – your muscles go all floppy and you fall down. The clonic bit makes me go stiff. Get them all at once and you shake and stuff. That's why I scream and grunt and bite my tongue.

I felt my face getting hot.

— And lose control of my bladder.

His eyes looking at me.

— Muscles going crazy in my chest and hands and legs. Everywhere. Even my eyes. My brain gets all mixed up. Messages flying round to all the wrong bits. Saying tighten and relax, tighten and relax. That's why I jerk. That's all it is. That's all.

Looking at me like the words were crawling out of my mouth.

— What makes your brain do that?

— Electricity.

— *Electricity?*

— Yep. But I'm not mad, Dave. It doesn't mean I'm thick, or a nutcase. It's not an illness. You can't catch it. It means I'm special. My fits come from right at the bottom of my brain. It's called the temporal lobe.

I took his hand and moved his fingers over my lump.

— The brain's split up. Four bits each side.

I curled my fingers over my thumbs, put my fists together. I showed him.

— These are called lobes.

I wiggled my fingers about.

— I've scarred this bit at the back, when I was a bairn. The temporal bit, this here, it's where the senses come from. It means I see and hear and smell stuff that's not there sometimes. Walk around like I'm drunk. It's just the brain talking to the wrong bits, mixing it all up. That's all.

He got down onto his knees in front of me. He took my face in his hands.

— I'm sorry, Dave, but I've got to know. Does this change anything?

— No.

— Don't bullshit me. I'm big enough to cope. I won't think bad of you if you want to finish things. I won't badmouth you or anything. I understand. Just be straight with me.

He kissed my words. He wiped the tears coming out the corners of my eyes with his thumbs. He kissed me and my tears were just my brain melting, leaking out.

— I think you're amazing, Lily O'Connor. You're a shining star.

— Give over.

— I mean it. You're the most amazing person I've ever met in my life.

He kissed my black eye really gently – it lifted a filthy cloud off my head. I could see him properly for the first time, and he could see me. No lies. Open. Bare-naked. No bullshit. It sounds cheesy, but we made love right there on the floor. That's how it felt: love. Not shagging or screwing or fucking: love. He even said it,

— I love you so much, Lily.

There were explosions.

Bright lights filled the room and I thought I was going. I felt the warm breeze inside, the shadows moving, and I was scared I was going to piss on him.

But it was just kids letting off fireworks in the street outside. Bonfire night was soon, and we held each other laughing because it was so perfect, the explosions as we lost ourselves.

But then I felt it: he'd come inside me.

8

Friday evening, the bathroom window was open, it was just starting to get dark out and I'm sat on the toilet listening to this bird in a tree outside. Its song getting louder, louder, too loud, until it filled my head and the singing was in the middle of my brain.

Two notes. One low one high going Li-*ly* . . . Li-*ly* . . .

And then all I could see were wings fluttering, feathers flapping about in my head, tickles, tiny scratches on the inside of my skull, like you want to sneeze but can't and the amazing thing is I can remember, remember it all so clearly.

Li-*ly* . . . Li-*ly* . . .

I got the light feeling, lightness like a wave but not going up through my body, this time it was all in my head, the bird perched on my tonsils digging its claws in tight. I let out a scream that wouldn't stop. No fizzing. No brain frying. No electricity zapping round my body in balls of light.

When I closed my eyes I could see it. An overgrown sparrow too big for my head, bits of its feathers were missing. It was minging and scabby. It clawed and flapped and the noise came out of my mouth in a siren

LI-*LEEEEE* LI-*LEEEEE*

gripping onto the toilet with the noise belting out of me

LI-*LEEEEEEEEEE* LI-*LEEEEEEEEEE*

All brown fluster, I saw the bird fly out of my gob and away out the window.

And I saw the room again. I let go of the toilet and put my hand up in front of me. I rubbed my fingers together and I could feel them, my small hands. White, bony hands. Bare feet dangling beneath my pink nightie. I touched my face and rubbed my eyes. The smallness. When I opened them there was darkness. And I knew.

I was back there.

I felt the cold door handle and pulled it down and the door hished on the carpet. Darkness, but I could see the bed and hear him breathing and I was so excited. I put my hands out in the dark and felt for the warmth between the sheets, slipping my hand in, feeling.

But then it was gone, quick-as. I was leaning my head against the bathroom wall, the tiles cold and the sound of a car driving past the road out front.

The bird on my tonsils, the room – it was gone.

I put my fingers to my nose and sniffed, but I couldn't smell him at all.

––––––––

Mel bought loads of food and wine and chocolate for our Friday night in. She was excited. She looked the happiest I'd ever seen her. I reckon she thought this was proper special. I bet her and Anna used to do it: Friday night in, bottles of wine, Channel Four shite and big bars of chocolate.

I wanted to tell her about the room, about the bird on my tonsils, but what could I say? I decided I'd tell the bright spark when I saw him in a couple of weeks.

My fits were taking another turn, I knew they were. They've changed a lot over the years. Maybe that's all it was. Pills, hormones. My dodgy brain. Or maybe I'd start remembering everything. Maybe I'd become that girl again.

Mel cooked some fancy grub. I only sipped at the wine but she'd started on the second bottle by the time *Friends* had started. She asked me if anything was up, said I was acting quiet. I told her I was just having A Quiet One.

— And my eye's totally knacking.

We could be like that together – quiet, not saying anything. It was nice, not having to talk shite all night. We watched telly but my mind was out the window, in the tree, on my tonsils and itching to sing.

I felt filthy inside.

————

In morning assembly my nipples would crease thinking about him. Thinking about the night before and how I sat in the bathtub behind him. He'd lie back and I'd reach around his sides and soap him up. His chest, his stomach, his balls. I was dizzy all the time with it. I loved it. I was his wife. He would leave Mam for me. The two of us would run away together. Whispering, sighing his name while the other girls talked My Little Pony. Every minute of the day, feeling like I could die with it. My Don.

I started to bud breasts. The first wisps of hair between my legs. He saw it when he was drying me down in front of the fire. He flinched and gave me the towel.

— I think you should dry yourself from now on.

That first push away.

I started raking the streets at night, keeping out of their way. I got in with a bad lot. I started robbing from shops, lying all the time, fighting, burning things down, swearing and spitting at people in the street.

And she's the girl that comes to visit me when nothing's real, when everything's a copy, when everything's reflections in glass. Swinging her legs and hissing. She's never gone away. The angry girl. She never left me and I wish she had.

Don came along and Mikey and Barry were gone, made to disappear. Then my pubes and blood came along and he wanted me to go as well.

Mam loved the angry girl. It was her excuse. Shipped off to the care home just because she could. Locked up until they could decide what to do with me. I remember my heart was hot with never wanting to see them again. The heat went from my chest to my body and I felt the warmth of myself because they were out of my life. But I wanted my brothers back. I wanted Mikey to look after me again. I thought he'd be there, waiting for me at the gates at the care home.

I never thought I'd never see him again.

———

— There's something I want you to do for me.

She raised an eyebrow and used the remote to switch the telly off.

— It'd mean a lot.

— What?

— I want to have a bath.

— You don't have to ask.

— No, I mean it's proper dangerous. If I fit I could drown. Thing is, I'll have to leave the door open. I haven't had a bath in years. I'll sing to you. I just want you to sit in the living room and listen to me, and if I stop singing or humming, then you have to come and get me. Is that all right?

She gave me the nicest smile, squeezed my arm, then left the room. I heard the squeak of the taps, water purling into the tub. I went into my bedroom and got undressed and put my silky nightie on, the black Calvin Klein one. The feel of my breasts against the silk, the swish and softness against my hips. I heard her go through to the living room and put the telly down.

She'd put some smelly in the bath for me, lit some candles. So sweet. I sat on the edge, moving my fingers in it.

— You OK in there?

— I'm just about to get in. Thanks for the candles. What should I sing?

— 'I'm Forever Blowing Bubbles'?

I turned the taps off, took my nightie off and got into the water. It was the best feeling. I went in slow and the sting was gorgeous. It was like a blanket slowly covering me up, and the bubbles and scent and candles – they made my head spin in a nice way. Kindliness, that's what it was. Mel was proper kind. I felt so close to her. Every muscle in my body going tonic. Everything resting in me, going loose. My head getting light. My black eye felt soothed. My scabs turning soft. All my fretting rising up and away in the steam. I lied down, slack and easy, and began. My voice is crap but I didn't give a shit.

And as I sat in the bath, singing away, I imagined the sparrow itch got wet in the steam and dribbled down my chin, into the water.

I lathered the lump on my head. Sometimes I think of it like a volcano and when I'm slamming and thrashing it spews all the bad stuff out of my head.

Since Mam died, I'd been thinking she gets inside me when I fit. She climbs down into my body to feel what it's like to be alive, and we slam and thrash together.

Only once did she touch it. I woke up and she was above the bed and I could feel her hands in my hair and smell the booze off her. I kept perfectly still and blinked up at her. She said nothing and then left.

— Lily?

I remembered folk's faces. The looks. Me a kid covered in bruises. Mum looking like a proper tart in her miniskirt and beehive, slapping me in the middle of the street. People's faces. You poor little sod. It made me feel pathetic.

— Lily?

I'm lying there in the hot water and breathing the steam and the memories are like sheets smothering me. Mikey's face, always there, shushing me, calming me as I came around, talking soft, the puffiness of his face looking down at me. Shush. You're all right now our lass. After Mikey and Barry were taken away, I got used to being on my own when I came round. Mam told Don it was best to leave me alone. They'd be sat watching telly, like I was invisible down there on the floor.

— Lily?

I washed inside with my finger, remembering Dave. I worked out how long I could leave it. It could wait until Sunday, safe-as. I pictured his tadpoles swimming around inside me. But I'd have my night out. I reckoned I deserved it. Me spewing my guts up with the morning-after pill – it could fucking wait.

Mel shouted all panicky,
— Lily?
— I'm all right. I'm OK. Thank you.
Liar.

⊗⊗⊗⊗

Dave answered the door with his blue overalls on and said a friend of his was there, helping him in his lab. Would I mind waiting in the living room for a bit until they'd finished?

— Course not.

I stuck the telly on while he went back upstairs. I went through to the kitchen to make a brew. The kettle started hissing. I tiptoed to the bottom of the stairs and cocked my head to listen, but all you could hear was heavy metal playing. No girly giggles. No screams going oh Dave oh Dave fuck me harder harder yessssss.

I made the brew and ran some cold water in. I sat on the sofa and watched some Saturday afternoon kiddies' shite on the telly. I was wondering how long he was going to leave me there, when I heard his clomps coming down the stairs. If it was a woman, I was out of there. No I wouldn't, I'd be strong. Act like I couldn't give a shit. I stared at the door and got the fright of my life when some fella stuck his head round goes hello there darling in cockney. Dave pushed the bloke into the room and they were laughing and slapping each other like they were the best of friends.

— Lily, this is Hank. Hank, this is Lily.

I put the mug on the floor and stood up, straightening my skirt. We shook hands and he eyed me up and down. He had the longest eyelashes I'd ever seen on a man. His gorgeous black eyes – they made me feel funny inside.

Dave elbowed him.

— I've told Hank you're epileptic.

I turned my back on them both.

— Nice to meet you, Lily.

I listened to them at the front door and I was sure I heard Dave talking foreign. I sat back on the couch and told myself not to be cross with him. But he'd nettled me. The front door slammed shut and there he was, greasing up to me, grabbing my breasts and kissing me with his scratchy face.

— I missed you last night, babe. I had a fantastic wank thinking about you.

I pushed him off me, but he wasn't having any of it.

— Oh come on, I've missed you. I really have. Let's go upstairs and make up for lost time. Let's consolidate.

He stuck his hand between my legs and I punched him, hard.

— Jesus.

— I'm not a fucking toy, Dave. Don't treat me like that.

He rubbed his arm and scowled at me dark. I picked my tea up and supped. He said sorry really quiet and gave me his puppy eyes.

— Who's this Hank, then? You've never mentioned him before.

He got up and started pacing around the room, rubbing his arm.

— He's a mate. Went to school with him. He's an

engineer as well. Really knows his stuff. Helps me with my inventions now and then.

— That's nice. You never said you were mates with a Paki.

His eyes wide.

— Jesus, Lily. What planet are you from? I didn't know you were racist.

— I don't know what you mean.

— You shouldn't go around calling people that. He's one of the nicest blokes you could meet. You're unbelievable, you know that?

— But it's all right, you telling him I'm *an epileptic*?

He squeezed his arm with his gob open.

— Don't you think that should be up to me? My black eye, is that what it was? Scared he'd think you'd knocked me about?

— I'm sorry.

— I'm not an *epileptic* but you're *an arsehole*. I'm important. I matter. I can do anything. I'm a sexy, strong woman that happens to *have* epilepsy. Do you get it? I *have* epilepsy but it's not who I am.

— I said I'm sorry.

— Just think.

He hunched up like a naughty dog.

— So anyway, why do you call him Hank? He's not American, is he?

— No. British through and through. Hank comes from hanky head.

— Hanky head?

— As in turban, you know.

He made circles round his head. I turned back to the telly.

— And you say *I'm* racist?

He tutted and slammed the door and went upstairs.

I put the cup of tea down and left.

☯☯

Inside the club it was all dark and sweat. Vibrating and the heat. The thump in your guts from the drums all boom boom boom. It was like something biting right into me. My insides being rearranged. Bondage gear, masks, crazy hairdos and make-up, you name it. Freak-a-fucking-delic. Men in too-tight clothes, dancing badly like the Gay X-Change Phoneline men.

We stood at the edge of the dance floor. Mel had leant me some shades that were red, not too dark. She said it'd help me see the evening through rose-tinted spectacles. You could still see my shiner, though, if you looked close enough. But who gave a shit? The dance floor was raised up and bits of it were spinning around. The floor was lit from underneath and it looked tops through the glasses.

— I'll get us a drink. Wait here.

— You're not fucking leaving me.

We went in arm in arm through the bodies and the sweat and the writhing. You couldn't tell whether they were lads or lasses. You could tell they were all off their tits, though – starry eyes and the massive grins you got back. Paggered, that's what Barry called it. Gurning like bastards. E'd-up, coked-up, looking for a fuck, a fling, a snog, a grope, a blowjob in the bogs. Something like last week but madder, better. No strings attached. No mobile number scrawled across a torn beer mat in Revlon lippy.

And the music was this huge mouth trying to eat us all up. My insides were pounding with it. That feeling though, I loved it.

The music had teeth. My senses were chewed.

We got the expensive-as drinks and went further into the club. The drinks were like treble measures. They made your eyes water. I wasn't complaining. But I knew I had to take it easy. I'd been drinking too much recently and my fits were getting worse. My own worst enemy, that's me.

We got to some stairs and up we went. We found some seats in a snug where we could hear ourselves think. It was nice to get sat. Mel was wearing this silvery top from Karen Millen. Silver and silky with mesh bits round the hems and these little jewels and pearls round the neckline. It was sexy-as. Showed her figure off good. Her cleavage looked even more ample than usual.

— Dave's asked me to move in with him.

She snorted and nodded like I wondered how long it would be.

— So what are you going to say?

— We had our first proper row today. I think so, anyway. I think I made it happen, you know. I don't know what's wrong with me. He's the first decent bloke I've met in ages and I want to get into a row.

— But you're going to say yes. That why we're here tonight? To soften the blow?

— I love living with you, Mel. I know I haven't been there much, but you're my first woman friend. I don't really like women that much. I'm not a girl's girl, you know. I know most men are pricks, but at least they're straightforward. You're my first proper woman friend and I *love* it, even if you are a big lezzer.

She laughed and we hugged.

— I feel exactly the same way. I think you're so great, Lil.

— So I'm going to say no. I know Hackney's another world, but it's only two stops away on the Smacklink. It's not like we hardly fucking see each other, is it?

Her face like a Christmas tree.

— I know it's none of my business, but I must say, I think that's the right decision. Not that I'm interfering, but you've only known him for five minutes. I wish you all the best though, I really do.

We raised our glasses and kerchinged. Hearing her say that – it was the best thing. It felt like all the tight feelings from the week before had totally gone. I was seeing how brilliant she was again. I knew she'd probably only invited me to live with her because she was lonely and all her friends had abandoned her, but it was great.

A fit had brought about some luck for once.

We drank and watched folk wandering about. All the men were really dolled up, mincing about like boys dressed up in their sisters' clothes. Most of the women were beautiful and had long hair and amazing dresses. They looked like they were on the pull for men, not women. But what the fuck did I know?

— Is this a lezzy bar, then?

She went no, she hates pure lezzy bars because most of the dykes are alcoholics and dogs and smoke rollies and have halitosis and look at you funny if you're fem.

— That's why I chose this place, because it's a good mix. Plus the music rocks.

I watched Mel watching them. She really is beautiful, but not in an obvious way. She has one of those faces you can just look at forever. One of the most beautiful women I've ever seen. I wondered what she was thinking. I'd pretended I was cool with coming. Mel shuffled closer to me and nodded at a woman. I was thinking this is it: she's going to pull and leave me all on my own with these fucking weirdos.

— So tell me. I know I'm a bit thick about these things, but I'm trying. Being gay, I mean when did you know? When did you first cop off with a lass?

She got all starry eyed and licked her lips.

— I was about twelve. I was sleeping over at a friend's house. We were in her bedroom with her younger brother, sat on her bed and playing Dare. The rules were simple: we had to do what she said. *Anything* that she said.

— I like the sound of that.

— Well, it started off pretty innocently, making silly noises, standing on our heads, flashing our bums, stupid kids' stuff.

— Usual night in.

— Then she said I had to kiss her little brother. He was only about eight and he had his pyjamas on and I could see he had a stiffy.

— Grim.

— I kissed him half on the cheek, half on the mouth. We laughed about it and he got all embarrassed and ran out the room, shouting at us to fuck off. Once he'd gone the atmosphere changed. I got butterflies and goosebumps. She pulled up her nightie, put her fingers inside herself, wiggled them around a bit, then pulled them out and stuck them in front of my face.

— Jesus.

— She said: I dare you to lick the juices off my fingers. I said no way and she said well I'll just lick them off myself. And she did.

I looked at Mel in the disco light. I didn't know her at

all. This posh little girl getting up to all that naughtiness. It was brilliant. I wanted her to tell me more. Disgusting stories. Total filth stories.

— So did you just get down and dirty there and then?

— We slept in the same bed that night, yes, but she scared the shit out of me and excited me at the same time. Let's just say we had a fantastic night that night. Boys seemed irrelevant after that.

We raised our glasses and kerchinged. The drinks kept coming. After my third I can't stop. I just get this thirst. It's stupid, I know. Mel was talking to me but I wasn't listening. I kept my eyes closed and turned my head to where the music was coming from.

And there it was: that sound.

The music was amazing. Whenever I hear techno, I think of my birthday night the year before with Barry. When we walked on the beach afterwards and, like a fool, I felt total love for him. I'd had half a Rolls-Royce and the music took over me. Music is different on E. Everything is. And some of the noises, the trance noises – there's one, a kind of farty squelchy noise; it did something to me. My hands were mouths and I screwed up my face like I was a monster and stomped about, laughing. I must've looked proper stupid. It did something inside my brain. I wanted to touch everything in the world. It was just like the lushness before you go. All in a little white pill.

When I was a kid, I'd bring fits on. I'd breathe hard and make myself hyperventilate. And that's what E is like, the same feeling, just before you go into the dark. Coming up with that rise in the stomach. Ecstasy, just like before you fall. The stillness and the world seems so perfect. Sounds and colours and shapes are so loud and bright and shiny – it does *everything* to your brain.

And I could hear it now, that sound playing downstairs. Rubbing my hands together, breathing fast, heart going like a nursery rhyme deDUM deDUM, deDUM deDUM.

I took my shades off and gave them to Mel to put in her handbag.

— Let's dance.

I grabbed her hand and dragged her down the steps. That's when it kicked in, that feeling. I was moving down the steps and coming up. Everything seemed so 3D. I dragged her across the dance floor until we found a gap. The rush surging, exploding in my gut, rattling up my backbone. I screamed, swaying. I kept opening my eyes and smiling at Mel. We'd never danced together before. I watched her and liked the way she moved. Her elbows into her sides, her hips going but her feet not moving. I spun round and around to speakers shouting *c'mon get up everybody* and something began to happen around my knees.

I began to worry. Began to seriously regret being there. Some weird drug thing was happening. Just being there, next to those people. I was breathing it in. Their skin touching me. Sweaty skin with drugs in, soaking into me. I grabbed Mel's hand. I was hysterical laughing. I span and shouted that I was loving it.

A tingling, burning, up and down my thighs. To my neck, along the insides of my arms. It was electricity flowing through me. I could feel it. I wanted to shed my skin and float around the club all blue and green and white lights. I squeezed Mel's hand and knew she could feel it, feel it running through me and into her. I opened my eyes and put my face right up to hers. I stared into her eyes and we were laughing. She could see it in the blacks of my eyes, at the centre there: she could see the fire and there was that fizz between us and I zapped her. Her eyes spread like night-time over her face. We span round and around. I stuck my arms up and pumped electricity into the air, shooting lightning out of the club and into the skies above London. Melting them all, all those bodies. Like the lights were stars and I was melting them in the night that was turning all milky swirls like dreaming. The stars were a thousand eyes watching me, winking at me. The sky loved me. The green and orange lights like God had farted, like the Northern lights. I'd seen them at home, out at sea, green fingers curling over the sky.

I span, shooting electricity from my arms
POWWWWWWWWWWWWWWWW . . .

And everything was going to go just right for me now. I was going to find Mikey. I realized I was going to see his face again and I think I started crying, but happy crying. I knew I was stumbling all over the shop, but everyone was moving and swinging, holding up the beat. The bad times were gone, that's what it was. Those times were never going to return. All the black shit, the dark shit in my life. Mam was fucking dead and everything she meant was gone. And I never wanted it to stop, that feeling. I imagined it was like being dead, drifting with no body. Out there, not attached to anything. And that sound in the music again, sending me off. I saw my life as a star. I was a shooting star, just like Dave said, and I missed him then, I wanted him. Wanted his arms around me, to feel him pulsing inside me, his electricity, his life.

But then I saw myself as a dark star, a black hole sucking everything in. It's because he was touching me in places I hadn't been for a long time.

I knew I had to close myself down.

The sound system said if house is a feeling then your house is mine.

Inside, I was the same, and I didn't want to be. I opened my arms and the bodies fell into me. Sweaty love. It was Mel. I felt her neck against my face. It was wet and hot with sweat. I felt her against me as we moved with the beat. I looked up at the mirror ball spinning up there, shooting off its lights, and then it came to me: her eyes on mine, that look.

I barged through the bodies and into the toilets. I went to the sink and splashed cold water onto my face. You could see the white of my bad eye now, but it was yellow inside.

I stood laughing at myself in the mirror. Two women were snogging against the wall. I watched their reflections. The woman next to me nodded.

— What you on?

And I laughed at myself.

— Electricity.

I could see the city lit up like a Christmas tree. It was lush: London at night from the river, four in the morning, going across Blackfriars Bridge. It gives me butterflies just thinking about it. It was to our right, all the lights and colours. St Paul's like a silver tit and the oranges and blues of Tower Bridge. The blue of Canary Wharf flashing away and the Gherkin's green diamonds like crocodile scales. And the Tate, a big brown monster with its slitty eye up there, all yellow and pink. We both said wow together and then it was gone. We leaned back and sighed.

— So did you pull, then?

She gave me the eyebrow.

— With you like a rash over me all night, I didn't stand a chance.

It wasn't meant to be like that, and I felt a sulk coming over me because I didn't have the words.

— It's all right, you don't have to say anything. I know the difference between a kiss and *a kiss*.

The cabbie was eyeballing us. Wondering if we were going to get it on for him, live lezzy sex show on his back seat. I got an urge to flash him my breasts and had to stop myself.

I was still getting used to being invisible. Being able to have conversations and not giving a fuck who heard. There's something about it, you feel free. No one knowing you. No one being able to spread rumours around town about you. You could ignore people and not be considered rude. I was becoming a rude Londoner and it felt great.

I remember thinking of home, and what I thought I knew, felt far, far away.

I stuck my tongue out at the cabbie, and that's the last thing I remember. Mel said I fell asleep, sprawled on the back seat, and she had to help me up the steps into the house. Good night. Fucking great night.

She said I was a star. A shining star.

———

Sunday morning, I went straight to the chemist at Highbury Barn. I was cutting it fine. I felt so wobbly. I was still pissed. When I got back home I necked the tablet and got straight into bed.

Morning-after pill – what a total fucking nightmare.

I've never been so sick in my entire life. Mel kept fussing. I told her it was the booze, that I shouldn't drink so much. She brought me a bowl to chunder into. I had three fits that day and pissed the bed a little. I told Mel I'd buy a new mattress and some rubber sheets. She didn't know what to say. I was out there, in a total state. She looked after me. She held my hair back and rubbed a wet cloth on the back of my neck while the hormone overdose flushed everything out.

I went without my pills that day. I couldn't hold anything down. All for letting him come inside me like that. And then going out and getting so pissed.

The price you pay for trying to be normal.

Every time I heaved it felt like my black eye was going to pop. I puked until nothing came up, just a dry retching like sandpaper up my throat, across my tongue.

I promised myself no man would come inside me ever again.

And that I would never get so pissed again.

7

I remember walking by Hackney Downs, up Queensdown Road under the line of trees that led up to Dave's, and you could see them everywhere – fluffy hops of squirrels. Dozens of them raking through leaves that were all oranges and browns. They let you get right up close to them. I wanted to pick one up and stroke its bushy tail. But then it was the wind that started stirring the leaves up. I couldn't feel it or hear it, just see it: a swirl in front of me. The leaves making a dry sound, scratchy on the pavement.

It tickled in my throat.

There was something in the leaves – it was trying to talk to me, I just knew it was.

I legged it across to Dave's and used the key he'd given me to let myself in. Safe. He'd left a note for me on the pillow on his bed, the page folded over and Lily written on it with a line underneath. A line and a kiss like a shooting star. I threw myself down on the bed. On his bedside cabinet were a few books and I remember one of them – it was called *Coping with Epilepsy*. I stared at the words but I was too tired to reach over and pick it up.

I started dozing, and that's when I saw it again: his face.

I'd gone to Camden Market that morning, thinking I'd buy myself some new clothes to cheer myself up after seeing that bastard bright spark. I was moseying between all the tight-packed stalls of hippy shit and leather jackets, stink of joss sticks and people smoking roll-ups. Just minding my own business, when I saw the back of him. The catch of his eye.

I followed him.

Coats and dresses and jumpers, tie-dyed sheets, battering them out of the way with my hands. I thought I'd lost him. He was speeding off, running away from me. It was him, I knew it was. I wanted to shout his name but I lost him. My head was already doing things, building a man around the twinkle there. I stood still, looking through the curtains of clothes, jacket filthy with stains. Smoke and rags hanging, Bob Marley singing 'No Woman No Cry' and people laughing, spliff stink and faces full of piercings, and then I saw his shoulder. I shouted it so loud my voice tore,

— Mikey!

Tears coming already.

— *Mikey!*

And bang, I ran right into him. His fingers digging into my arms.

— Fuck you after, girl?

The patterns in his eyes. Booze breath on me.

— Fuck you want?

I fought out of his hands and legged it, pulling things off the stalls, battering into people with swearing and shouting behind me. Onto the main road with cars and buses and motorbikes. Men with masks over their faces, coming at me all horns and anger. Suddenly I'm in the middle of the road and London wants to kill me.

I thought it was him, Mikey. I thought it was him.

But my head did it. My head made a picture of him, just from that glint in the dirty face. It's the picture I had of him. It's who he was to me. Someone that'd given up. I'd seen him so many times in shop doorways, passed out on the footpath with folk stepping over him, no shoes on in the freezing rain. So hurt they forget who they are. Scraping the bottom of themselves. Rolling around in chip wrappers and dog shit. His life all ice, black, sopping in misery. It hurts too much to remember that. It really fucking hurts.

Then something woke me.

I stared out of the skylight for ages. It was getting dark with the nights closing in. I watched the clouds moving up there and felt like I was floating underwater.

I sat up and read the letter from Dave. I read it a few times, and finding it like that – it reminded me of something I didn't want to think about. Love letters in my pockets, finding them at school. And anyway, I heard the music straight off, just that one line in my ears.

'Thank you for loving me'. Bon fucking Jovi. I went into the living room and looked through his CDs. His Bon Jovi one wasn't there.

When he came home, I said it to him teasing,

— I found something on the pillow before.

He looked away.

— It's nice, Dave, thank you.

I gave him a kiss on the cheek and he seemed to be about to tell me he'd copied it, but then he just looked shy and said nothing.

He cooked us a meal. It was the first time I'd ever seen him cook. I checked the bin afterwards and found the packets: stuffed pasta from Tesco's. Boil For Three Minutes. And I saw the herb salad bag: Washed and Ready to Eat. He'd lit candles and laid the table and everything. He even made dessert: slices of melon with sugar on.

It's the thought that counts.

— You're a dream come true, Dave Electrics. That was yummy.

I leaned over and kissed his scratchy cheek.

— Wined dined and . . .

He grabbed my breast.

— Don't spoil it.

Too late. He let out a massive burp and I felt it hot on my face. The garlic made my eyes water. He said he was sorry; I said he was a pig.

— So anyway, how come I've never met this flatmate of yours? You talk about her all the time. Are you sure she's not your imaginary friend? Were you just putting on a posh voice when you rang for me to fix your wiring, eh? Were you?

He was drunk. He was being a twat.

— You can meet her whenever you want.

— So what does she do? She must be minted with a flat like that in Canonbury.

— She works in the City with a capital C. Banking.

— She stuck up?

— No. She means a lot to me. She's my best friend . . .

I don't even know why I said it: but.

— But what?

It felt like a risk.

— Well, you'll find out sooner or later: she's gay.

I thought he'd go all moody. Thought he'd start getting sus, but he just hummed and started playing with his wine glass.

— I didn't know at first, like. I freaked out a bit when I found out. But I'm all right about it now. She's the nicest person I've ever met, really. She's tops.

He looked far away. I cleared the pots and he shouted through,

— You can invite her round, if you like? I'll cook for you both.

I went back in and smiled at him. He said should we have an early night and gave me his saucy look. I told him I was on my period and I wanted him to sigh a big sigh of relief. I wanted him to have said something about coming inside me like he did. That he knew it wasn't OK, that he was really sorry. I just wanted him to say something, anything, but all I got was,

— That's all right, you can wank me off instead.

ⓐⓐⓟⓟ

All bright sparks are twats. Consultants are no better, they're just pushier. I'd waited fucking ages for that appointment. The waiting room was crammed and I had to stand for forty fucking minutes with my feet burning. You tell yourself you won't take any shit from them this time, you'll make them listen without interrupting, and they'll do as you ask. But as soon as you're in that room with them you know it: you're stupid and they fucking hate you for it.

No time to say what you want to say. He was a fat greasy bastard with words bumbling out of him like spew. He looked stressed-as, like he wanted to slap me, like he wanted to kick me round the room shouting there's fuck all wrong with you, you dozy bint. I wanted to tell him about the morning-after pill, about the accident, about my periods going doolally. I opened my mouth but he didn't give me a chance.

He told me some figures. It didn't make sense. Nothing

he was saying had anything to do with me. I usually write down my questions before I get there, but I was so confused lately. I felt my life wasn't mine any more. I wanted to tell him, but he spoke to me like I didn't know what the fuck epilepsy was, like I didn't *understand*.

I said no, wait, but he didn't hear. He looked at the clock on the wall and sighed and wrote something down. I wanted to shout LISTEN TO ME YOU FUCK.

He gave me some leaflets and bits of paper.

— Why aren't you on an oral contraceptive?

— It makes me fat.

— It could help control your periods.

— They're not catamenial.

He looked at me properly for the first time.

— I had a bird on my tonsils, doctor. I've been seeing things that aren't there.

He looked me up and down. What he saw didn't please him. He stood up.

— When changing medication from one drug to another, you decrease one gradually whilst introducing the new one. Any change needs to be done carefully to prevent your kidneys and liver from reacting badly. These are non-enzyme-inducing, but as you're not on the Pill that won't matter as much.

I thought wonderful. Great. What he meant was that I was now going to have two lots of side effects, instead of one. Whoopee.

— Halve the dose of the existing drug every two weeks until you reach a small dose, which is when you should stop completely. And the reverse for the new one, start small, double after a fortnight until you get to the dose recommended.

Words like snow falling on my brain.

— I've charted it all down for you, in case you forget.

— *Forget?*

He sighed, brows in the air. I went,

— You know, one of my first memories is of taking grains of Phenobarbitone. And then being confused-as when they moved me on to Zarontin. I didn't know what day it was. Then they stopped my Zarontin and put me on Mysolin. I didn't know my arse from my elbow, but I can name every drug I've ever been on.

— I'm sure you . . .

— And every side effect.

— Listen, Miss . . .

— They reduced the Mysolin and increased the Sodium Valproate. Then they stopped the Mysolin and Zarontin and replaced it with Epilim. On and on and on. I can give you years, dates. I can give you dosage.

— That's why I've made an appointment for you at the hospital. There's a chance surgery could lead to a seizure-free life. No more drugs.

I didn't say no, I didn't argue.

I bowed and said thank you and closed the door gently behind me.

———————

A week after and we were getting ready to go to Dave's for tea. I was telling Mel all of this, and she tried to say the right words, I know she did, but she didn't understand. She said some of her friends were doctors and she was sure I was just mistaken. She wasn't even fucking listening.

— I'm really nervous about meeting Dave.

I thought she'd have dressed up a bit, but she didn't and I was relieved. Worst thing would've been if she *had* dressed up. Tight black top and shortish skirt. Nightmare. He told me he didn't like big breasts. He'd said they're all fat and what's the point of that? I told him they weren't fat they were milk tissue and he said more than a handful's a waste and I went that's true. But men like them big – he was just saying that to make me feel better, I know he was.

Who can argue with big breasts?

We took a taxi and I was jabbering on, trying to tell her all of the nice things he'd done and how special he made me feel because I was nervous-as that she'd hate him straight off.

He opened the door with a big smile. I could tell he fancied her – men can't hide it. That twitch in his face, his eyes looking everywhere but at her. Acting like a boy. Who wouldn't fancy her, though? She's fucking gorgeous.

He had his hair down, all sleeky. How come I was jealous of my boyfriend's hair? He took our coats and hung them up. Then he showed us through to the living room. He'd candles lit and was playing his eighties compilation on the stereo.

Kajagoogoo singing 'Too Shy'.

— It's a lovely house you've got here. And it's so nice, being next to the park. It must be really quiet.

— That's one of the benefits, Melanie.

Melanie?

I realized the place was stifling hot. We sat down on the couch and Dave stood over us. He looked smart, like the night we went out on our first date. He was wearing a suit jacket with his jeans. He said it showed he was relaxed but making an effort. I was thinking if he rolled the sleeves up he'd look proper *Miami Vice*.

— So what can I get you ladies? Gin and tonic, wine, beer?

He was looking at Mel with his hands in the air. His voice was funny – he sounded posh.

— Gin and tonic would be great. Thanks.

— Ice and slice?

— Lovely.

He walked out. I shouted after him,

— Nothing for me, thanks.

Mel stood up and started nebbing at pictures on the walls. I realized how badly painted the place was. He might have been good with a screwdriver, but he was shite with a paintbrush. In fact, I'd never seen him clean, not once. I noticed bits of wallpaper were coming away. I wondered if he'd decorated since his mam and dad had died. I coughed and she looked at me.

— What do you think?

She stuck her thumbs up and then turned back to the pictures. I didn't know what to do with myself. Dave came back in with Mel's drink.

— That's for you, Melanie.

— Her name's Mel, numb nuts.

He gave me a dirty. Mel sat down next to me again and Dave went and sat in his chair by the fireplace, his forehead wet. I'd never seen him drink gin before.

Cyndi Lauper singing 'Girls Just Wanna Have Fun'.

— I'll go through and keep an eye on the dinner. You two make yourselves at home.

When he'd gone I stared at her.

— He seems nice, Lil. I like his hair.

I didn't want to think about his fucking hair. I told her about the consultant again. It was nagging at me, the thought of what they wanted to do. Take my skull apart, ice and slice me. Open me up and take a chunk of me away.

They've told me the brain has no feeling. No nerves. They said it was like the brain is under anaesthetic all the time. It doesn't make sense. This thing that causes my body so much pain – it can't feel pain itself.

I told her about the scan and that I was scared. That I thought it was fucking pointless. I told her about the new tablets and the consultant not listening to a word I'd said.

— I'm sure he's only looking out for your best interests, Lil.

I wanted her to agree with me. I wanted her to go yes he sounds like a right twat. It wasn't *her* head they wanted to saw open. Wasn't her blood they were poisoning. I wanted to be better, of course I did. I wanted them to take my fits away forever, the slamming, the thrashing, the ugliness, pissing myself and grunting. So you had to trust them or what else was there, eh?

Dave called ready and we went through to the kitchen. Candles, wine, he'd even bought flowers and had the nouse to put the salad in a bowl. He'd put some small tomatoes and olives on the top. The food was steaming on the plates. He sat me and Mel next to each other and put the lights out, but it was too dark so he put them back on again and looked flustered.

— Tuck in, tuck in.

There was cheese in a bowl. Mel sprinkled some on her pasta.

— This looks nice, Dave. Lil didn't tell me you were a cook.

He smiled. I could hear the words running through his head: Good cook, and a damn fine fuck. Dave the poet. Bon fucking Jovi.

I watched them both get drunker and drunker. I felt sleepy. I let their words slip in and out of my head like fish.

The fork was so heavy that my arm ached. The pasta was like wet pillows in my gob. I wanted to get down on all fours, roll my forehead on the cold lino.

They were laughing about something. I was pleased. Of course I was pleased – they were getting on together. Great. But my head was elsewhere. I felt suffocated. I went and stood beside the sink and watched them.

Dave refilled Mel's glass. He loved to talk when he drank. He was telling her things about himself I'd never heard before. He was talking in that funny voice, telling her about school and his mam and dad. He rabbited on for ages. Me me me. How come he never told me stuff like that?

I turned my back on them and looked out of the window. I could see phone wires, black lines sagging and trees swaying, rooftops, birds settling for the night. Electric blood across orange-peel sky.

— No, Arsenal.

— Lil told me your surname was Levine. I thought you'd be a Spurs fan?

Shadows in the garden, it was all spooky out there. I heard the *poop* of a cork being pulled, then splosh and glug. The second bottle of red. I turned back around.

— I could take that the wrong way. But I'm a Gooner through and through.

Terence Trent D'Arby singing 'If You Let Me Stay'.

Mel gave him a sly look. She ran her fingers through her hair. Her eyes looked dark. She lifted the bottle of wine and poured herself some more. Thirsty gulps. She rubbed the back of her hand across her mouth. I thought she was going to burp.

I didn't feel right. I was missing bits. Someone was pressing Pause and Fast Forward. Dave coughed, then coughed again, louder; Mel ignored him.

Something had been said.

They were both staring at their hands. Was it about me? Then Dave's off again. Me me me. Mel's looking at him, her palms on show. I went to the toilet and sat there for ages, listening to their mumbly voices through in the kitchen.

Something had changed. Something had been said and I didn't cop on.

Those pills. It must have been my new pills kicking in, making me feel weird. I looked at my watch and two hours had flown by. I don't think I'd said a single word since we'd sat down to eat. I went back in.

— I can hear it sloshing round your balls.

Dave snorted and looked at the wall.

I said it slow,

— What. The fuck's. All this. About?

I might as well have been invisible.

— I can hear your sex, Dave. It's screaming out for me and Lily to get down and dirty, right here in front of you, isn't it?

— Mel!

Dave staring at the wall, his shoulders going up and down.

— Sixty-nine each other on this filthy lino?

She was the other side of the room to me, but I lifted my hand like I was going to slap her. She stood up, her hands on the table, and leaned over to him.

— Isn't it!

I left the room.

I walked down the hallway and closed the front door behind me.

I went down steps and to the end of the street. A group of kids were playing Kerby with a tennis ball under the broken streetlight. I looked back at the house and imagined them inside, throwing things at each other. I had to keep moving. The children stopped to watch me as I walked past. I looked at them and smiled, and one by one they all smiled back

two

three

four five

six smiles lighting the dark street.

I walked into the park and stopped at the first bench I came to. A breeze was whooshing up cold against my cheeks. I was thinking I shouldn't have done that, shouldn't have just left. I spread myself out on the bench and looked up into the sky that was ribbons of black, of purple. The problem was clearer than the branches up there or the cold wood beneath me. I don't know how long I was lying there for. I knew it was dangerous, but when I closed my eyes, I became invisible. I was cold and the bench was wet and it went right through me. I started juddering. I could hear a drip in my head and my teeth chattered.

I don't know how long I was there for.

The front door was open when I got back. The kitchen was empty, stuff left on the table. Mel had gone and the Thompson Twins were doing 'Hold Me Now'. I turned the stereo off and could hear the clock tick-tocking on the mantelpiece. I waited as long as I could, then I went upstairs and climbed in next to Dave.

I lay in the dark, listening to him snore.

The tap in my head going drip . . . drip . . . drip . . .

I was looking at the new foil packets. Ready to up the dose again. But I decided I'd wait. Just a few days. See if the feeling went because I just wanted to sleep all day. It felt like it was draining the life out of me. Some part inside that had been put to sleep. Life – it was suddenly like watching TV, but it was the worst soap-opera shite you've ever seen. So you're staring at the screen but not really watching. I was scared it was going to get worse. A lot more of the new drug and still a lot of the old. Poisoning me. My system wasn't coping.

So I decided: wait. Do it how *I* want to do it for once.

It's my fucking body, after all.

〜〜〜〜♪♪♪♪♪〜〜〜〜♪♪♪♪

BENCH OUTSIDE HAYWARD
GALLERY SOUTH BANK
NEAR FESTIVAL PIER
NOON TUESDAY SYLVIA

I had to write it down. I had to write it on scraps of paper. I left them at Dave's and explained he wasn't to move them. I left them all over the place. I wrote on the walls in thick black marker pen. I asked him to remind me, remind me, remind me. Remind me NOT to miss that date because I need to sleep now, I really need to . . .

〜〜〜〜♪♪♪♪♪〜〜〜〜♪♪♪♪

There was a strange woman in the flat. She went ooh when she saw me and struggled to stand from behind the kitchen table.

— You must be Lily?

She sang when she spoke. She stuck out her hand and came towards me. Tiny shuffling woman, grey hair in a little helmet and her hand hard in mine. Cold, like she'd been running it under a tap. And dry like paper. She looked me up and down.

— Well, I must say, it's lovely to meet you at last. Melanie's told me *so* much about you. I feel like I know you already.

A mole on her top lip, two black hairs sprouting out. They all had moles – Dave and Mel and this woman.

— All good, don't worry.

She was a witch with paper hands. The toilet flushed and I showed the woman my teeth. Hiss of taps, bathroom door opening, and thank god there was Mel. She pointed at the old woman.

— My mother, in case you're wondering.

All the air had gone out of her. I tried to give her an it's-OK-smile. Mel went,

— Let's go through to the living room and get comfy, eh?

I followed them in, thinking I hope Mel told her I wasn't gay. I pictured her having a right good nosy in my bedroom, just to make sure. Looking for a calendar of naked women, dungarees hanging up, a pair of Doc Martens in the corner, a poster from that *Flashdance* film. Whatever.

Mel sat next to her mam and they held hands, looking at me. It made me feel weird seeing them do that. Something cold on my back, like a slab. Mel's mam started talking about Mel's sister. She was going on about Lucy's husband's new job, all blah-fucking-blah. I watched Mel's eyes rolling around. Then her mam glared at me.

— Melanie tells me you're epileptic?

Mel put her head down.

— I *have* epilepsy. Yes.

— My, I must say, I do find that surprising.

— Why's that, then?

— Well . . .

— Mother.

— You just don't *look* like you're epileptic.

— Mum!

— Really? And what do people with epilepsy look like?

— Well, you just seem so . . . pretty. And bright.

— *Mother!*

— Excuse me.

I went into the bathroom. I could hear them hissing at each other. I flushed the toilet and ran the taps.

People are so fucking stupid. They're not interested in who you are, just what you're not. I remembered that list Mel got up on the Net, of famous people with epilepsy. Julius Caesar. Agatha Christie. Alexander the Great. Van Gogh. Napoleon Bonaparte. Ian Curtis.

It made me feel so tall.

I leaned over the sink, looked at my face in the little mirror and thought if epilepsy does have a face, it looks something like mine: a bit lopsided, scars on the eyebrow and forehead and chin. Leftovers of bruises and black eyes. Inside the mouth: scars and holes where chunks have been bitten out. Teeth missing, gums cut. And the eyes: that buzz. That fire hiding just behind the eyes – it's like a telephone ringing, waiting for someone to pick it up. That person, that thing I never get to see. The shadowy figures. I just feel their hands there, their fingers sliding into my skull, and then there's the dead tone. There's never any message on the answer phone, just God shouting BOO down the line and having a right good fucking laugh at my expense.

I looked at my head, my skull in the mirror, and touched it with my fingers. I tried to picture what was in there. My brain, that lump of meat – I imagined I could see it. A lump sat in its juices, buzzing away. The electricity like a far-off humming. I imagined it went very dark in the bathroom and I took the top of my skull off. I tilted my head forward and the lights filled the room. Oranges and reds and purples. That was me in there. Me. And I was every colour of the rainbow.

It was beautiful, like the Christmas lights along Blackpool seafront. Glowing and twinkling like multi-coloured stars. I suddenly remembered words from my *Night Sky* book. Blue stars are hot. Red ones are cold. Leonids. Andromeda. Nebula.

I looked inside my head and saw galaxies and constellations in there.

I saw electric meat.

Mel was all apologies. Her mam just looked surprised she'd said anything wrong. We sat and drank tea and I wondered if they could see the lights in my head. My mouth was going and their faces said it made sense, what I was saying, but I had a Blank One that went on

and on

and on.

I wanted to lie down on the floor. I wanted to curl up and go to sleep. Then her mam was saying it was funny to think she gave birth to Mel thirty-seven years ago to the day. She looked at her watch and I wanted to go over to the couch. I wanted her mam to hold me like she was hold-ing Mel. I said Happy Birthday and then I heard myself crying and the floor slammed right into me.

⊘⊘⊘⊘♪♪♪♪⊘⊘⊘⊘♪♪♪♪

The place was packed with tourists, joggers. The river full of boats. Trains rumbling over Hungerford Bridge. Seagulls whipped by the wind. Strings of lights between the tall lamps, swaying. The river was choppy milky coffee and I was starting to feel really cold.

Sylvia was late and I hardly recognized her. She had on a blue mac and a white headscarf that made her look old.

She smiled half-arsed and sat down next to me.

— These shoes are bloody murder.

She leaned down and took one of them off and rubbed her foot.

And so there we were, sat on a bench looking out over the Thames. Me and Sylvia. Me and Mikey's old girlfriend. Me and my nephew's mam. She put her shoe back on and just came right out with it,

— I think Barry was glad your Mikey disappeared.

It was a punch in the gut.

— Well, *I'm* looking for him. And I'm doing it *proper*.

— That's good.

She sounded like she couldn't care less.

— I can *feel* he's OK, Sylvia. You know what I mean?

— Whatever.

— I can feel it inside. I can feel he's alive.

A family stopped against the railings and had their pictures took. We watched them posing, hugging and smiling, and I wondered if they touched each other when there wasn't a camera shoved in their faces.

— I'm sorry for hitting you, Lily. I was just scared.

— Of me?

— Of you doing an O'Connor and ruining everything.

— Oh.

— Everything's how I want it. I've a great husband and a darling son and I thought you were here to ruin it.

— I'd never do that. Never.

— I'm glad to hear it.

— There's just stuff I need to know. Stuff I want to hear. Stuff that doesn't make sense.

— Life doesn't make sense. You've just got to get on with it.

She was putting the brakes on. She rummaged in her handbag.

— Like Mikey's reptile house. I mean?

She pulled out a packet of Marlboros and laughed.

— He broke some rules. Thought he was above all that.

She tapped out a fag. Lit it. Sucked on it like she wanted it to choke her.

— It was the borstal that started it all. Sent him to Flamingo Land I think it was. Work-placement thing. He told me he was always capturing animals and birds in the grounds, sneaking them back into his room. Kept them in his wardrobe. He thought he was looking after them. They called him Bird Man.

I remembered the rabbit in his bed, the mice in the shed.

— Then he got a job in one of the zoos when he left. Did well. But don't ask me where he got the money to set up on his own. Your Barry would know the answer to that.

She blew out smoke, shaking her head. Her leg was going.

— So how come it got shut down?

— It was a bacterial thing that started it. Some kids fell ill. Really ill. It was closed for a while until they'd sorted it. But it reopened. Then some charity got involved. Campaigning the council to close it for good.

A woman pushed a pram through Sylvia's fag smoke. I tried to concentrate. I stared at some pink chewing gum on the path in front of me.

— So it was the bacteria thing that shut it?

— Mikey broke some rules. This team moved in because he didn't have a licence and the snakes and whatnot weren't endangered, you know. Plus he didn't supervise the visitors properly, when they were handling the lizards and snakes. Absolutely stupid of him. He was soft like that.

She looked at her fag, burning to the butt. She dropped it and stood on it and turned away. I thought she was looking out over the river at something, but then I saw her shoulders going. She was sobbing and I was surprised.

I folded my arms and leant back. She went,

— A part of Mikey . . .

Something stopped me from touching her.

She took a tissue out of her handbag. Her eyes were pink with tears.

— But you're going to tell Simon? That Mikey's his dad?

— That's our business. None of yours.

— Sorry.

— Either way, he might hate us. We'll have to see.

She sniffled, dabbed her eyes and nose. She stood up and went over to the railings. I followed her. We looked down into the water. I went,

— Last time I saw him and Barry, I was just a kid. No one mentioned his name after he left. Out of sight, out of mind. Mam used to say lock them up and throw away

243

the key, and they did. But they were only sticking up for her. And Barry suddenly appeared after she died last year.

— I'm sorry to hear that.

— I'm not. But Mikey, I want to find him more than anything. What was he like?

She got a little grin on her face and I realized what she was staring at: her wedding ring. She was turning it slowly on her finger with her thumb.

— He's my biggest regret.

She told me she met him when she was on holiday up North with her mam and sister. She was wandering around the shops when she found the reptile house. And he was sat inside, on his own, stroking and talking to a huge snake draped around his shoulders.

— I adored him. Never met anyone like him before. But I hurt him when he needed me most, all because of that *bastard*.

— What?

— Simon isn't Mikey's kid, Lily.

I heard her say it.

— He's Barry's.

I saw the look on her face.

— We had a fling. Big deal. It was nothing. It didn't mean anything.

— You're lying.

— I'm not surprised Barry didn't tell you.

— You're a lying fucking bitch.

She put her eyebrows up and I remembered where I'd seen her face before: in that photograph, the one on Barry's sideboard in the living room. The one that went missing.

— I never wanted it to happen, but Barry wouldn't take *any* responsibility. We both broke Mikey's heart. Barry was my biggest mistake – I'm not going to make any excuses though. It still hurts to admit it, but I knew what I was doing. His reptile house getting closed down – it ruined your Mikey. He pined. Didn't touch me for months. I thought it was over. I really did.

I put some space between us and looked up into the clouds. I imagined Barry away over the sea, in America, sitting at a table in some glitzy casino, covered in jewellery with a bimbo on each arm, dollar signs in their eyes. And at that moment, I hated him like I've never hated anyone before.

I went back over to her.

— So how was he? Mikey. Last time you saw him?

She winced.

— Beside himself.

She clung on to the railings.

— He put Barry in hospital.

— Eh?

She snorted snot back up her nose.

— Mikey did him over, when he found out what we'd been up to. Did a good job and all. Was in for a week or so. Barry wouldn't say anything. Just that it was over and he couldn't see me any more. And that was that. I haven't heard hide nor hair from either of them since.

I tried to imagine my brothers fighting, but I couldn't. I wanted her to tell me something that would point straight to Mikey.

— You know, he was very fond of you. Always spoke about you.

She touched my arm.

— I'm sorry, Lily.

And she walked away. A police boat vroomed down the river. A seagull let out a squawk. The sky began to spit. I watched her until she became a tiny dot.

A full stop.

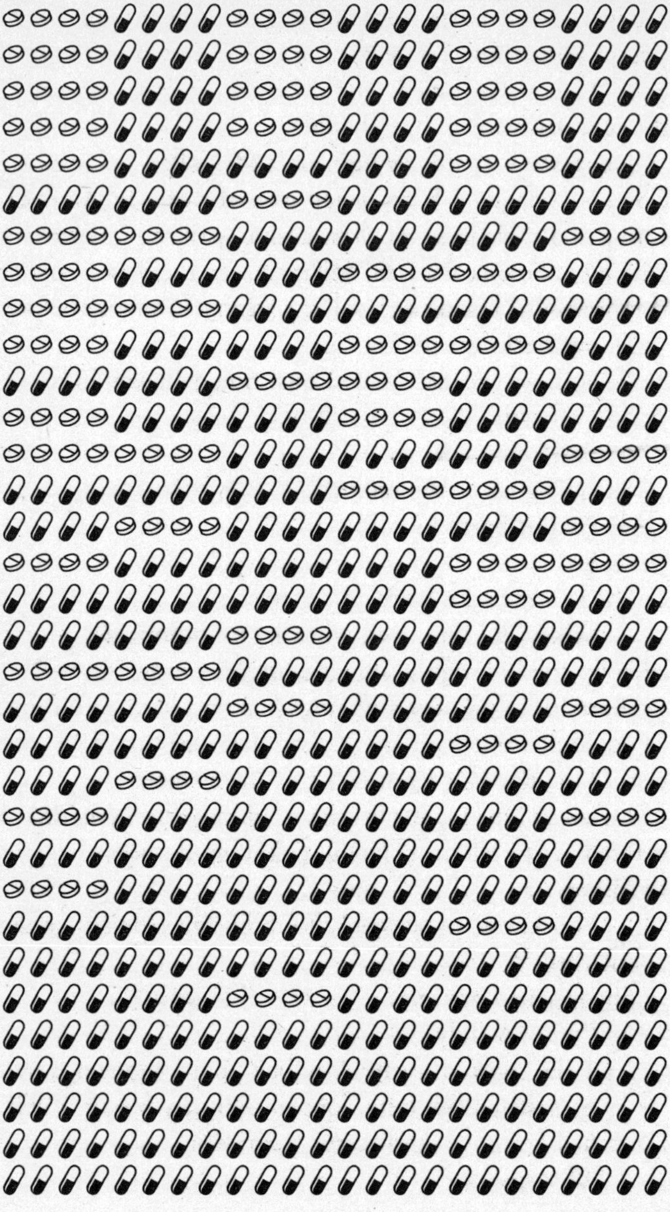

6

You make a list of what you need, what you want, then you make your way out the house and along the street looking at the list and the words on the top: **THINGS I NEED FROM THE SUPERMARKET** so's you don't forget why you're walking along the street. It takes forever getting there because you know there are things in shop windows to stare at and people you want to talk to. But then I was there and I surprised myself.

Drip.

And then you're inside and you start finding the things on the list. Easy peasy. You place them in the trolley, ticking them off the list until the paper is all scribbles and no words. But you have to go slow, one step at a time. First you look down one shelf, then the other, then a step forward. It takes fucking ages, but it's the only way. And it's the place itself, with its smells and voices and faces and trolleys. The things that fill it. The actual way the place is laid out. Aisles being so long and straight. Everything organized. Lines of cans and packets and brand names and best-before dates. And the floor, it might look like it's shiny, but if you bend over there's dust there, people's dirt. And the different voices you hear, the smells of the place, the moves you have to make to go around the people and the trolleys and the aisles. You struggle through. You keep your temper and hands and thoughts to yourself. You have to.

And then when you make it to the end, there's the queuing. The things to place on the conveyor belt. The knackered-looking man or woman with their nametag and their robot questions about cheques, cash cards, loyalty cards, signatures, cashback. And there's the bags, the packing of the bags, deciding what to put in where and with what.

Fuck me.

Then you have to carry the bags home with the plastic digging into your fingers, your shoulders and arms stinging from the weight. All these things ganging up on you and you can't even fucking think.

— Lily?

I was in the veg section. I was holding a tomato in my hand and staring at it so totally without thinking that when I heard this voice saying my name I thought it was the tomato talking.

— Lily?

I turned and looked into those eyes, listened to that voice. It was like I had to untie my tongue to let the word slither out,

— Dave.

There, I'd done it. I'd said his name without having to scrape the bottom of my memory.

— Dave.

And my body rang DINGGGG. It was Dave, the man I shared a bed with. It thumped through my brain, the image of his face against a pillow, his naked chest.

— Hello, Dave.

Drip. Drip.

He put his arm into mine, saying something. I wanted to disappear. To make myself invisible. I wanted to hide behind the stack of pink loo rolls. I remember laughing and hearing myself going,

— Daft as ever, daft as ever.

He just shook his head.

— Come on, Lily, I'm taking you home.

I looked at him and saw the silence behind his eyes. It was big. It had muscles. It could read my thoughts. It wanted him to swallow me up. I opened my mouth and tried to bite him. He moved away. I ate the music coming from somewhere in the ceiling instead. I ate the Beatles. I ate a Yellow Submarine and it tasted like bananas.

My face was boiling. I made him stop pulling me and turned. My hands were white from clasping the trolley handle so tight. I said it loud,

— Stop.

I looked at the other shoppers shuffling by. I watched a woman clout a small boy round the back of the head and hiss at him. The child started screaming and the woman hit him again. She wore a long blue overcoat and her hair was in rollers covered by a flowery headscarf. There were snakes under there, I knew there were. She hissed again and we both shouted at the same time.

— STOP!

It was my mother.

— You've had me worried sick, Lily. But you left a note. That was good, Lily. That was good.

Talking to me like a bairn. I was angry so reached out and started putting tins and jars and packets into the trolley, but there was Dave's big hand stopping me, peeling my fingers off.

— Leave the shopping here. Let's go.

Drip.

I was trying to concentrate, I was. With my face aching with a smile and I looked at a sign for two-for-one special offers and I read the labels on some of the cans and packets with the drip, drip. I moved in jerks, leaving the trolley behind and Dave was pulling me like I was on ice. At the end of the aisle I counted the cash registers out loud and I pointed one . . . two . . . three . . . four . . . five and squirmed because people were looking at me. I looked down at my clothes and thought I must look like a witch.

I saw I still had my slippers on.

— Silly me.

I gave Dave a filthy look and it dangled in the air, then I glared at the cashier because she was looking at me with a little smirk on her face and I wanted to kiss her cheek, I wanted to bite the bitch.

The doors swished open and the cold slapped my face. It made me suck air through my teeth. Home – I was thinking of home and wanting to run my fingers through my hair, but Dave had my hands. He'd been talking to me the whole time. Mumble Dave.

I remember wanting to say, well, it was nice seeing you again, and just walk off, like the life I was in wasn't my own. I lived somewhere else, that house on the corner there with the net curtains. I wanted to live there. Be quiet. Watch telly. Be warm and invisible in a house that never had visitors.

DavELECTRICS. What a stupid fucking thing to have on the side of your van.

It smelled new inside and the seat farted when I sat down. His seat had bead things on, like cab drivers have. One of those Magic Tree things hung from the mirror, but I couldn't smell it.

Dave's van. I'd never been in it before.

I liked it. It made me feel special. Don't know why. I noticed cigarette butts on the floor and one had lipstick on. As he reversed the car, he looked over his shoulder and my face was close to his. I could hear him breathing. I wanted to remember kissing him, kissing like it would never stop. How kissing him seemed to cancel everything out.

I leaned over, licked his cheek.

— Jesus, Lily.

— Put some music on.

He tutted and twiddled a knob but it was just talking on the radio.

— Switch it off.

He huffed, shaking his head. He pressed something on the dashboard and the loudness shook the car. He pressed something again and it stopped.

— You trying to deafen me?

— Shut the fuck up.

— Oh deary me.

I laughed into my hands. I looked at what he was wearing: a black shirt with pointed collars, tight black jeans, black boots and a black leather jacket. He looked dangerous. I closed my eyes and saw him: a black figure disappearing into the shadows of trees. I imagined I was in some bushes in a park, and my breasts were hanging out and a cold wind blew on them. He'd had me in the bushes.

— You dirty bastard.

— Let's just get you home, OK.

I cleared my throat. He drove fast but it felt safe. He drove with one hand on the wheel, the other on the gear stick. His hand was close to my leg. I watched his long fingers gripping the gears and the steering wheel. I watched the streets go by, thinking how disgusting and dirty Hackney is. My breath was fog on the glass. I wanted to suck his dirty fingers clean and lick the windows.

I put my hands over my eyes and said my name.

———

He was asleep, turned away from me. I stood bare-naked beside the bed and looked at the sweat across his back, glittering like a slug had been there. And it had: me. I'd forgotten about the big mole on his backside, the ones on his back. It looked like he'd been rolling in currants and sultanas.

Whenever he touched me, I felt like he was measuring me, weighing me. It made me feel horrible. I felt flabby, fat, ugly. I used to be so thin. I had the greatest legs and bum. Now look at me: a slimy lump. I craved the spoons to make me feel loved, his knees tucked under mine, the tickle of hot breath on my shoulder. Two bent spoons under a warm sheet. My breast, sitting in the curl of his palm. It makes me feel safe, he'd whisper. But now all he did was squeeze and probe and eat me.

I went over to the mirror and looked at my breasts. They looked larger and heavier and hang-low. The nipples were a dull purple and bigger, like round bruises. Beneath them waves of stomach – two, three folds. I turned around: two large dimples on my backside, plain-as. I felt ugly. I felt fat-as.

Fucking pills.

Dave said I was dopey. Docile, like a cow. He said going out with me was like going out with a sleepwalker. I told him it was the drugs.

— I can hear them dripping in my head, Dave.

— So stop taking them.

— Yeah right.

I hadn't had a fit for weeks. You've no idea.

But the drip.

I dressed as quickly and quietly as I could and left the house. I passed his van outside and ran my keys along it and laughed. I pulled up the hood on my jacket and walked stooped against the wind.

The sludgy path.

I passed a restaurant and I stopped and looked in. The light looked soft in there. Candles and flick-flicker of a fire. I moved closer to the glass and could just make out a couple of faces. They were pale discs moving behind a candle. I could see their smiles, their hands together. I stood in the cold looking in. It seemed like another world. I could feel the damp on my skin, the jacket getting heavier, the wind smarting my cheeks and tip of my nose. I watched the couple smiling then kissing behind the glass. I wished them luck. I wanted to see Mel. I wanted to slither into bed.

So I slept. And I slept. And I slept. And when I woke up one morning, I'd turned into a fat fucking ball of slime.

JJJJJJJJJJJJJJJJJJ

Three Sisters. There was a big bonfire in the park over the road. Screaming kids everywhere. Pushchairs and sparklers. I stayed away. I sat in the pub while Dave and his mates went and watched the fireworks and smoked some spliffs.

I watched the locals.

The skinny one, always at the bar, skinniest bloke you've ever seen. Must have been nearly seven foot tall, no shit. It was like staring up a waterfall. And the cross-eyed bloke. You never knew whether he was drunk or just backwards. And the landlord – what a knobhead. Total laughing boy. He never shut up. Loved the sound of his own voice. Like everything he said was funny-as. Making the worst jokes you've ever heard. Thought everyone loved him.

And Jesus the music in there, and the carpet, and the barmaid – that old hag with a punk haircut and the biggest bottom lip you've ever seen. She always put silver lippy on it, heavy-as, her tongue always licking it, keeping it moist. Clarted up to the eyeballs. She needed a good fucking scrub. And the cross-eyed spaz guy that kept going: It's OK, I'm going after this. All the time. *It's OK, I'm going after this.* Like a parrot. Like a stuck fucking record. And the bloke on the crutches who always put Elvis on the jukey. Just the one song: 'Suspicious Minds'. His legs all bent and spazzing out when he walked – you couldn't tell whether he was doing an Elvis impression or just couldn't help it. Suspicious Pete they called him: *We can't go on together.* And Déjà Stu: *It's OK, I'm off after this.* And laughing boy pissing himself. And whenever I heard Elvis, I always thought of Barry and wanted to gip.

Always a fug in there. Smell of bacon, fried egg, fags and man-piss. The streets outside were never quiet, sirens coming and going, the sound bouncing off the high-rises. Some old dearie that's fallen over and broken her hip. Or some woman pregnant to the eyeballs, about to burst. But I always pictured some woman who looked a bit like me. She'd had a fit in the kitchen and fallen onto a knife, straight into her gut, and the knife always had a bit of butter on – to make it go in easy.

I went over to the window and looked out, trying to

see the fizzing lights. Where was Dave? Black shapes against the fire, and those ugly bloody tower blocks marching away there. The street outside littered with dog shite, broken bottles, scrunched-up cans and pages of newspaper.

I didn't know where he was. I kept forgetting things. Forgot how I got to places. I went to the bar and asked laughing boy.

— You seen Dave?

— I think you've had too much, darling.

I tried explaining, but the words came out like vomit and fell on the carpet between my feet. Some had gone down my top and were wriggling about in my bra. I started to undo my blouse. Laughing boy pointed.

— Come on. *Get out!*

———

The smell of burning wood. Explosions of light in the sky, like soldiers dying.

I screamed and ran down a path down by the water: black in the orange street-lamps. I pat-a-caked along the canal wall, in case I fell in. The water was all oily and slow. It sounded like treacle glooping. Stench like burnt toast. I remember imagining it: a few seconds to sink below the surface. My arm, hand, fingers disappearing. Glop.

Up ahead a train rumbled and rattled over the bridge, the light in the carriages flick-flickering. The wall opened onto a snicket and that led onto some wasteland. I found a burnt-out car and realized I was lost and on my own and in the dark. I couldn't see anything to tell me where I was and the thought: I'm going to die.

I climbed up on the car bonnet, wobbling a bit until I

got my balance. The hood made denting noises. I looked over the rooftops, across to the lights on the tall office buildings twinkling away, house lights and cars and pylons like matchstick giants with their hands on their hips. And beyond it all was hanging a big white moon.

And there it was: Three Sisters sign, lit up. I thought I'd walked miles.

I filled my lungs and screamed blood to my throat.

I got to the road and walked back. Dave was at the bar, having a row with laughing boy. Dave's mates looked at me like dirt.

— Gin and tonic, please.

— For fuck's sake, Lily.

I remember snippets. A conversation with Al, crying down the phone. He told me the news going round town about Barry's win, on the local news, and I think I told Al he'd murdered Mikey.

And I spoke to the woman at the Helpline. I remember her silence. I remember her tone of voice, trying to be comforting. I even rang the consultant's a few times, just to hear his secretary tell me he was out or busy. I wanted him to tell me it was OK, it would pass, that I wouldn't be a docile cow forever.

And I remember thinking I'd blown it again with Dave. Pushed him too far. He'd asked me not to go round on particular nights, that he'd set them aside to work in his lab and I should respect that. But I kept getting the days wrong. One night there was a man with Hank and a big van, taking boxes into Dave's. We had a blazing row, and I was telling Mel all of this while she held my hand. I was having a Clear One, but I knew I didn't have long.

— So will you ring them for me?

— The Helpline?

— And Al. And Dave.

She looked away.

— What did Dave say to you that night?

— Lily.

— Tell me.

— You really want to know?

— Yes.

— I think I might have overreacted a little.

— *What* did he say?

— We'd both had too much to drink.

I grabbed her arm.

— He propositioned me.

— Eh?

— I don't want to cause any trouble between you. He was really drunk.

— You can huff and puff all you want, just tell me.

— He said he'd like to watch.

— Watch what?

— You and me. You know.

She nodded at me and looked embarrassed.

— Shite and like.

— Do you want to talk about it?

— What's to talk about? He'd've been kidding.

I stood up and stared at the blankness of the wall.

— Don't worry about it, Lily. If anything, it just makes him completely normal. Men are always trying to get in on the act. It's me that lost it. Because I *care* about you.

— Will you ring them for me and tell them I'm not well. They're not to worry. It'll pass. Will you do that?

I told her about the meeting with Sylvia. I told her about all of the bad thoughts I was having about Barry and Mikey. I told her not to tell the Helpline about the fight. I didn't want the police involved. Not yet. I told her what Sylvia had said about the reptile house and Simon and it was her that started to cry, not me. I hugged her with the drip in my head like a clock ticking away, keeping me company.

———————

When I woke up the next day, she was there. There was sunlight coming through the window and I could smell the cup of tea on the bedside table and she was stroking my hair. Birds were singing in the trees outside. I kept my eyes closed for ages, listening to her breathing, feeling her fingers in my hair, on my bump. I rolled over and looked into her eyes: she went on forever in there. My voice was crackly when I spoke.

— A month, Mel. I haven't had a fit for a whole month. It's weird.

— But that's good, surely?

— You're beautiful. Do you know that?

— I've run you a bath. Are you hungry?

I sat up and rubbed my face and flattened my hair down.

— A bit, aye. This past month's been fucking weird. I think Dave's at a loss.

— Well, I can look after you. I've taken the day off especially.

— I don't want looking after.

She leaned over, kissed my forehead, then left the room.

I supped the tea, listening to her in the kitchen. I went into the bathroom, checked the water, and got in.

We hummed to each other through the open door.

♪♪♪♪

— Listen, I want you to call them for me. I want you to pretend you're me. I want you to ask them to check the whatdyamacallits?

— The embassies? Consulates? See if he's gone abroad.

— Aye. Tell them to see if he applied for a what's it?

— Where's his case number?

I went and got the numbers: the Helpline's, Al's, even Dave's.

I couldn't remember the names of things. I looked at my hand and said to myself: What's that called? And it terrified me because I didn't know. A space in my head like a windy tunnel.

I went to bed and could hear her on the phone. I'd've been lost without her. She was an angel. I could hear rain outside. I opened the window to listen to the drops falling through the leaves of the huge conker trees.

There were kids in the street. I closed my eyes and listened to them but I kept getting pictures of Dave in my head from the week before. I remembered staring at him, burning a hole through the sheen on his bald patch. I was thinking of that word he used: shtum. I think I heard him say it when he was on the telephone to someone. I can't remember. Keeping shtum. I was having all of these lunatic thoughts, about what he was doing in that fucking lab of his.

The kids in the rain in the street outside. Off the council estate down the end of the road there. Pissing it down and they were loving it. Better than being plugged into the PlayStation. One of the kids was screaming blue murder. I got up and went to the window again. There were about ten of them, and some had towels wrapped around their heads, bushwhacking each other with twigs and branches. They were arguing over who would be an American and who would be a Muslim.

— You be a Muslim. You look like a Paki anyway.

— Yeah, you be Bin Liner and I'll be Bush Man.

— I don't look like a Paki. *You* do!

I got back into bed and closed my eyes. I remembered trying to picture what was going on inside Dave's head. I saw a picture of him putting down his beer, taking a deep breath and going into the garden. I remembered watching him mosey down the crazy paving and thinking he wants to dump me. Who could blame him? I could hear him humming 'Money for Nothing'. He reminded me of Fred Flintstone crossed with that Laurence Llewelyn-Bowen bloke off the telly.

I was chuckling away to myself when I heard it. Not the kids arguing. Not the rain in the trees. Not Mel talking on the phone in the kitchen.

The brown feathers rustling in my gob, like scratches in a paper bag.

I sat up and started spitting. I was choking. I coughed and gipped, gagging on it. I couldn't breathe, my head was filling with it.

And then I saw them on the duvet. Dirty feathers. Bits of claw.

It was fucking coming out of me. It was coming out of my head.

It flapped and swelled. I retched good and hard.

LI-*LEEEEE* LI-*LEEEEE*

Gripping onto the sheets, nails snapping. But it was black, the stuff coming out of me it was black treacle.

LI-*LEEEEEEEEEEE* LI-*LEEEEEEEEEEE*

I jerked forward and spewed like a hose. My sheets sank with the weight of it and I could feel it on my legs, burning and heavy, the smell of metal and blood. Just a shape in the black, twitching, trying to get out and fly away. The bird was drowning in the black and then

I'm in the room. I'm in the bed.

I feel the heat of the body beneath me.

And I screamed my lungs empty until blackness filled the room.

———

I'm not sure. I imagine snippets.

— You've been talking to me for some time.

— Am I?

— Shush.

Mel dabbed the flannel across my face. I was in her bed and wet, but not with piss, the smell on my fingers was sweat. Yes, and I remember it was like wet soil and trees, like I was in some woods somewhere, some memory of woods.

— No doctors.

Then I could hear her walking about on the wooden floor. I went to shout her name but my voice was a breeze. I got out of bed. I stretched my arms to the ceiling and my back cracked. I felt my height. The muscles in my legs were powerful stones, standing on a hill somewhere for thousands of years. I went into my bedroom. She'd stripped the bed and you could tell from the wet patch she'd scrubbed the carpet. She made a little noise when she saw me and we had a long hug and her heat was like a blanket and I tried to speak, I tried to say I was sorry.

— Don't. As long as you're all right. Go sit down and I'll bring you a drink.

The telly was on with the sound turned down. She came back through with some orange juice. I drank it down in one gulp and opened my mouth again, but nothing. I made a scribbling sign. She came back through with pen and paper. She sat next to me and I think I wrote *don't know what happened*.

— How do you feel?

A smile, a nod.

— You were making the most awful noise.

I shrugged. She squeezed my arm and looked really sad.

— You kept going on about some man being in the room with you. In your bed. You were going on and on about him. Like you were seeing a ghost.

I shook my head and she looked at the TV. She wasn't convinced. I elbowed her and made a phone-hand next to my ear and she sighed.

— Later, Lil.

I leaned close to her so she could hear me. My lips touched her hot ear.

— Please.

— Are you sure?

I nodded again.

— Well, they said they've checked all of the hostels' records in London. They've checked with the DSS. It appears he never stayed in a hostel or claimed any benefits over that period. They even wrote to his old address back up North that you gave to them. It was returned 'not known at this address'.

I whispered,

— I could've told them that.

I'm not sure how many days went by. Not sure how many pills went down. How long I sat there fretting, waiting for the right moment. Like I was escaping from something. There's a gap like a pillow in my face. But then I remember the poster on the wall scaring the shit out of me, the body at the bottom of the escalator and the words,

PLEASE BE CAREFUL AFTER A FEW DRINKS

I was down in the bowels again. The zapping tapping noise was coming along the rails and I knew there were sparks there. The hiss and breeze of the train coming and my back against the wall, eyes shut tight, feeling the whoosh as it sped in. I went right to the front, next to the driver's door. I stared at the handle behind the glass.

PASSENGER EMERGENCY LINE
– PULL LEVER TO ALERT DRIVER
BREAK GLASS FOR EMERGENCY ACCESS

He'd worked behind a door like that. Working in the tubes, must be like being a miner. Down in the dark guts while I was wishing away up there. I got the little map out of my purse and checked the stops. South all the way on the blue Victoria Line. And I got a sense of his body like when I was a girl and I could feel him in the house. Could tell whether he was in or not. Like he had some weight, something tugging at you, pulling you down. Like he had his own gravity.

I looked at the paper Mr Morris had given me. Maybe I should've told Mel or Dave where I was going. I was sleepwalking with the drip keeping me company. But I told myself you'll be all right, Lily. Don't be daft.

I checked it against my *A–Z*. Two squares from the Brixton tube. I wanted a walk. Wanted the time to change my mind if I had to. I watched the stations go past. King's Cross. Euston. The amount of times I'd been back to that place. Staring at tramps all over the city. Warren Street. Oxford Circus. Green Park. A posh voice going alight here for Buckingham Palace. Mind the doors. Victoria. This is the Victoria line train to Brixton, change here for the District and Circle lines. Pimlico. Alight here for the Tate. Vauxhall. Stockwell. The train getting so loud, so fast I'm sure it's going to come off the fucking tracks and then I'm there, I'm there. Last stop. I'm there.

My legs are leading me up and out and I let the people barge past me, running up the escalators. The light hits me in the face.

I stared at the empty market stalls, shutters down on shops and I thought of home in winter, the seafront shut down. Just one stall was open, playing reggae really loud, but the record was stuck, scratched, repeating the same line over and over again and when I walked past I saw two guys in the back with Afros like thunderclouds, nodding their heads to the scratch. They were enjoying it, too stoned to notice. Arches under the railway line all shuttered. Lock-ups. Garages. Shops selling tropical fruit. Grey net curtains and tacky gold jewellery and dusty wedding dresses in windows. One of the shops called Just Yams and there was a woman head-to-toe in a black sheet, just a slit for the eyes. She was rummaging through the boxes outside, looking for scraps. Jesus. The left fork called Barrington. Two men pushing a cart like Steptoe and Son. A black man walking towards me, his little Afro with his comb still stuck in it, dressed in leather and a string vest on – his muscles like cuts beneath. It was spitting on and parky but he didn't care, he was rapping and it fitted with the rhythm of his walk. He was buzzing off something, you could tell. I smiled at him and he winked . . .

I almost turned around. Almost ran back to the station, right there and then. The wink. But something pushed me on. The tickle in my throat.

I found the road, I turned the corner, the sky got dark. Rows and rows of massive high-rises. The buildings so big, lined up in blocks marching away – they were all you could see, they were taking up the sky and people fucking lived there. It was brutal. Buildings the colour of exhaust fumes and when you looked up at them, with the clouds moving behind, it made it look like they were falling, a sick feeling in your stomach mixing with the butterflies and hotness all loose inside.

In between all the high-rises were rows of dirty sheds, but they weren't sheds, they all had doors and the doors had numbers on and the rows all had names. I kept having to get my *A–Z* out. I should've had a big sign on my head: COME ROB ME, STUPID WHITE GIRL.

That one sound going round in my head – her bastard voice: *You should learn to keep your legs shut, young lady*.

I wanted Don to stop her saying it. I wanted him to say yes, we're in love. Me and Lily – we're in love and we're running away together and there's fuck all you can do to stop us. Try, and I'll fucking kill you. But the day they came to take me away – he wasn't there. He never wrote. Never came to visit.

Never rescued me.

I'd started my period and hey presto: he didn't want to touch me any more. The bedroom door would be shut on a morning. No more baths together. No more sitting behind him, soaping him up. No more sitting on his lap watching telly, hands all over. No more love letters in my pockets when I went to school. That glow of thinking about him all day. Don. My Donny Don. Lily Blackman. The ache of it. I was ill with it. She looked so pleased that I'd started bleeding.

I found his street.

———

He was just another one we had to avoid, be polite to, so's not to piss Mam off. We always called them wankers or bastards. She's got another fucking bastard home, keep it down. We'd sit in Mikey and Barry's room and listen to them in the house, planning how to kill them. Mikey and Barry hated Don's guts, but soon after he moved in, they were gone.

Mam was always a tight bitch. Always going on about money, about bills, trying to make us feel fucking guilty because she had to feed us and keep us in clothes. I was always wearing Mikey and Barry's hand-me-downs. I looked like a proper tomboy. I had to lump it, she said. Hair full of cotters, pissy skirt, scabby knees. She never ironed. Tea was always fish and chips in newspaper. She hated washing anything but her miserable fucking face.

She would take light bulbs out, in the kitchen, the front room, the landing, in the bathroom, even.

Saving electricity, she said.

It was the middle of the night and I needed a piss. I was pat-a-caking along the landing wall in the dark when I smacked right into him. I yelped and he said Jesus and grabbed me. He put his arms around me tight. I think he thought I was going to go flying down the stairs.

It felt like I already had.

He put his hand against my head, pressing my cheek into his bare chest that was hairy and hot and the smell – I can still smell the smell off of him, hear the cistern hissing in the toilet, the snoring coming from one of the bedrooms. He always had his hands in soil, and he stunk of it. Wet soil and trees. He held me tight and kissed the top of my head with a soft sound. His other hand was on my back, pressing me into him. We were both breathing hard and I knew I had to be quiet. I put my arms around him but I didn't squeeze.

I was eight or nine but I was tall by then. I looked up, trying to see into his eyes and he kissed my face. Then he let me go and left me there on the landing. He couldn't see me smiling at him in the dark.

He couldn't see me winking at him.

His house, like a rabbit hutch it was. One door and two windows, one above the other. Flat-roofed. Must've been tiny inside. My head would touch the ceiling. It was falling to bits, dirty, shabby-as.

It was enough. I was there. It was enough.

I pulled my hood up and walked by, and then I got the fear and legged it across the road, stopping next to a wall. I started breathing again. That was his house and I just sank inside. It was like a flower opened up inside me and I fell inside it, into the black bit in the middle where the insects go.

I felt a flesh flower blooming away in the pit of my stomach.

It was his gravity pulling at me, and I wanted to fall.

I knew it was his house because you could see it was like a jungle in there. All the plants pressed up against the glass panels around the windows and door, big leaves, small leaves, all green behind the glass. He loved his plants. Loads of them filling the house. Always tending them, touching them, talking to them, kissing them.

Big fat soily fingers inside me.

When I started walking back to the tube, I told my brain to lock that door. I begged my brain, never think about it again. Never send a bird to sing, that dirty bird on my fucking tonsils. Never make me puke the black stuff of my life onto Mel's clean white sheets. Another twenty years he'd be food for worms, in the soil where he always wanted to be. The thought made me smile. I tried not to think if there'd been others. Other girls with love letters in their pockets. And as I walked back to the tube, I tried to imagine a door slamming shut in my head. The echo would go all the way back through the years. I screwed my eyes up and made my hands into fists and squeezed everything inside of me so hard, so tight, waiting for the slam.

But I knew it wasn't over.

It was when my hair started to come out in clumps, mats of it on my hairbrush. I think this is why I looked at them in my hands: *🥚🥚🥚🥚🥚🥚*. Looked at their shape, like eggs. I pictured them in my stomach breaking up, getting dissolved and going through my gut and into my blood. I saw my heart fizzing with its burst of lights, pushing the poison along the tunnels into my brain. I saw the colour of the meat in my skull change, like turning down a dimmer switch, and I didn't want to be dimmed, I didn't want to have to wear a fucking wig like Al.

In my hands. I knew I'd get struck off the doctor's list. He'd say I was refusing the recommended treatment.

I put the pills in a drawer. No more. I'd see what would happen.

I was cleaning my brain of that poison.

I was turning the lights up full.

It was the Saturday of the week before Christmas. I think I convinced Mel to go shopping with me, Covent Garden, somewhere round there, and then we got cold and bored and I think this is what happened.

We went to London Zoo. I told her I was going back home for Christmas and she said I was welcome to spend it with her. Then I remember a giraffe, and I remember seeing these little signs everywhere saying: PLEASE ADOPT US. I knew what Mel was thinking and she was right: I was proper gutted.

Yes, I remember the giraffe with the love-heart shape on its back, and then we were in the aquarium and it was empty in there.

I stood looking at her face. Yes, I remember her face lit up in the bluish light, flickering, moving. She's looking stern and she's asking me why I got put in a home. Something like that. First time she'd asked me straight out.

It felt like a risk and took me long enough to say it.

— I had a bit of a thing with my mother's fella.

She moved off, saying nothing. I followed her around the tanks, watching her silhouette, waiting for something. Anything.

But that's the last thing I can remember.

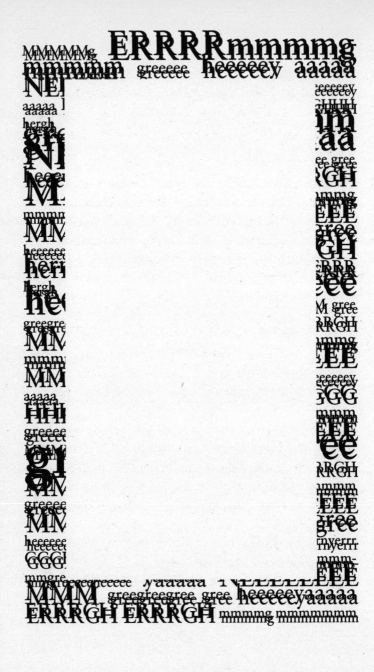

5

Whiteness. Cold. There were no machines in heaven. Nothing to keep me breathing. Nothing to check my pulse with a bleep. In heaven there are just quiet voices in the distance. And curtains. Green curtains with red flowers all over, like poppies in a field. To remind you of the place you just left. And the place you will only see again in memories that keep on fading.

I held up my hands, white hands, and turned my head. I smelled the white of the pillow, like sleep. I lifted my arms and they throbbed like Jesus. I was wearing something with white sleeves. But it was the buzz of neon frying in the white tube up there – it brought me back to Earth.

I closed my eyes. I wanted to go back to the white.

I wondered how long I could stay like that. Pretending I'd died. Pretending I'd gone to heaven. No need for electricity. Electricity is life but electricity is an invisible fist punching up your spine, knocking your brains right out of your skull.

Electricity is pain.

I closed my eyes.

They would be in here soon, with their white gowns. Touching me. Asking me questions. My history. Making shapes with their hands, nodding like dunces. Writing things down, noises in their throats, and all I wanted to do was sleep.

Maybe they would inject me? Maybe they would stick their needles in and send me back into the white?

I knew Miss Lily O'Connor was written in thick black pen above my head. I didn't have to look.

Where was Mel? Where was Dave?

I touched my face. I passed my tongue around my mouth. No snapped teeth. No chunks taken out. I moved my stiff arms, my legs. I touched my head. I tried to remember where I was. My last bit of memory before my time got chopped out.

But nothing.

I wanted to float out of that room. I wanted to get rid of this useless battered body, because I didn't want the stuff inside to be always coming out. I didn't want to be slammed into the ground any more. The poppies were too red on the curtains. I was sick of seeing my own blood splattered everywhere, sick of thrashing, getting up, getting on with it.

They'll be here soon. To spoil it all.

And there I was, thinking I'd escaped me.

————

— What day is it?
— Tuesday. The twenty-third.
— Two days.
— Sorry?
— Christmas.
— That's right.

I closed my eyes to see the sea again. To walk along the beach and feel the sea swelling like a migraine. To taste the salt on my lips.

— We're keeping you in for a few days. Try not to rub them.

My arms full of stinging water.

— We had to do some tests when you came in. Glucose, serum calcium, some toxicological tests before we could order additional electrolytes.

Electrolytes. I saw green lights out at sea. I saw a shimmering just under the waves. They're turning me up. Turning the lights up full.

— They've helped us determine your drug levels. One of our doctors will be in shortly to discuss this with you.

She meant the head-doctor. She meant psychologist.

— Try to get some rest.

To walk into the Nugget and see the booth where I'd sat, reading magazines, counting change. To see Al's face lighting up like a Christmas tree.

— Death is white, you know. Not black.

— That's very nice dear. I'll be back in soon.

———

— We see from your records that you've been reducing your blah and increasing the blah? How successful have you been with this?

Not again.

— It was turning me into a slug. I want to go back onto the old stuff. I was fine with the old stuff. Leave me on the old stuff.

A sound in his throat; pen scratching paper.

— Where are my friends?

— They'll be back this evening.

I closed my eyes to see my old flat again, to see if I could still see the writing on the walls, underneath the paint.

— What day is it?

— Tuesday.

I could see straight through his white coat. I could see the curtains with my blood on. I stopped listening so that I could hear people with my accent around me. To see some familiar faces. To have a gin and tonic in Davy Jones Locker.

— We need to get you back on your medication as soon as possible.

Maybe see Ridge Racer? Maybe go back to Barry's flat?

— Why don't you wear an identity tag, Lily?

— Because I'm not a dog.

———

— Status epilepticus. One in five die from it, you know. I could've been a goner.

Mel cried into her hands.

— They say I'm lucky there's no lasting damage.

Dave looked at the floor.

— They know I'd stopped taking them. They said I was treading a very fine line. I laughed. I said ha: like a trapeze artist?

I rolled over.

— Can you turn out the light? The buzzing's doing my fucking head in.

The buzz stopped and the white lifted. The light in the room and on the walls – it was grey now, and the grey settled on my face and sleep took me away again.

I slipped inside the grey.

The sound of doors, hundreds of them, blowing open and shutting all at once. I knew I couldn't sleep too long, but it was so nice. Breathing was easy. I didn't have to concentrate on anything. It just took me away, voices far off, grey light and my lungs filling and emptying.

But that one thought snagged at me: don't sleep too long.

What woke me was that picture of her, like a knife slicing into my eyeballs. Her lying there, waiting for us to come, for the police to find us, to bring us back. Knowing she was going to die. I never asked Barry what her last words were? They wouldn't have been what I'd wanted to hear. She wouldn't have said sorry. Tell Lily I'm sorry for everything. For being a selfish bitch. No apology. It would've been some last bite, one last chunk taken out of me. Just so I knew how much she hated me. She would have chewed me up and spat me out again. Just like she did when I was eleven. You're nothing but a little fucking slut. Good riddance.

I remember it was night-time. My room seemed so cramped and the furniture too high. I got out and wandered down the corridor in my white smock and found another little room like mine. I peered through the glass. The curtains were brown but without flowers on. I could see there was a man in there, sat in bed talking, the lamp above his bed making his eyes look hollow. He was old, his hair stuck out in clumps like white grass. I walked around the side and pushed the door open, but there was no one else in there, no one on a chair listening to him, no nurse keeping an eye on him. I stood in the doorway and watched him, watched his mouth going. The sign above his bed said Mr Charles Parkin. Nil by mouth.

He pointed towards the bottom of his bed.

— He's here.

I looked, but there was no one there. I whispered it quiet,

— What's he saying?

Mr Parkin looked at me. He squinted and smiled all gummy.

— He says: You've kept me waiting too long.

He leaned back into his pillow, closing his eyes with a little smile on his face. His skin looked like pastry. Pale and chewed up. Like the inside of a pork pie. I watched for his chest rising, falling, but I couldn't see any movement.

I closed the door dead gentle behind me.

———

The buzz started, the white fell. I came awake.

— The positive EEG you had back in ninety-two confirmed genuine temporal-lobe epilepsy. Your consultant

276

has put you forward for more tests. He thinks you're an ideal candidate for surgery. The blah tests will include an MRI to see if there is a specific structural problem in part or parts of your blah-di-blah. Over seventy per cent of people who have surgery become completely seizure-free.

— What about the other thirty?

I could see his tongue inside his mouth.

———

I waited until it must've been two or three in the morning. It was dark in the corridor outside and quiet. I got dressed, got my things together, pocketed the stash of pills and tiptoed down the corridor.

I looked in on Mr Parkin. His room was empty.

I went into the toilets and opened the window and looked down. Shit. I was about three floors up. I went back along the corridor. There was a window with a light shining out, the sound of typing inside. Thirty per cent, I kept on saying to myself. Thirty per cent. I took a deep breath, ducked down, and tiptoed out into a longer corridor. Two nurses walked past me, but I might as well have been invisible. There was no one at the nurse's station either. I took the lift down the ground floor and I was out, simple-as. There was a man sat on a bench outside, having a fag in his dressing gown and slippers. Signs lit up: Whittington Hospital, a big black cat perched on top of the W.

I got to the edge of the hospital grounds. I could see the city lit up like a galaxy away down the hill, and I realized – I hadn't a fucking clue where I was. I turned back. The smoking man had gone. I went into the hospital foyer and took down one of the cab numbers on the little cards next to the phone.

───────

I was half expecting her to scream, to kick up a fuss, but she just put her arms out like a little girl, blinking up at me through jumbled hair. I took my jacket and jeans off and climbed in next to her. It was hot and smelt of sleep in there. She rolled over and curled her legs around mine and we fell asleep like that, holding hands. Two hot spoons under the covers. I was free, but my brain felt like a cold lump of metal in my head, weighing on me.

☙☙☙☙

I was stood next to the window with Mel's backpack at my feet.

— You'll phone me when you get there?
— Course.
— And what do I say if the hospital ring? Because they will.
— Tell them anything.
— Are you sure . . . ?
— Don't.
— Sorry.
— Just tell them I had a moment of . . .
— Clarity?
— That's the one.
Her face said she wasn't sure. Her face said you're making a mistake. Her face said I'm scared for you. The

phone started ringing and it made us jump. But it was just the cab driver saying he was outside. We hugged quickly and I told her to have a great Christmas and I'd see her in a few days.

— And if Al rings, tell him you haven't seen me. I want to surprise him. Here.

I shoved the present into her hands and kissed her cheek.

— But wait, I haven't . . .

I ran down the stairs and out into the cold. She waved as the cab drove me away, her face sad behind the window up there.

————

There were just a few stragglers hanging about King's Cross. It was the last train I could get and I had a fifteen-minute wait. I bought some chocolate and a magazine from the shop and went outside, trying to remember my first night in London and how scared I was. That was my first view: from outside King's Cross. I thought that's all London was: the Euston Road. Like the Euston Road was London's high street.

And now I was going home. And I was scared I wouldn't come back.

I turned to go back into the station when someone hit me hard on the shoulder. I turned around and they ran round the back of me, laughing. My heart swelled in my chest and I was thinking this is it – I'm a goner, knifed dead in the station for the change in my purse. Then I saw the blonde hair and her face in mine shouting BOO.

— Fuck me.

— Lily. Loopy Lily.

It was freezing cold and she only had a blouse on. It was

dirty and ripped and I could make out the dark shapes of her nipples in the wetness. Matted hair in clumps and her lips with brown bits on.

— Loopy Lily, remember me?

She threw her arms up and whooped.

— Rachel?

Snot running down her top lip. Chewing chuddy in her gob like a tart.

— Me, I'm fucking great I am. But hey, this is fucking mental. I've someone here for you to meet. Oh, and I'm sorry and all that, about your stuff, but check this.

— I haven't got time.

— I saw him and I was like no way, it can't fucking be. And then I'm looking around and it's like I fucking magic'd you from thin air.

She clicked her fingers in my face. I thumbed over my shoulder.

— I've got a train.

She looked me up and down, put her face up to mine, her breath cheesy.

— You are real, aren't you?

Spittle on my cheeks. She grabbed my arm and pulled me hard.

— Come on. He's just round here.

It was dark and litter blustered about. She pulled me to a phone box and pointed at the door, laughing her head off.

— I found him, I found him for you. Do I get a reward?

I was sucked into the picture. *Can you help?* His eyes blurring into squares where they'd blown it up.

— Can you lend us some cash for some tamazzies?

Michael O'Connor has been missing from his home in . . . His smile, the squares of colour, it was like he was laughing at me. I don't know. I put my fingers up and touched his face. Voices behind me. I turned around and a man in a suit was dragging Rachel away, his arm around her neck.

— Lily?

I sprinted back into the station, across the shiny yellow floor and the voice in the speakers was too loud to hear. A whistle was being blown. I jumped on and ran down the aisle and the train juddered off. I was breathing hard with blood in my throat and I tried smiling at some woman opposite me, but all I saw was our Mikey's face, his blurry face on a phone box in London.

And here I was going home. Leaving Mikey behind.

4

I walked across the road and leaned against the railings. Even before I saw the fishing boats, before I saw them perched on their sides on the wet sands, I could tell the tide was out – just from the sound. The wind was proper belting out there. I licked my lips to taste the salt and the wind was trying to get down my throat. The sea smelt black, angry, and the flashing green from the lighthouse – it said home.

I turned around and looked along the front. A feeling took shape. What I was seeing was too small. Those dark shapes that'd held me so long, they looked so tiny.

I walked back over the road and stood looking at the number 83 on the blue door. I took the three steps up, those yellow tiles slippery-as when it's pissing down. I flicked the light on and clomped up the stairs. The same smell of nothing and everything, of home and being safe. I thought about the last time my hands had been on the banister, sliding down and out to find Mikey in London where we'd be together and happy.

I saw the new furniture and bed and lamps. He'd even fitted new units in the kitchen and changed the sink in the bathroom that I'd cracked when I'd fallen on it one time. On the bed was a little card with my name on.

Mel had spilt the beans. Al had rung just after I left

London and he was there, waiting for me at the train station in his Elvis outfit. He'd come straight from the karaoke and reeked of booze. He drove slowly in the old yellow car he calls Banana, his hands shaking on the steering wheel. He looked so made up I was back home.

And I could still see them. Faint like memories under the paint. All of my words, trapped there.

DON'T WORRY HOME BED SLEEP BE OK LOVE LILY X X X

I went over to the window. Just below one corner, below the sill, there's a hole. Stuffed inside the hole was a brown envelope. I rummaged inside with my fingers and pulled it out.

I waited to feel something.

I opened it up, took the bangle out. It was one of those elastic ones, with orange plastic cubes around it. I slid it over my hand, onto my wrist. I thought that seeing it again would upset me, gut me. But I felt total nothing.

I turned the little heater on, got into bed, and turned out the light. Ursa Major in yellow star shapes – they were still up there.

I rolled the little cubes in my fingers. It was the only thing that I had from Don. I was wearing the bangle when they took me away, from her, from him. I remembered the day I found it in my pocket, in the brown envelope, and remembered the warmth inside me when I slid it on the first time and whispered his name. Don.

I felt safe in that bed again, looking up at the plastic stars, playing with the bangle. London was just a dream. I knew I'd wake in the morning and I'd be eighteen again, starting over again. Eighteen, in my new flat on the seafront. Feeling that I'd made it. Feeling that I'd survived.

My phone beeped again, another new message.
I switched it off.

⊖⊖⊖⊖

The fire was lit in the dining room and he had jazz play-ing on the stereo. He was made up when I gave him his Elvis CD.

— It's got remixes and digitally-whatever on it. The works.

— It's cracking, lass. Just *bloody* cracking.

He pecked me on the cheek and then he went into the hallway. I heard drawers opening and closing, grunting noises. When he came back in, he had a massive bin bag in his hands.

— Look, I've kept this stuff for you. It's been bothering me to no end having this lot here. It didn't feel right, me opening it.

I looked inside: boxes wrapped up all fancy.

— I don't want it.

— But it's from your Barry. What going on with you two, eh?

— Nothing. I just don't want it, that's all.

I scrunched the bag up and kicked it behind my chair.

— Give it away to charity.

— Ee, I don't know.

He tutted and huffed about for a bit, then he went into the kitchen and played his new CD and started singing along.

The inside of Al's house is like a charity shop – though he says it's all antiques. Paintings, old chairs, rugs, kettles, fur coats, cabinets full of crappy trinkets, and he has this jewellery all over the place, and lamps, old record players and his stinking cats, sleeping and licking themselves everywhere.

He cooked us the usual with the trimmings and was quite pissed by pudding time. He'd told me the same old stories about his family and the stuff they used to do at Christmas.

It always left me feeling empty. The silence after he finished, me looking at the floor, thinking of something to say.

Barry was always up before it was light, waking us. We'd go downstairs into the front room and wait. Mam would always get up late. She'd have our presents in a carrier bag. She'd put the bag on the chair, three sets of eyes staring at it. We sat still, saying nothing, scared we'd upset her and she'd throw the presents in the bin like she'd threaten to. Sat there freezing, waiting for her to light the fire. Sometimes she didn't get up until the afternoon, she was so pissed the night before.

Christmas Day was the only time we ever used the front room, too expensive to heat she said, even though it was the size of a matchbox. Sometimes she'd have wrapped the presents, sometimes she wouldn't. Sometimes there were a lot of presents, sometimes just one each. Most of them were second-hand, we knew because they were usually broken and dirty, but we didn't care. If we looked disappointed she'd beat us and call us selfish little bastards, so we went over the top when we opened them. Then we'd go back up to our rooms and stare at them, feeling cheated, you know. And she was usually blotto by dinner, asleep on the couch with the telly on loud. Never any crackers. Never any tree with an angel on the top. Never any silver-glitter cards. Never any funny hats or jokes round the dinner table. None of that shite.

We never had a Christmas dinner, not that I can remember. Barry and Mikey used to go to their friends' houses and eat there. I just stayed in my room with my shit present and a jam sandwich, glad to be on my own and out of her road.

I never got any cards from her when I was in the home. Never got any post. She never visited or phoned. Not once.

But I wasn't the only kid in there whose mam or dad couldn't give a fuck, and in a way, that made it easier.

Al saw I was uncomfortable and started talking again. He got onto the when-are-you-moving-back malarkey and he seemed happy enough with what I told him.

— How are your fits doing? You still coping?

I told him about the hospital, about the scans, and he seemed pleased. He was over the moon they wanted to take a piece of me away. I almost said something, but I stopped myself. It was the first time I realized I was scared that if they took my fits away, there'd be nothing left.

— So who's this fella you've been seeing?

— Oh, him. It's nothing.

He got a serious look.

— It takes *everything* you've got. You've got to put in *every* part of yourself. You know?

He shook his head like he was trying to get the thoughts out of his brain.

I tried to change the subject,

— Anyway, how's Bird Brain Brian doing? You didn't mention him last time we spoke.

— He died, lass.

— No?

— Pneumonia. It's a bloody shame, right enough. There

was only three of us at the funeral. Me and old Tom scattered his ashes off the pier.

— Who's feeding the birds, then?

I was being serious, but Al laughed his head off.

He got up and put that Slade Christmas song on and started to jig about. I tried really hard not to piss myself. He was usually such a good mover, but his beans had run out, and by the time the song finished he was in his chair by the fire with his gob open, snoring.

I tiptoed over to the mirror and put loads of lippy on. Then I watched him sleeping for a bit. His wig skew whiff and his hands twitching, brown spots all over them like freckles. His fingers moved and he made little moans. It's a shame he never married or had kids of his own, he's such a lovely bloke. Heart of gold. Maybe he did have a love years back. A sweetheart, that's what he'd call her. My sweetheart.

I leaned down and I could smell him: Brylcreem and damp jackets. I kissed him and pictured him waking up, looking in the mirror, and how he'd laugh at the red lips on his forehead.

———

I hung the bin bag over the sea wall and closed my eyes. I saw Barry's eyes behind his purple glasses. I saw something evil there and thought fucking Slick you prick. I opened my hand and let it fall.

———

I stood and looked up at the sign: Golden Nugget Arcade. The neon was out. It was the only day of the year Jim shut the place down. I put my hands up to the glass and peered inside. I couldn't see the change booth – a new DANCING STAR EUROMIX machine was in the way. There were a couple of other new machines, but everything else was as it was – the large row of MEGA CRANER machines with the orange balls of teddies in, and the same signs, same swirly carpets, the blue and red and pink neon of it all. CASH CASH CASINO switched off in the gloom.

I couldn't believe that I'd worked there.

It felt like yesterday. Felt like years ago.

Not working was like a relief, but there was something about it that I missed. Just having to do it, I suppose. Give your days some meaning. I'd never thought why don't I do this or that? I just hadn't. I knew I was lucky having a boss who didn't mind me having fits, who didn't care what the customers thought when the shadow figures came. But I'd still get that feeling: Tuesday blues. I always worked Sundays because it was the busiest day, and so Mondays were my Sundays. And I'd be lying in bed Monday night thinking how long was it since I last chucked a sickie? Sat in bed with that knot in my gut. But I didn't mind the job, not really. Besides, traipsing the streets of London and staring at tramps – that was my job now.

I think I was looking for something. I wanted to see a change. It didn't seem possible – me being down there with all of that going on, and back up here: nothing. I looked. I looked everywhere for change.

Everything along the front was shuttered, dirty sheets over the kiddie's rides. The streets were empty. I passed a car and I could hear it ticking. I put my hands on the bonnet and felt it hot through my gloves. I remembered summer trips to the seaside when I was a bairn, weekenders clumping along the seafront and cars driving slow. Sunshine on my back, tilting my face up to it. Gangs of skinheads with their tops off, bright red chests and tattooed arms, dogs on studded leashes. The smell of the salt – the frowsy stink of it. The rattle of shells in the bottom of buckets. The surprise of jellyfish on the beach, seethrough dollops that I loved to prod with sticks. Whooping sprints into the sea. Crunching sand in your chips. Huge sugared dummies on ribbon that you tie to your wrist, and clouds of pink candyfloss that made you feel sick. Headachy donkey gallops along the sands. The rude mugs with tits and willies on that always made me giggle. Topless fat slags, saggy breasts out, beside the seaside beside the sea. Piles of deckchairs. Seagulls nicking chips straight out of your hand.

I walked back to the flat, and the only people I saw were an old woman hunched over, her face so grey it was almost white, and a cockler – a black shape out on the sands.

I pressed MEL. There was a lot of screaming, like someone was being murdered. She went just give me a minute I'll call you back.

I sat on the bed and waited. The silence was like water in my ears.

— Sorry about that. I've had to come upstairs to get out of the way. The kids are being so horrible. They're spoilt little shits. Lucy lets them get away with murder.

She whispered: I want to wring their fucking necks.

— Anyway, Merry Christmas. How is it up North?

— Usual: cold, wet and miserable.

— Nothing changed, then?

I hummed, I harred, I went what did you get, then?

— Oh, Lil, thank you so much for my things. The

necklace, oh my God, it's absolutely *gorgeous*. It must've cost a fortune. You really shouldn't have.

— Oh, shush. As long as you like it?

— I adore it. I *love* it. I've got it on now.

— Great stuff.

— By the way, has Dave got hold of you? You just missed him by a second when you left. He looked worried. He'd gone to the hospital and you weren't there.

— He's left umpteen messages on my phone.

— What's going on? Do you want to talk about it?

— I don't know. I think I want him to dump me. He deserves better.

I could hear her breathing.

— Has the hospital rung?

— Not that I'm aware of. I came here straight after he left.

— Fair enough. He didn't, you know, say anything to you again?

— No. But he didn't apologize either.

— I'll see about that.

— So how's Al? How's your day been? Tell me tell me.

⊘⊘⊘⊘

The doorbell went. I was lying there watching sparks jump and dance around the room. Whoever was ringing, they went away. In the afternoon, I got my strength back and went to Davy Jones Locker and I remember I tried to drink a lemonade but it tasted of piss. I didn't see Ridge Racer like I was hoping. I don't know why. I don't know what I was going to say to him.

I went back to the flat and slept and it was getting dark when I woke up.

I stretched out on the bed and rolled the bangle between my fingers. I arched my back and a burn spread in my guts and shot up my throat like a flame. I ran to the toilet with the heaviness under my chin and fell to my knees. I hammered my guts down into the water, struggling with it.

⊖⊖⊖⊖

'Hound Dog' booming downstairs. It was stifling hot in the room. I opened the windows and the sharp air was tickles of ice on my face. It took me ages to fold my clothes into the backpack. I felt exhausted and had to lie on the bed. I didn't think I had the strength to carry on, thinking maybe I should just forget it all, get my old job back at the Nugget and act like nothing had happened.

My phone was saying there was no room for any more messages. I read through them all and deleted them. All from Barry. He'd been sending me about one every week. Was I OK? All right? Something wrong with the phone? Numbers for hotels in Vegas – call and I'll call you right back.

Are you OK, are you OK, are you all right?

Then just before Christmas, it went quiet, and that scared me.

I heard footsteps coming up the stairs and the four knocks. Al looked at me, at my backpack.

— You're not?

I propped myself up on my elbow. He came and sat on the edge of the bed and stroked my hair.

— I've hardly bloody seen you, lass.

— I'm not feeling too good. Really.

— You've got to look after yourself. It's hard for me, not being able to keep an eye on you when you're *down there*.

He said down there like it was someone he hated.

— I'm big enough to . . .

— I *mean* it. You've got to be careful.

I let my head drop onto the bed and he carried on stroking my hair. We were both quiet, listening to the hish of wind and waves outside the window. Then I let my lids go and he was sat in the chair at the other side of the room when I woke up.

— I was just resting my eyes.

He smiled at me slow and warm.

— I've heard that one before.

I got up and ran some water into a mug. Then I told him what the consultant had said again, about me being a good candidate and all. I wanted him to tell me don't do it, it's too big of a risk, but all he said was that's good news, isn't it?

— I'm not sure, Al.

The phone went in my pocket – Mel ringing from the home number. Al picked up my backpack and said he'd wait in the car. I listened to her voice. She never said what I wanted her to say.

Outside, I looked up at the flat thinking *for the last time*.

I got in the car.

— Good news?

— The hospital wants me to go back. If I don't, I'll be struck off.

He tutted and gave me a look: stupid girl.

— We've still got a couple of hours yet. You sure you still want to go?

— I'm sure.

———

The coast road took us close to the edge of the cliffs in places. You could see it down there, rough and angry, whipping itself into a right state. It took nearly an hour to get there with the way he drove, singing his head off and banging to the beat on the steering wheel with his hand.

Mikey's old house. I was hoping it would tell me something. We parked up outside, across the road on the gravelly bit with the sign on.

VIEWING POINT: DO NOT LITTER

The house was big and white with curved bits at the front and huge windows. Must've been worth a fortune. And I know it's stupid, but I thought I'd see Mikey's face at the window, looking out, waving. I did.

— Should we get out?

— Just a minute.

I couldn't see anyone in there. Children – I thought I'd see children and coloured lights dancing around the window, pretend flickering candles. And the thought: it should've been Mikey and Sylvia in there, with their kid. A kid that would've looked something like Simon. They'd be in there playing games in front of the fire, and laughing.

That's when I saw the sign.

SOLD.

— Al, wait here for us, will you?

I got out of the car and crunched down the gravel driveway. I pressed the doorbell and used the knocker. I could hear distant music. Someone was in there. I turned to look at Al in the car and he nodded at me and waved. I pressed the bell again and clouted the knocker a few times.

A shadow moving behind the glass. Thud of footsteps getting closer. Then the door opened.

My blood screamed.

His face was like an explosion when he saw me. He whooped and flung both his arms around me tight, making a laughing noise. I struggled out of him.

— My not-so-little sis.

— Barry?

I felt like I'd fallen for the electric handshake. He was breathing hard, looking me up and down. The front door slammed shut behind me and the sound off the walls – it was my heart banging. We stood in the hallway, the sound of music coming from somewhere and the sweet stink of weed. He spoke fast,

— Where've you been? I went to the flat and that. Al said you'd gone.

— Bollocks. Al would've said.

— I've been worried, Lily. What's wrong with your phone?

He didn't wait for my answer. He told me about how successful he'd been, had I heard? How he's got an online sponsor, paying him shit-loads and all he's got to do is what he loves. He went: imagine it. Then he took my hands and stared at them, turning them over, frowning.

— Did you not get my presents?

— Yes, I got them.

— Where's the ring?

— Swimming with the fishes.

— Eh?

He put his hand to his mouth and I noticed the thick gold bracelet: WPO written on it in sparkly diamonds. And the knuckleduster ring that said SLICK. He shone all over with expensive bling and his pasty skin looked like it hadn't seen the sun in months. The whites of his eyes yellow, teeth turning brown again.

— So you've bought his house?

— Li-*ly*.

— You've bought his fucking *house*?

— I've been trying to call you.

— You're the lowest.

He put out his hand and I flinched.

— Come in, come on. Come in and have a drink.

He walked on, waving me further into the hot of the house. I followed him down the hallway and into a long room with the dark figure of someone sitting on a sofa.

— Mikey?

The laugh was a boom and I heard Barry tut.

— It's fucking Lamb chops.

I watched him get slowly to his feet, like his video was on slow motion, and I thought smack. This guy's a fucking smackhead.

— Lily. Nice to see you. How's, you know, tricks?

I span and pointed at Barry.

— Me and you need to talk. Alone.

I could sense Lamb's big arms flapping, like no worries no worries.

I followed Barry into another room that had a big

kitchen at the end with patio doors. He pulled up a chair and nodded at me to sit.

— I'll stand, thanks.

He sat down and I watched him fidget, taking a fag out of the packet on the table and passing it between his hands, between fingers.

I kicked him in the leg hard-as.

— Jesus fuck.

— So?

— So what?

— So do you know where I've been the past six months?

His face told me: no.

— I've been in London. The day after you left.

He lit his fag, smirking, nodding his head. He huffed smoke out and tried to smile but it looked more like a grimace. Then he tried to hide his hands.

— He's better off without you, you know.

— Who?

— Simon.

An evil laugh, like who gives a fuck.

— He's a grand bairn. But sometimes any dad is better than no dad.

He stared at the floor, sucking on his fag. Sucking. Sucking.

— You must think I'm stupid, Barry? You must think I'm fucking thick?

He shrugged.

— And I started a search for Mikey. A proper one. Nothing.

— But you'll know how fucking pointless that's been. Will you at least fucking *look* at me.

He stood up, put his face close to mine, his breath on me. I thought he was going to head-butt me, but he went over to the sink and flicked his cigarette in, spat, and turned on the taps.

— So what, Simon's mine. So *fucking* what? I only fucked her because she was begging for it.

— I don't want to know.

— Oh, I think you do. I think you *do* want to know. He folded his arms and leaned back against the sink.

— You want to look closer to home, Lily.

He nodded.

— Aye. Look at yourself before you go accusing others.

— And what's *that* meant to mean?

— You're not my proper sister.

His eyes drilled into mine.

— Whatever.

— You and Mikey, you've a different dad to me.

— Don't play your mind games. We all look alike.

— My dad's your uncle.

I ran my hand through my hair and took a deep breath. I turned a full circle before looking at him again.

— So what, fucking history repeating, is that it?

— But the difference is, *your* father's alive, Lily. Mine fucking died before I was born. I had to live with that. Live with that from early on.

— I don't . . .

— Mam told me when I was eight. Told me to keep it secret from yous two. That's when I started looking at things differently. But I never hated her, not like you and our Mikey did.

— She can rot in fucking hell.

— You only have one mother, Lily.

— She died for me a *long* time ago.

My fingers went to the plastic bracelet on my wrist and he went,

— Anyway, that's all water under the bridge now.

— I'm afraid it's not that easy. I want our Mikey's share of the money.

— That why you're here?

— I want to keep it *safe*. Give it to me now, or get a cheque to Al. I don't care how, just do it.

I threw my arms out, looking around the massive empty room.

— Because I *know* you can. I know you're loaded and you've probably fucking spent it all on some cheap tart. I want it soon-as. Forty-two grand, and whatever else is left. Whether we hated the bitch or not, it's our money, Barry. Ours.

A snort down his nose, an eyebrow up.

— Or else I'm going to the police.

That was the first time he looked at me properly. The room was heavy with it.

— You wouldn't want them snooping into your affairs now, would you?

— Doesn't mean fuck all to me. I'm *legit*.

— And when I tell them about the fight, and Mikey going missing. Kind of says one thing and one thing alone, doesn't it?

— I never laid a fucking finger on him. It's *him* that attacked *me*.

— *Really?*

There was real fear slapped across his face. He looked over my shoulder, searching the other room for Lamb. He said quietly,

— He's abroad.

— Don't fob me off.

— He's in Ireland, Lily.

Like a speeding car, coming towards me, mounting the pavement.

— Five years ago. After I got out of hospital. I suppose you know?

— Know? I know *fuck all*. What do you think I've been doing for the past six months, you wanker?

He tried to touch me. He tried to put his hand on my forearm and I punched him in the chest, my full weight behind it. He gasped and took a step back and glared. I wanted to hurt him. I was exploding inside.

It took him a few seconds to gather himself.

— After his breakdown, he went looking for your dad. Mam never lied to you two. *Never*. She told you he was alive, didn't she?

— She told me he was a useless Irish cunt and nothing else.

— But Mikey knew him. Remembered him. And so do I. He lived with us for a while, and so did Roddy.

— Roddy?

— My dad. But he came off his motorbike the month before I was born. Fucking killed himself.

He said dead quiet,

— I never got to meet him.

I tried not to smile, not to laugh.

— So how will I find him? If I go, I mean. To Ireland.

— Charlo has a pub.

— Charlo?

— Your *dad*, Lily. Fuck sake. Charlie, Charlo, Chick, Chucky, call him what the fuck you like. He owns a pub. O'Connor's. You'll prob-ly find Mikey behind the bar.

— Prob-ly?

— What?

— You thick, ignorant cunt.

He looked me in the eyes again and I had to turn away, fighting the smile. I heard him say it behind me, but I couldn't believe it. Like a little fucking girl,

— Can we still be friends and that?

— Fuck you.

I saw his arms shake in the corner of my eye, and his glass bounce against the floor, but it didn't smash. He went,

— There was always a part of me that *hated* you two.

And I let the smile free on him, because I felt like I'd landed.

— Goodbye, Barry.

I walked straight out of there, and it took all the strength I had left inside, not to slam that front door behind me.

ERRRRRmmmmg
MMMMMg
mmmmm greeeee heeeeey aaaaa
NEEEEE MMMMgreegreegree gree heeeeeeey
aaaaa ERRRGH ERRRGH hernyerrrGGGHHH
hergh HERRR hergh mmmmm
greeeeheeeee yaaaaa
NEEEE MMMMM greegreegree gree
heeeeeyaaaaa ERRRGHERRRGH
MMMMMg ERRRR mmmmg
mmmmm greeeee heeeeey aaaaa NEEEEEEE
MMMMM gree gree gree gree
heeeeeeeey aaaaa ERRRGHERRRGH
hernyerrrGGGHHH hergh HERRR
hergh mmmmmmgreeeee
heeeee yaaaaa NEEEE MMMMM gree
greegree heeeeeyaaaaa ERRRGH ERRRGH
MMMMMg ERRRR mmmmg
mmmm greeeee heeeeey aaaaa NEEEEE
MMMMMgreegreegree gree heeeeeeeey
aaaaa ERRRGH ERRRGH hernyerrrGGG
HHH hergh HERRR hergh mmmmm
greeeeheeeee yaaaaa NEEEEE
greegree gree
gree aaaaa
MMMMMg ERRRR mmmmg mmmmm
greeeee heeeee aaaaa
aaaaa NEEEEE
MMMMMgreegree gree gree
heeeeeeeey aaaaa ERRRGH ERRRGH hernyerrr
GGGHHH hergh HERRR hergh mmm-
mmgreeeeheeeee yaaaaa NEEEEEEEE
MMM greegreegree gree heeeeeyaaaaa
ERRRGH ERRRGH mmmmg mmmmmmm

— Mel?

Shush-shushing me, stroking my hair, her face above me, the bright light up there on the ceiling like a

— You're an angel.

like a halo over her head, and I could hear me, smacking my lips like mwa mwa, pulling my face, fingers dancing over my cheeks, noise revving up out of me like a banshee and the shadows – I *won't* let them knock me off my feet any more, I WON'T.

— Mel, *hold* me.

Burnt winds blowing around inside, crackles and coughs and

— Mel.

I couldn't look Mel in the eye because her face is dripping down all purple and reds and yellows and

— HOLD MEEEEEEEEEE

her arms closing around me and the lushness, the weakness, clouds ripping open my eyes, white smoke blowing, turn off my eyes, fading dim, yes turning

and it looks like
and smells like
and feels like

MMMMMg ERRRRmmmmmg
mmmmm greeeee heeeeey aaaaa
NEEEEE MMMMMgreegreegree gree heeeeeeeey
aaaaa ERRRGH ERRRGH hernyerrrGGGHHH
hergh HERRR hergh mmmmm
greeeeeheeeee yaaaaa
NEEEEE MMMMMM greegreegree gree
heeeeeyaaaaa ERRRGHERRRGH
MMMMMMg ERRRR mmmg
mmmmm greeeee heeeeey aaaaa NEEEEEEE
MMMMMM gree gree gree gree
heeeeeeeey aaaaa ERRRGH ERRRGH
hernyerrrGGGHHH hergh HERRR
mmmmmmgreeeee
heeeee yaaaaa NEEEEE MMMMMM gree
greeee heeeeyaaaaa ERRRGH ERRRGH
MMMMMMg ERRRR mmmmg
mmmm greeeee heeeeey aaaaa NEEEEE
MMMMMMgreegreegree gree heeeeeeeey
aaaaa ERRRGH ERRRGH hernyerrrGGG
HHH hergh HERRR hergh mmmmm
greeeeeheeeee yaaaaa NEEEEE
gree greegree gree
MMMMMg ERRRR mmmmm
greeeee heeeeey
aaaaa NEEEEE
MMMMMMgreegree gree gree
heeeeeeeey aaaaa ERRRGH ERRRGH hernyerrr
GGGHHH hergh HERRR hergh mmmm-
mmgreeeeheeeee yaaaaa NEEEEEEEE
MMM greegreegree gree heeeeeyaaaaa
ERRRGH ERRRGH mmmmg mmmmmmm

MMMMMMg ERRRRmmmmmg
mmmmmm greeeee heeeeey aaaaa
NEEEEE MMMMMgreegreegree gree heeeeeeeey
aaaaa ERRRGH ERRRGH hernyerrrGGGHHH
hergh HERRR hergh mmmmm
greeeeeheeeee yaaaaa
NEEEEE MMMMMM greegreegree gree
heeeeeeey aaaaa ERRRGH HERRRGH
MMMMMMg ERRRR mmmmg
mmmmm greeeee heeeeey aaaaa NEEEEEEE
MMMMM gree gree gree gree
heeeeeeey aaaaa ERRRGH HERRRGH
hernyerrrGGGHHH hergh HERRR
hergh mmmmmgreeeee
heeeee yaaaaa NEEEEE MMMMM gree
greegree heeeeyaaaaa ERRRGH ERRRGH
MMMMMMg ERRRR mmmmg
mmmm greeeee heeeeey aaaaa NEEEEE
MMMMM greegreegree gree heeeeeeeey
aaaaa ERRRGH ERRRGH hernyerrrGGG
HHH hergh HERRR hergh mmmmm
greeeeeheeeee
greeeeeheeeee yaaaaa NEEEEE
gree greegree gree
gree mmmmg ERRRR mmmmg mmmmm
MMMMMg greegree gree gree
greeeee heeeey aaaaa ERRRGHERRRGH
MMMMMMgreegree gree gree gree
heeeeeeeey aaaaa ERRRGH ERRRGH hernyerrr
GGGHHH hergh HERRR hergh mmm-
mmgreeeeheeeee yaaaaa NEEEEEEEE
MMM greegreegree gree heeeeyaaaaa
ERRRGH ERRRGH mmmmg mmmmmmm

3

Coming back down to London, I realized I'd stopped noticing it all. The mad rush. The traffic noise. The building site of the place. Sky full of engine noise. The colour of people's skin, foreign voices, the funny get-up people wear. The argy-bargy of footpaths and buses, on the tube, the aggro of it all. Kiss goodbye to your personal space. The smell of man-piss in doorways, alleyways, that tang that makes your eyes itch. And the smell from shops, food smells I've never smelt in my life before. Music and shouts and screams and sirens belting out of windows and streets and doorways. Sweating on the tube.

The fucking madness of London coughing its guts up, spitting you out.

But I did notice the writing on the walls everywhere. Bright fuzzy colours, silvers and golds and blues, electric-looking. I saw kids in baseball caps and hooded tops and I imagined it was them spraying their names all over. Secret words making them feel safe. Just like I used to do.

And I wanted to tell them: one day you won't need to.

On the wall outside Mel's house, sprayed in silver and black on the white wall: *Chocolicious Bubali. This house is shit. Yellow bitch.*

I pointed them out to her and she shrugged.

— I never really notice graffiti any more.

I felt sorry for her. Felt sad that everything becomes so everyday.

We got on the bus and I tried to find the right words. The house. Barry. Ireland. But it was stuck like that fucking bird in my throat.

— Mel.

She looked at me and I coughed.

— Thanks for saying you'd come. You're a sweetheart, you know that? And thanks for the other stuff.

She'd been online and found a company that does special bedding. Waterproof stuff that's really nice and doesn't look or feel anything like rubber sheets. I could never imagine a man doing that. Not that I'd want one to. The sheets don't crinkle when you sleep on them. Don't make you feel like food wrapped up.

She smiled a warm smile, took my hand, squeezed it. Our gloves felt massive together. I could feel the ring, her Christmas present to me, digging into my finger.

— I'm here for you. Whatever you decide.

— They'll probably handcuff me to the bed this time. You *will* let us drug you. You *will* let us saw your skull open.

— Who got you that bangle?

— Al. Al gave it to me.

My second lie. I stared out the window. The bus rattled and farted up Holloway Road. It was snowing up in the sky, you could see it falling, but it never reached the road as flakes, just became wet stuff that made the streets slimy – you could hear the tyres of the bus hissing in it.

Our breaths steamed the window. I wrote my name in it and Mel wrote hers beneath. I drew a heart around it and we laughed. I rubbed it away when we got off the bus.

The black cat perched on top of the W. I showed Mel

the card. She read all of the signs and arrows, led us through the long corridors. I read posters showing different types of skin cancers. Signs everywhere saying Switch Off All Mobiles. It was busy in there and had that stink – Germolene and TCP. We passed a Ladies and I went and sat in the metal light, fretting, feeling hot and loose inside, but nothing would come out. I strained so hard my face throbbed. If they tried to put me back on those fucking pills, I'd tell them where to stick them.

We found the Neurology Department. I thought the big black nurse would suck her teeth and shake her head at me, but she smiled and singsonged: Come this way, the doctor's ready. I put my arm through Mel's and followed the nurse's big behind.

I recognized him. He stood up and shook my hand and said his name, something foreign. And there was a woman there as well, sitting down, reading something. She didn't look up.

— This is my best friend, Mel. I want her here.

Fine fine, he said, and shook her hand. He pointed at the chairs for us to sit. Then he pointed at the woman. This is Dr So-and-so who's a . . .

Mel stared at me like I was going to pounce, her eyes flick-flickering.

— Following status epilepticus we run a blah-di-blah. Standard procedure. One showed a high percentage of whatever in your blood. We followed this with another test, but when the results came back the next morning, well, you'd gone.

I watched their mouths move. I listened to their voices. But they weighed on me. The words queuing up to stampede me, kick me about, jump on my head. Words like clods of soil, burying me alive.

303

I looked at a picture on the wall of a sunset and the sea
– it needed a good dust.

The woman had crow's feet and little sags round her
mouth that made her look stern. I couldn't tell what age
she was. She could've done with some make-up. I listened
to her going on about counselling. They said that word
again and that it was OK, there was no risk. Smiles all
round, their arms going up and down like puppets. The
woman looked at her clipboard and wrote something
there. She was rubbing her ankle against the leg of her
chair. Mel bit her fingernails and looked scared and ran
her fingers through her hair and sighed. The doctor's face,
the woman's ankle, I could see Mel's eyes getting wet with
tears.

— Are you OK, Lily?

The laughter – it came crashing right out of me.

————

I didn't mean to start crying. Didn't mean to stay the night.
I'd gone round to finish him, but as soon as he touched
me, I started unpeeling. I wanted him close, but not for sex.
My whole body stinging with it, but I wouldn't let him
inside. I wanted to feel the roughness of his body, something that would take the numbness away. It was all the
waves I'd been watching back home – they came flooding
right back out of me. I cried into his chest and I hated
myself because Barry had finally done it – he'd broken my
heart and made me weak.

And now I had this to top it all off.

Something woke me up. I opened my eyes and my arm
was trapped under Dave's neck. The sky glowed red in the
window. I pulled my arm out, leaned over him, and put my

lips over the suck of his breath. Then I watched his chest rising, falling. My voice croaked,

— Dave?

His eyes twitching. I kissed his scratchy cheek and kept my lips there, smelling lager and cigarettes in his long hair and the smell of his skin. I kissed him because it was so real.

He blinked, slowly curled and uncurled his hands.

— Dave?

A noise in the back of his throat.

— Dave?

His breathing slow, heavy. I shouted,

— DAVE!

— *Hermmma?*

He shot up in bed and looked around the room, brushing his hair back from his face. He looked down at me, eyes glass marbles. They closed and he went soft, lay back down. He rolled onto his side away from me.

— Dave?

I made a circle on his shoulder blade with my finger.

— Dave?

He mumbled something like fuck and shrugged me off, pulling the covers over his shoulder.

I waited. I kept opening my mouth again and again, but the word kept getting stuck. I wanted to blurt it right out in a scream. But it was like a whisper,

— I'm pregnant.

———

They mentioned something about the effects of my pills on the unborn baby. I went you're joking? The man's face said no and the woman glanced away again. I looked down at my hands in my lap, then at my stomach.

— I think you've made a mistake.

— When was the first day of your last period?

— I don't know.

Three blank faces.

— Those drugs the consultant put me on, they proper messed me up. I didn't know what day it was.

— Roughly, when do you think it was?

I looked up to the ceiling, poked around in my head.

— December. First few days. No, before that. Week before. I don't know.

I put my head in my hands, rubbed my face.

— I don't know, but I can't. My fits. I just can't.

Mascara on my fingertips.

They began again, about the risk of injury if I have a seizure. The skeleton, the organs, the other stuff. Development, that was it – the development of the unborn baby. The word bounced off my ears and came out as a laugh again. A door slamming in their faces.

— What we'll do is take you to a lower level. Reduce the risk but still control the seizures.

— I'm fucking pregnant?

Mel frowned. The serious woman sighed through her smile and said that word again: folic acid. She was telling me how it helps the baby's spine to form, helps reduce the risk of blah. Free of charge, on prescription. Go see your GP as soon as possible. Nodding away, noises in throats.

I saw bones, tiny splintery bones, dissolving in acid.

— What do you mean *defects*?

Gritty bubbles, white.

— Developmental abnormality.

— What do you mean? You said *no risk*.

— Cleft lip. Cleft palate. Very low chance. And neural-tube defects.

They said spina bifida. They said learning difficulties. They said problems with behaviour. Ultrasound scans. Something-feto something-protein blood test. That word again: spi-na bi-fi-da. They told me percentages and I thought of maths at school. The genetic counsellor – he said my type of epilepsy wasn't hereditary.

I could smell the dust on the painting up there. Mel's fingers threaded into mine. I wanted her to hold me. I wanted to climb into bed with her, curl up, and go to sleep.

— I estimate you're seven weeks gone. Approximately. Morning sickness usually occurs around week eight, so you must remember to take your pills *after* you've been sick.

She said it like I was some kind of slag. I was waiting for her to say do you know who the? I'd've slapped the bitch. She shoved leaflets into my hand and I saw Dave's face in my head: drunk, shouting at me.

They said the thing inside me – it had buds of arms and legs. Buds. They said it would be the size of a raspberry by now. Smiling, like this was the best fucking thing on Earth. A fucking raspberry.

— Are you all right? Would you like some water?
— How soon can I have the abortion?

———

I put the telly on and stretched out on the settee. Mel switched it off and came and sat down beside me. I turned away from her.
— Lil?

307

— I'll dump him. He won't know fuck all.

— You wouldn't do that?

— I'm tired. I'm off to bed.

— You don't have to push me away.

— I'm tired, for fuck sake. Remember what they said?

I looked at her, at her chin creasing, eyes shining.

— I can't have a baby. How *can* I? I can't hold a bairn in my arms. How do I breast-feed it? Wash it? What if I fit and fall on my stomach when it's in there? I'll kill it, simple-as. It'll be deformed and I'll end up killing it and I don't want a spastic baby, Mel. I don't.

— But I can help you.

I lifted an eyebrow at her. She went,

— This leaflet, it says the risk is *so* small. There are ways of coping. You can feed and change and sponge bath the baby on the floor. There are strategies. Loads of women with epilepsy . . .

— I'm sick of coping. I'm sick of fucking strategies.

— Lil?

— And what: I get married to Dave and we live happily ever after?

Our eyes like two magnets – when she looked away, I nearly fell off the settee.

— I was thinking about finishing him, back home. I kind of decided. I can't see us making anything of it.

— Well, maybe you should discuss it with him, whatever you decide.

I stood up and went to the door.

— Exactly: what *I* decide.

Sometimes that fizz between me and Mel – it becomes a burn. I screamed at her and stormed out, knowing I'd done the wrong thing.

I wandered around the streets. And there they were –

young mothers with prams. The noise a baby makes – Jesus. And that stuff they carry around with them under the prams – nappies and creams and shit. Stuff I know nothing about. I wanted to shout at them all to keep the fuck away.

They looked so knackered. The energy sucked right out of them. Zombies in comfortable stretchy clothes. One woman blowing her fag smoke into the pram as she marched along, like she was wondering where to ditch the screaming little fucker.

But then I imagined the warmth of a baby and the smell of talc, and it made me think of her. Mam. When I saw her lying there, dead, I felt safe for the first time in my life. Safe, but with just this one niggle of something unfinished, like a broken promise.

———

He stopped breathing. I waited for him to turn around, for his eyes searching mine. To say you're joking? For him to throw his arms around me, I don't know. But he just spat the words right out again, snoring like a car engine starting. I whispered it into the dark of the bedroom, words like clods of soil,

— Seven weeks gone.

⊘⊘⊘⊘⊘⊘

They looked like they kicked dogs. They looked like they swore at old ladies and spat in the street. All swagger and tattoos as coarse as their gobs. Everyone but us is

INVISIBLE. Everyone but us is SHIT. That included me. So what else was there to do but sit there and look stupid? Sit like a stuffed bird with a gormless fucking grin while Dave played another game of pool with his mates, prancing around the table, twirling his cue whenever he made a good shot like a twizzling-girl – a majorette.

— Come on, Lily, just one more round. Be midnight soon.

I could've been at home with Mel, having a nice New Year's Eve. She thought I was crazy. She knew something was wrong, other than this fucking *thing* inside of me. Knew something had happened back home. And I don't know why, but I just couldn't tell her. I couldn't think about it properly, and coming back to London was an escape from it all. Leaving my old life behind, starting again. But there I was in the pub with Dave and he kept giving me looks, winks and roving sex-eyes. He'd sit down next to me and put a hand on my knee and I couldn't help but flinch. Each time I got up to go to the loo they all stopped what they were doing and said things under their breaths. I took longer and longer in there. I wasn't going back to his house without him. I didn't want to sit there on my own, in his living room, thinking thoughts. I eyed the toilet window and pictured myself sliding out if it.

But I went back in, hoping the others had gone, praying he'd be sat there on his own. But no: there was another game to be played, and another round to be bought.

I could hear Suspicious Pete singing we can't go on together. Elvis blaring out of the jukey and I felt nothing.

I caught Dave staring at me. Like I was prey. Like he was trying to get inside me. I wanted to tell him, he already had.

This hole growing in me, getting bigger, darker.

I put my jacket across my stomach and avoided his eyes. In a few minutes we'd hear Big Ben chiming in the old, chiming in the new, and I knew that it'd be painful: pretending my life wasn't going in reverse.

⊘⊘⊘⊘⊘⊘⊘⊘⊘⊘⊘⊘⊘⊘

I got out of bed and looked at my pills. They wanted me to halve my dose right away. *Halve* it. It scared me shitless. I was going to get rid of it, I knew that much, because it was this solid thing in my head that told me it was the right thing to do.

Get rid. Get fucking rid of it.

It was an accident, a mistake. Me and Dave – a mess of whatever, growing bit by bit, sprouting this and that. Buds. Arms and legs like buds on a tree. It made me feel sick, dirty, like I'd been invaded. Like he'd given me some disease. I was trying not to think about it, but it was there and it was real, and what was I doing poisoning it more than I had to?

I got Mel's laptop out of her room put it on the kitchen table.

I Googled the word. Abortion.

The more I read, the more I felt a pain inside of me.

With what's called suction-aspiration, the abortionist paralyses the cervical muscle and then stretches it open. It's difficult and painful-as, because the cervix is what they call green. It's not ready to open.

I sat there forcing myself to breathe.

The abortionist then inserts a plastic tube thing into the uterus. The tube's hollow but it has a knife edge on the tip, and it's that that tears the baby's body into pieces. The abortionist then cuts the deeply rooted placenta away from the inner wall of the uterus and the scraps are sucked out into a bottle.

I closed my eyes and what I saw was my naked legs, during my last smear. My legs up in the ankle straps, thighs twitching, I was so scared.

Speculum. Box of vaginal disposable specula. Clear jelly.

— This is going to be cold.

You feel the giant egg with the sharp point they put inside. Shaped like two hands together, a pair of lips. You hear the squeaks of bolts as they unscrew it, and it gets bigger, bigger inside. It's never gentle. They whiz it around, cranking it up inside, and you're gaping wide open with the wind blowing up your cervix. Then they get the torch out and have a proper gander.

— Vaginal discharge. Completely normal. Just have to wipe that away.

Swab. And then they get the spatula out of the box and start scraping. You try not to make a noise. They're in the most secret part of you with a torch and spatula. And I was thinking the bastards wanted to do this with my fucking brain. Scrape me away. Bit of bleeding. Pull it out with a plop.

I rubbed my eyes, read on.

The other method, which they use at a later stage, is similar except that the abortionist inserts a loop-shaped knife into the uterus to shred the placenta and baby into pieces. The bleeding is full-on. As is the pain.

I'd gone to see the bright spark the day before – that's why I was putting myself through all of this. First thing he asked about was the surgery, and I went do you have to be a heartless cunt to be a doctor? You tell me I'm pregnant to a man I don't want, with a baby I don't want, then you ask me if I want you to take a piece of my brain away. I went no fucking way. I went the risk is too big. Write it in my file: Lily says no. En, oh. And don't fucking ask me again. And then we got on to the baby business and he said I had to see a doctor at the abortion clinic and that they *both* had to agree that it was the right thing to do.

It wasn't just up to me. It wasn't that easy.

Heartbeat begins after eighteen days.

Electrical activity in the brain after forty.

So I goes to him,

— Make the appointment with the other doctor, then.

— I want you to think about it, Lily. You still have time.

— I've thought about it.

— Maybe you should think some more?

I slammed the laptop shut and ran into the toilet and rained my guts down into the bog. And then I began sobbing loudly, lying there on the bathroom floor. I couldn't stop.

It was later on that day that the thunder and lightning started up. I could hear the rumbles far off and there was this queer light in the sky, all yellowy and electric. I moved back from the window and the picture started to freeze on the telly. Faces breaking up into coloured squares. The telly said no satellite signal is being received. Then rumbles, but no rain. I sat on the couch, watching the telly struggling to get its picture. I wasn't watching it anyway; I just wanted something to numb me. But the sky was having a fucking fit.

The first crack sounded right above the house – a big metal crashing in the sky.

I went to the window again: it was grey and blue now, but with that yellow still in it. It didn't look right. I could feel it in my head, my body. I could feel it dancing, pulsing in my blood, making my heart skip beats. Then the flickering came. The sky strobing, it filled the room with fast blinking. And then there was the sound of the rain coming down hard, hissing through the trees, making them sag. Raining so hard the rain held the light.

Four or five stabs of white light.

Then silence.

Then the almighty crack.

I ran into my bedroom, climbed into bed and got under the covers, listening to it outside. Light sliced through the room. I could see each drop of rain out the window, fat and white, like the sky had cracked into a million pieces. I put my hand in front of my face and *flash* – I could see the veins inside, dark purples and oranges.

That's when I pictured it so clear. A small pink thing hanging in its sack, its see-through skin, the veins beneath. The heart beating, pumping. Electrical activity in the brain after forty days.

And something solid filled the hole, filled the darkness.

It was light. Electricity.

I heard the thuds of steps coming up. Keys scraping the lock. Her heels on the floorboards and her voice singing hello?

She knocked and came into the room. Her hair was plastered to her face.

— Did you check the phone? The message they left?

I put out my hand and she came and sat on the bed. I

gave her a T-shirt from the floor and she dried her hair
quick. She was out of breath, bubbly.

— Did you?

— No.

— The Helpline, they said they . . .

— I know.

She swept her hair back from her eyes.

— What?

— I know, Mel. I know where Mikey is.

2

I turned the corner and the blocks of buildings marching away – they took up the sky and made it dark. I found the road and stood at the end of the snicket. I twizzled the bracelet in my fingers, round and round my wrist, pulling it, letting the elastic snap back. I was about to make a move when his front door opened.

An old man stepped out.

I hid behind a bush and peeked out as he struggled with his keys, his back bent over like a hook, his long coat stained, his face close to his hand as he closed the door, half blind. It seemed to take him minutes just to fit the key into the lock, just to shut that door. Then his hand went to his pocket and he began to turn. His stick tap-tapping on the path, legs shuffling one at a time like he might fall, and I almost went to help him, this old man, whoever he was. He got to the gate and seemed to straighten. I imagined his back clicking into place, bending like a metal bar. He turned his head, looked up into the sky, and then started to move towards me, clickety-click.

I pushed my back against the wall, waiting for him to pass. Click and wheeze, click and wheeze. I held my breath.

He was tiny in front of me. Face down, eyes watching his feet.

But then he stopped.

He turned and looked at my legs, my stomach, my neck.

I saw his eyes and felt a hand on the back of my head, pressing my cheek into a hairy chest that smelt of trees, of wet soil. The old man looked into my eyes and I was eight years old again, on the landing, trying to see into his face as he kissed me, so close to my lips, but he couldn't see me winking at him.

It was Don. He looked at me for one tiny second, and the flesh flower came up out of the soil again and bloomed in the pit of my stomach. His gravity pulling at me so hard I thought I was going to puke and fall over.

But he just squinted, turned, and shuffled towards the end of the snicket.

The heat went from my chest to my body and I felt the warmth of myself because Don was an old, sick man. He looked like he was about to die. Mr Morris's words came back to me: I suspect illness of some kind. The wattles on his neck, his chewed-up nose, his milky eyes, he looked proper fucked. Like food for worms. Into the soil he loved so much. Where he belonged.

I closed my eyes and waited as long as I could, until I heard a bird fly overhead, letting out a high note, and I smiled.

I walked down the snicket and up his garden path. I ripped the bangle from my wrist, snapped it in two, and shoved the bits through his letter box.

He'd know now. Know who the tall woman was, pressed long and stiff against the wall, holding her breath.

And maybe his head would start opening doors, doors that wouldn't shut.

I knew that it was over, with just one more door to visit.

I stood on the landing, staring at the padlocks. I'd been doing it a couple of minutes, enjoying the thump, the crack. I still hadn't decided what excuse I was going to make, what tall story if Dave came back from work early.

I had a right to know now anyway.

I stopped punting the door with my toe-end and started hitting it full whack with the bottom of my trainers, black marks on the white paint. Thwack it went. Thwack. But the door felt totally solid. The locks rattled and that was it. I stepped back and this time I twisted as I kicked, full force behind it. Uma fucking Thurman kicking some bastard's arse. A deep smacking sound, but not enough.

I walked around the house, eyeing things, weighing them up. The telly, the table, his bedside cabinet, chairs, the metal bin in the kitchen. And then I found it, in the cupboard under the stairs.

I lifted the sledgehammer onto my shoulder and climbed the stairs.

It took me a while to get the swing right, to get the grip right. I found that if I didn't lift it too high, just swung it like a cricket bat, got the swing going until it got as high as I could manage, and then lunged at the door with it – well, it started making a right mess.

The bottom panel came out with splinter noises. I expected light coming out of it. A blast of white light like something out of *Raiders of the Lost Ark*. But it was dark in there. It sucked the light in.

I kept smashing at it. Sweat ran into my eyes. The wood was coming away in chunks. I didn't care any more, about Dave coming and finding me. My cares had gone because I just wanted that fucking door opened, to be at the other side. That's all there was in the world: me and that sledge-hammer and that fucking door.

I swang and smashed and swang the bastard.

I crouched down, climbed inside, and found the light switch.

Stacks of boxes. Not just a few but a hundred, more, stretching away down the room, a little walkway down the middle. I'd imagined the room to be small, but it was long, tall. It didn't seem like it was Dave's house at all. It seemed like it belonged to the folk next door.

Boxes. Different-sized boxes up to chest height. I couldn't see any lab stuff. There were no benches with Bunsen burners or jars full of liquids, no vices or drills, just box after box after box.

I opened one. Then another. I don't know how long I'd been in there when there was a noise in the house somewhere.

I could hear rain hissing.

I could hear wind rattling the blacked-out windowpane like a naughty kid.

I tiptoed to the light switch and clicked it off. I heard another noise, coming from downstairs. Then footsteps thudding up. I stood in the darkness next to the door and saw the shadow go across the light.

— Lil?

I opened the door.

— The front door was . . . what?

I pulled her in and turned on the light.

— I'm pregnant to a fucking thief, Mel.

And I don't know why I said it,

— Who only ever fucks me in the missionary position.

I laughed and she put a hand to her face.

DVDs. Laptops. Computers. Cameras. Stereos. Drugs, bags and bags of pills and brown stuff. You name it. A fucking safe house.

— He's an inventor, Mel. An inventor of *bullshit*.

At the back of the room were a desk and a computer and some files. Mel went over to them. I was still busy with the boxes when she went Lily, you should see this.

It wasn't the emails from other women. I saw them and an image surfaced from my head and it popped: a fag end with red lipstick on.

It wasn't the unopened letters in the shoebox next to the PC. Begging letters from his mother in the nursing home. Please, son, I just don't understand.

It wasn't the fact he was a liar and a cheat and his mother wasn't dead at all.

It wasn't that. I didn't give a flying fuck about that.

It was the photographs.

Not of other women, but me. A hundred photographs. More.

The first one I saw was of my arms floppy, breasts on show.

I stood next to Mel and we went through them in silence.

I remembered his visits to the lab, always after we had sex. I remembered a flash. White light. A shadow passing over me.

He'd been taking photographs of me asleep.

But it wasn't even those.

It was my face that did it. Pushed me to that place beyond caring.

So ugly and twisted. Frothing. I could hear the grunting. Bugged-out eyes and my first thought: I looked like her – I looked like my mother, dead.

He'd taken pictures of me having a fit.

There I was. That's what I look like. The struggle there, like dying.

Like my dead fucking mother.

Like I didn't have a brain inside.

We stood outside in the drizzle, underneath the trees. Mel slid her arm through mine and we stood watching the end of the road. I finally stopped heaving and wiped my face. Make him invisible, that's what she said.

— You've just got to make him invisible now, Lil.

I watched the end of the road and wondered where he was, what he was doing, who was he with, why I'd been so fucking stupid. I wasn't upset. I didn't burst into tears and shout why me?

It was just another door slamming shut in my life.

I was disappointed they didn't have the sirens going, lights twirling. The police pulled up outside the house. Cars, and a van. We stepped towards them.

— You need to ask them, Lil. To check the computer files.

And I saw it in my head, my face on a website some-where, my horrible face and a man in a dark room, his arm pumping.

The light of my twisted face shining onto his sweaty skin.

1

Mel sat down at the kitchen table and sighed and rubbed her face.

I went over to the side and lifted the kettle off its stand. I sloshed the little bit of water around in the bottom and thought: that's just how I feel, like there's nothing left inside me, just this little slosh in my guts and the rest of me is empty.

But that wasn't so true. My breasts ached – they still do. They feel enormous and I've got a cramp in my gut and I need to piss all the frigging time, and at four o'clock every day, I puke. They said it was completely normal. To be expected. The skin around my nipples is going so dark, purple almost, and there are these flecks of blood that keep appearing in my knickers. The baby burrowing itself into me.

Don't worry, they said. Your body's changing.

I went over to the sink and took the lid off the kettle. I ran water inside and I was talking over the sound it made. For some reason, I'm telling Mel about wishing I had photos of her, of me as a bairn. I carried the heavy kettle back over to the side and clunked it down on its stand.

— Photos of me crawling, having my nappy changed, first tooth, missing teeth, on the beach in summer, you know. Me and Mikey. My big brother looking after me, looking out for me.

I closed my eyes and imagined the photos in my hand, me looking at them, and I'm wondering would I know her, that girl?

I flicked the switch and turned to look at Mel.

— I wanted him to look at me. To love me and not her. Love just me.

She closed her eyes.

— We were in love and Mam knew it. She's lying on the settee and she's pretending not to hear. Watching the telly, pretending to be asleep. He's touching me and I'm laughing. He's touching me and I *love* it.

Mel said fuck under her breath. Her hair curtained her face.

— And I've always wondered, what I'd've been like if I wasn't her kid. If she'd wanted me. If she hadn't thrown me down the stairs and I never had my fits. If fucking if.

— You were abused, Lil. By both of them.

She got up and went into the corridor. I heard the toilet door go and I saw a quick flash of Dave, cowered and handcuffed in the back of the police van. I shouted in my head: MAKE HIM INVISIBLE.

I leaned back against the side and my hand went to my stomach, fingers stroking. It felt tight. I wasn't imagining it. Sometimes it burns inside and the burn is so heavy it's like hot metal. Dave's gone and I'm on my own again. But of course rubbing myself like that, I knew I wasn't.

He was still inside me. He's still inside.

The kettle hissed to the boil, rattling and popping on its stand. She came back in and gave me the smallest of smiles. She looked at my hand on my stomach and I pulled it away. The kettle clicked and steamed. I wanted to put my hand on it, to feel the scald, to feel something that isn't this fucking numbness inside. I asked her to get the laptop running

> and here's the breath
> here's the breeze
> here's the shimmer

I grabbed onto the side, fingernails scratch-scratching the wood.

— Sorry?

She looked at me and we smiled and the bolt, it snapped my hand away like fire and the planet tilted, burnt wind blowing around inside me, skin suck-sucking the dust in and her face was a blank, trying to see what made my hand just do that, leaning over. I turned around, reached into the cupboard and pulled two cups out. I clanked them on the side heavy-as and she goes,

— You mean?

The crackles, the coughing, saying they're here again. Shadows moving all around me, breathing static breath, smell them in the buzzing as they sliiiiiide their long fingers in, tickling the switch and the colours, the sweet colours are here, wrapping their arms around me like they love me.

The steam puffed and curled under the units. She was quiet behind me.

— I want to book a flight.

I turned and saw her mouth curl to one side. Thoughts dropping like Tetris blocks in her head, and it was coming on strong now, such strong motion.

The room cracked and shattered, the colours wrapping their arms around me but I couldn't hold them back, it was like rain running down windows, the air melting in front of me, colours like feelings inside, suffocating but nice

like storm clouds up there

like bullies, black lightning off and on in their fat bellies and I need to pull at everything, need to touch and tug and twist and poke and push because it was all slipping away from me

and I knew

— Mel?

I knew she was there in the room, but I couldn't let go of the chair, my fingers crack-cracking the corners and I

can't catch my

can't catch my

— Mel?

— I'm here, I'm here.

— Help me.

I climbed down onto the floor. Reaching down, the wood cold on my palms and knees. Onto my side and over, flat onto my back. I could breathe again. I could breeeeeeeeeee

— Mel?

Shush-shushing me, stroking my hair, her face above me, the bright light up there on the ceiling like a

— You're an angel.

like a halo above her head, and I could hear me, smacking my lips like mwa mwa, pulling my face, my fingers dancing on my cheeks, noise revving up out of me like a banshee and the shadows – I *won't* let them knock me off my feet any more, I WON'T.

— Mel, *hold* me.

The burnt wind blowing around inside, it crackled and coughed and

— Mel.

I thought it was the baby coughing and I couldn't look Mel in the eye because her face was dripping down, purple and reds and yellows and my hands, my hands clasped over my stomach to protect *to protect* it inside

— HOLD MEEEEEEEEEE

because this is me falling through life, and I have to learn how to fall now, learn all over again to protect, to protect *it* inside

we're turning electric

zap-zapping it in its juices, Mel's arms closing around me and the lushness, the weakness, clouds ripping open my eyes, white smoke blowing, turn off my eyes, fading dim, yes turning

and it looks like
and smells like
and feels like

not the squealing the aaaaaaaaaa slow soft aaaaaaaaaa feel the sag, yes the dip, the lull, the nodges of my scars turning soft, glowing with light, the smoke clearing, eyes fading, hands clasping, holding it inside because I'll zap them both, fill them with my light yes fill them with my

the shadows flick-flicking my switch with their long crackling fingers
and I feel the twitch inside of me
a flutter
a spark
and it's so beautiful, it's so

But it doesn't come. I stare up into Mel's face and
everything snaps back into place. Hard edges. Light
and dark, solid. They said it might happen, during the
pregnancy, the seizures might stop. A possibility.
Likelihood. A chance. I can't believe it: I didn't go
into the black.
Mel helps me get to my feet. I walk over to the kitchen
table.
— Are you all right?
— I can't believe it.
I'm laughing. I was going full tilt and then I felt this
thing inside me and I knew: it was the baby, zapping
me right back.
I hold out my arms and we hug and I hear myself say
it into Mel's hair,
— I need to find my family.

O

So here I am. Today's the day, and though I'm not saying
it out loud, I'm saying it in my head: Dad. But it just
doesn't sound right. As much as I want it to, it doesn't
and I'm trying to get used to it, the word in my head.
Dad. I sat in bed last night whispering it to myself.
Such a tiny little word but it's impossible how big it
is. My dad. Father. Dad.
It just feels so totally weird.
It's the fear that's been holding me back. Fear that he's
just like her, like mother. Why he's never tried to find
me. A man that loved her, had me and Mikey with
her, that must've loved her at *some* point. And the
thought that he might be like her, and the whole
disappointment thing will start all over again. It'll be
hard not asking it, not getting angry.
Why did you leave us with that bitch?
What if Mam was right? What if he is a useless Irish
cunt? There's something that's not real about it.
I can't imagine it, seeing him for the first time. I really
can't. I try to picture what he looks like and I see our
Mikey, but Mikey's still a young lad in my head. Then
I see a big man with huge sideboards and long black
hair, and I want to see if his eyes are like a summer's
sky, but I can't and I don't know why.
— What if he doesn't like me?

— He'll *love* you, Lil. Who wouldn't?

— What if I don't like *him*?

We're watching the huge planes making their way across the motorways of tarmac. They seem too big. I watch them take off and they're going too slow. Huge chunks of metal nosing up there, up and away like something in a slow dream, like trying to run but you can't.

I stroke my belly, picturing it inside, bubbling, fizzing away, and I remember it zapping me and how powerful it felt. And I wonder if Mikey has any kids, whether he's married. I wonder if my dad's got someone? I might have this huge family in Ireland that I know nothing about.

I keep thinking about the past year, about the police coming to the Golden Nugget and then meeting Barry and then coming down to London, looking, searching. I stroke my stomach and look at Mel and think: it wasn't all pointless.

And I keep thinking about yesterday – my day of thank yous. Al phoned saying that some bruiser had been round to the shop with an envelope. I said how big is the envelope and he said like there's nothing in it. A cheque. Al said the bruiser told him that if he lost it, his life wouldn't be worth living. So Barry had done it – coughed up Mikey's share. I told Al not to fret and gave him my account number and told him to pay it into the bank.

And then I told him about Ireland. He was quiet on the other end of the phone. I told him that whatever happens, he's the nearest thing I've ever had to a dad, and that I'll always think of him that way. Always. I tried really hard not to cry.

After I picked up my passport, and me and Mel had pissed ourselves at my photo – startled rabbit in car headlights – I rang the Helpline to thank them for being so brilliant. I told them they could shut the case.

Then I put a card in the post to Sylvia.

And now I'm bricking it. A lot of people seem to be moving about. I check my handbag again, make sure I've got all my pills, though I haven't had a fit in two weeks now and I'm so excited I want to run in circles screaming.

— You know, Lil, I really . . .

— Oh shush.

— And I just . . .

My elbow in her ribs and we're laughing.

— I'll be there for you, whatever, you know.

There's that fizz between us again and I don't know why, but I'm embarrassed. I want to tell her that I love her. Really love her.

She stretches her arms and yawns, looks at her watch, and my guts are turning and squirming like worms again.

I take the bits of paper out of my handbag and read them for the umpteenth time, looking for god knows. We'd Googled pubs called O'Connor's in Dublin, but it kept coming up with nonsense. There seemed to be a pub called O'Connor's in a place called Doolin, but that was on the other side of the country. Mel said there's a good chance the pub isn't on a website. But we'll find it. I know we will. And I'll tell Mikey about the spark inside, and that I knew he was all right, that I could *feel* he was alive.

I look at my boarding card. 56-A. Mel said it's a window

seat and that I'll be able to see the land disappear as we take off.

— What you asked before, about the doctors and that.

Rubbing her mouth.

— I don't know whether I can go through with it.

Her eyes searching mine.

— The abortion, I mean.

She bends a little smile and I wonder when I'll start showing. I wonder what my father'll think when I tell him. Dad, I'm pregnant.

It just doesn't seem real.

But Mel's saying something. She's getting to her feet, lifting her handbag off the floor.

— They're calling us. Our flight.

This is it.

I stand up and we walk slowly towards the gate. There's a crowd moving forwards with us, fumbling, looking for passports and boarding cards. We join the queue and I wonder if everyone here feels the same spark inside.

I'm thinking this is the place, here and now, to start all over again, from the beginning, right from the start. And suddenly I'm inside me again, and I feel the miracle of it. The power.

I take Mel's hand in mine, and we walk towards the gate.

Opening doors of our own.

Debt of thanks

To Madi Ruby, Nicola Broadbent, Ryan Painter,
Dave Goodwin, Janet Rowson, Jodi Melssen,
Sally Gomersall, Derrick Souba, Julie Cooper,
Hannah Frost, Elizabeth Coombs, Gemma Baxter,
Rona Gibb, Peter Suchin, Christopher Crouch,
John Sansick, Linda Anderson, W. N. Herbert,
Sarah Robinson, Esther Davis, Karl and Paul Harder,
Mollie Baxter, Robbie Smith, Dr Gonzalo Alarcon,
Dr Helena Bligh, Dr James Nicholson, Dr Paul Broks,
Neil Channing, Devilfish, Dr Graham Mort,
Lancaster University's Research Studentship,
Issy Cowburn, Veronique Baxter, Sam Humphreys,
Paul Farley, Dr Anna Rowe, Wilf Dickie, Sara Maitland,
National Missing Persons Helpline, Epilepsy Action,
National Society for Epilepsy,
and most of all, to Lynne.

Grateful acknowledgement is made for permission to reproduce
extracts from the following:

She's Lost Control written and composed by
Curtis/Hook/Morris/Sumner.
Published by Fractured Music/Zomba Music Publishers Ltd.
Used by permission. All rights reserved.

'Electricity' by Paul Farley from *The Boy from
the Chemist is Here to See You*. Published by Picador.
Used by permission. All rights reserved.

Every effort has been made to contact copyright holders of
material reproduced in this book. If any have been inadvertently
overlooked, the publishers will be pleased to make restitution
at the earliest opportunity.